The price of success

"I can rewrite the translator program," Lucas said. "I can do that!" And he hurried back to his station.

Graves started to join Lucas, but Henry put a hand on his shoulder. "Let him do it, Air," he said in a low voice. "He needs to."

Carter watched the conversation between the two, catching Henry's unspoken innuendo concerning Lucas. More going on there than Carter knew. But he also noticed the look on Graves's face. It wasn't one of elation . . . not the face of a scientist who was now closer to achieving his goal. That look said he'd seen enough in this place.

No. Graves looked . . . worried.

About what?

That the translator still wouldn't work?

Or that it would?

EUReKA

BRAIN BOX BLUES

CRIS RAMSAY

ACE BOOKS, NEW YORK

THE BERKLEY PUBLISHING GROUP
Published by the Penguin Group
Penguin Group (USA) Inc.
375 Hudson Street, New York, New York 10014, USA
Penguin Group (Canada), 90 Eglinton Avenue East, Suite 700, Toronto, Ontario M4P 2Y3, Canada
(a division of Pearson Penguin Canada Inc.)
Penguin Books Ltd., 80 Strand, London WC2R 0RL, England
Penguin Group Ireland, 25 St. Stephen's Green, Dublin 2, Ireland (a division of Penguin Books Ltd.)
Penguin Group (Australia), 250 Camberwell Road, Camberwell, Victoria 3124, Australia
(a division of Pearson Australia Group Pty. Ltd.)
Penguin Books India Pvt. Ltd., 11 Community Centre, Panchsheel Park, New Delhi—110 017, India
Penguin Group (NZ), 67 Apollo Drive, Rosedale, North Shore 0632, New Zealand
(a division of Pearson New Zealand Ltd.)
Penguin Books (South Africa) (Pty.) Ltd., 24 Sturdee Avenue, Rosebank, Johannesburg 2196,
South Africa

Penguin Books Ltd., Registered Offices: 80 Strand, London WC2R 0RL, England

EUREKA: BRAIN BOX BLUES

An Ace Book / published by arrangement with NBC Universal Television Consumer Products Group

PRINTING HISTORY
Ace mass-market edition / December 2010

Copyright © 2010 Universal City Studios Productions, LLLP.
Eureka TM & © Universal Network Television, LLC.
Cover art by Syfy Network.
Interior text design by Kristin del Rosario.

ISBN: 978-0-441-01983-0

ACE
Ace Books are published by The Berkley Publishing Group,
a division of Penguin Group (USA) Inc.,
375 Hudson Street, New York, New York 10014.
ACE and the "A" design are trademarks of Penguin Group (USA) Inc.

PRINTED IN THE UNITED STATES OF AMERICA

10 9 8 7 6 5 4 3 2 1

Published by arrangement with NBC Universal Television Consumer Products Group

NBC UNIVERSAL
TELEVISION CONSUMER PRODUCTS

To my father,
whose ability to find a sense of wonder in
this world still inspires me to this day

ACKNOWLEDGMENTS

First I'd like to thank my editor, Leis Pederson, for giving me the opportunity to write in the *Eureka* franchise. It's a dream come true! To Jaime Paglia, whose talent and insight now guide me in other work—thanks for creating such a rich and incredible world. To Chris and Steve York, for their encouragement, talent, and all-around friendship during the project. To Dr. Ernest Steele, for his support and patience with this creative profession. To Matt Bassett, without whom I'd never have been able to tell the difference between the DoD and DoE (it's good to have friends in Washington!).

And, finally, to Aircom Graves, Second Life's own little version of an average sheriff caught between the lines of the normal and the fantastic. I'm glad we met online—*and* you kept the faith, kiddo.

CHAPTER 1

"Fargo!"

The bell over the door of Café Diem jingled as Eureka's sheriff, Jack Carter, stepped inside. He nodded to patrons as they turned and smiled. To his right sat the elderly android twins playing chess. Just past them sat a few men in business suits, their heads bent down, focused on their PDAs as one of the local's biomimetic dogs barked.

A step behind Carter was Deputy Sheriff Jo Lupo. She grinned down at the pooch and gave it a pat on the head.

Spotting Fargo, Carter strode purposefully toward a small group huddled around the back table. Douglas Fargo, the assistant to the director at Global Dynamics and Eureka's brilliant but accident-prone problem child, sat among friends and co-workers, including Carter's daughter, Zoe.

Home on a short break from Harvard, Zoe had offered to help bus and wait tables again at the café, only this morning she looked more like a patron than an employee.

Vincent, Café Diem's stout and ever-helpful owner and proprietor, waved at Carter as he entered. "Morning, Sheriff—hey, Jo. The Thank-God-It's-Friday Fritters are fresh."

Carter shook his head. "Morning, Vincent—maybe not today. S.A.R.A.H. says I still need to cut back on the fried foods."

"Oooh . . . Vincent." Jo diverted to the counter. "I'll take one, and a Bavarian Hammer."

"Coming right up, Jo. Your loss, Sheriff. They're guaranteed to make your Friday go smooth as silk."

Though the idea of having one of Vincent's delicious fritters sounded wonderful—especially to Carter's growling stomach—he really was trying to cut back a little on the rich food he'd enjoyed since moving to Eureka.

Café Diem boasted an eclectic and entertaining array of interior decor, much of which reflected the town's history, as well as her more famous scientific residents. Vincent himself held a reputation that he could fill any order asked of him, and he prided himself on having a freezer stocked to suit anyone who came through the door.

Also seated at the table with Fargo and Zoe were Julia, Fargo's girlfriend and researcher at Global Dynamic, and Henry Deacon, the town's most versatile scientist, mechanic, and mayor.

"Morning, Carter," Henry said.

"Good morning, Sheriff Carter." Julia's smile was incredibly bright and chipper for a Friday morning.

"Morning." Carter stood in front of the table, his hands on his hips. "Fargo—about this complaint against your neighbor—"

"Yes." The diminutive assistant pointed at him with the pencil in his hand. "That noise has *got* to stop. The lights, the yelling, the moaning . . ."

Carter frowned. *Moaning?* "You said they were making

a movie." His eyes widened as he felt a smile tug at the corners of his mouth. "What *kind* of movie are they making?"

Julia sat up straight and pushed her dark-framed glasses up higher on her nose, blushing just slightly. "Nothing as brash as that, Sheriff. They're reenacting *Contact*—making a satire out of it."

Carter blinked and frowned as he tried running as quickly as he could through the list of movie titles he could remember. "You mean like *Star Trek*?"

Fargo sighed, lowering the pencil and his shoulders. "Sheriff, that's *First Contact*. This is *Contact*, the beloved book by Carl Sagan, where man's first contact with extraterrestrials is—"

Carter held up his hands. "Okay, okay. Sorry. My bad. The movie with Jodie Foster—"

"Awful." Julia sniffed.

"Totally not the book," Fargo echoed.

Zoe moved from her seat beside Julia and touched her father's arm. "Hey, Dad . . . something for breakfast? Fritter?"

Carter smiled at her, feeling the soft affection he always had when he was with her. He was thrilled she was home from school even if it was only for a long weekend. But he was also aware of something else in her expression. Something sad.

He moved a few steps to the counter, away from the others, as Zoe joined him. "Hey . . . you plan on telling me what's been causing you to walk around like a zombie? S.A.R.A.H. said you called her *Lucas* twice this morning." He lowered his voice as he watched her face.

Zoe shrugged and looked back at the others as they talked among themselves again. "It's nothing . . . really."

"Uh . . . Zoe . . . it's me . . . remember? Your dad? The one who always embarrasses you? The one who's always right but you never admit it?"

Her gaze immediately moved up to meet his, and she gave him a half smile. "I know, Dad. . . . It's just that"—she glanced back at the group—"I look at Fargo and Julia and I feel . . . kinda . . ." Her shoulders rose and lowered. "I don't know. Sad?"

Frowning, he glanced back at them. "Well, I know it's kind of an odd pairing . . . but they seem to go well together." He grinned. "Kinda like spaghetti and meatballs."

"But that's just it." She sighed. "They're so happy together."

"Uh . . ." He sighed and straightened, now understanding his daughter's seemingly listless behavior since arriving in Eureka. "This is about you and Lucas."

She nodded. "Dad . . . he's just so . . . At first we were keeping up with each other. Texting, e-mail, calling . . . And then I got busy . . . and then he got busy . . . and now . . ." She shrugged. "Now it's so hard to even get a response out of him. I told him I was coming back to Eureka for a few days—but he never responded." She turned a pained expression to him. It broke his heart. "I miss him."

"Oh, honey." He reached out and gave her a quick hug. "I'm sorry. I should have seen this. Look, I'm sure Lucas is busy at MIT. Why don't I pick Henry's brain later, okay?" He tilted his head from side to side. "Maybe kinda see if I can get information?"

"I wish I could pick Lucas's brain sometimes. I'd do anything to know what he's thinking."

"Trust him, okay? Like I said, he's probably just a little preoccupied with school. And I'll see what I can find out for you."

"Thanks, Dad," she said in a whisper. Then she lowered her voice and said, "Just don't let Henry know I'm the one that wants to know."

Carter grinned. "I promise." He moved back to the

group with Zoe beside him. "So what exactly have we got going on here? Some kind of game?"

Jo joined them, a to-go cup in one hand, a napkin-covered fritter with a bite out of it in the other. She chewed as she looked at everyone. "What's up?"

Henry was the one to answer, looking Carter directly in the eye. "Remote Viewing."

Carter pursed his lips, nodding. "Annnd . . . by that I'm assuming you're not talking about binoculars or, like, a telescope."

Jo shook her head and swallowed. "Nope. Like the Morehouse book, right?" She looked at Henry.

Julia's and Fargo's expressions slipped into surprise as they looked at the deputy, their mouths dropping.

"How did you know about that?" Fargo said. "Morehouse's book? *Psychic Warrior*?"

Jo's eyebrows arched high into her smooth forehead. "It's called reading, Fargo. You should try it sometime." She looked at Julia. "Though I'd always assumed it was fiction. So this Stargate thing was real?"

"Very much so." Henry grinned.

Carter looked from Jo to Henry. "Anyone care to give me a book report?"

"Remote Viewing, or RV as it's called, is the science of gathering needed information about a remote target," Henry said. "The means of the gathering is what's always been called into question because it relies on the mind and its connection to all things. The term itself was introduced by parapsychologists Russell Targ and Harold Puthoff in 1974."

"Harold Put-off?" Carter grinned at Henry, and then straightened his face when he realized Henry wasn't smiling. He cleared his throat. "So parapsychology?" Carter made a face. "Uh . . . so you're into psychics *and* tarot cards now?"

"Of course not, Sheriff," Julia piped up. "RV is actually based in science. Our own government believed so in the seventies to the tune of about twenty million. They called it the Stargate Project."

"Stargate?" Carter looked at each of them before looking back to Henry. "You mean like the TV show?"

Jo chewed on her fritter.

"Oh, hardly," Henry said. "There's always been a fringe interest in using psychics and psychic sciences in other countries. Germany was more of the leader in this research, until the United States got involved. A lot of interest in the idea of actually 'seeing' something from a distance with the mind—without having to risk operations or teams, manpower or weapons and time—always appeals to those in charge. You just have to prove to them it works."

Carter shifted his stance and glanced down at Zoe, then over at Jo. "You two know about this stuff?"

"Not really." Zoe smiled. "I offered to help him teach it—be a test subject."

"Teach it?" Carter's gaze whipped back to Henry. "You want to *teach* psychic mumbo-jumbo to smart kids? You know you're gonna get laughed at, right?" He looked at Zoe. "And you're going along with it?"

"Dad . . ." Zoe began.

Henry frowned. "Carter—do you even know what it is we're talking about?"

Carter opened his mouth, paused, looked at each of them, then closed his mouth. "No—no, not really. I'll admit I'm thinking of crystal balls and voodoo dolls."

"Well, first off, voodoo dolls are a part of a religious practice called Voudoun." Henry shook his head. "But that's not what we're talking about. Back in the seventies, Puthoff and Targ were working at the electronics and bio-engineering laboratory at Stanford Research Institute, or

SRI. They were studying quantum mechanics and laser physics."

"Okay, now, that sounds like *real* science, right? With lasers and quantum . . . stuff . . ." Carter looked from Henry to Julia to Fargo and then to Jo, who was smiling around her fritter.

Fargo made a frustrated noise and looked up at the ceiling.

"Oh, now, don't *you* go all 'I believe in this crap.'" Carter pointed at him. "Go on, Henry."

"While they were doing that work, the two of them also created a few experiments in the paranormal, which were funded by the Parapsychology Foundation." He smiled as he leaned over the table next to Fargo. "Puthoff found a prize subject in a man named Ingo Swann, back in 1972. Work with Swann brought in a CIA-sponsored project."

"So." Carter frowned. "What did this Swann guy do that brought in that kind of money?"

"He created the procedure used in Remote Viewing." Julia piped up. "The steps Viewers took for later, more successful experiments. He and Puthoff were able to train other gifted Viewers." She grinned.

"Procedure?"

Jo arched her eyebrow. "You guys are using the SRI method? Descriptives and set-asides?"

Fargo nodded, though his expression was still confused. "Yes. But still"—he made a face at Jo—"how did you know about that procedure?"

"I took a class in Remote Viewing, Fargo. Not that hard."

Carter opened his mouth, but Henry interjected, "Swann came up with a series of motions used for better results in tapping the mind for answers. Like Jo just said"—he gestured to the blank paper in front of Fargo and the pencil in the assistant's hand—"the pad is the blank starting point, the pencil the tool."

"And the target"—Julia lifted the paper, retrieved a sealed manila envelope, and held it up—"is in here."

"See, Dad," Zoe said, and Carter looked at her. "The target is hidden from the Viewer. It can be a person, place, or thing. Let's say this particular target is—" She looked at Henry, her eyebrows raised, seeking an answer.

"Ah, this target is a thing, an item. Now, what Fargo will do is close his eyes and start writing down on the pad every adjective that comes to mind. But if a noun pops into his head, then he'll write it to the side."

Carter crossed his arms over his chest and shrugged. "Why are the nouns being sent to the corner?"

"Well, what we're trying to tap into is the subconscious. That part of us that's interconnected to everyone else on the planet."

"So our subconscious hates nouns?"

"Come on, Carter." Henry half grinned. "After everything we've been through in this town, including the shared dreaming, can't you even for an instant imagine that we're all connected somehow?"

"Some more than others," Jo said as Zane walked by. She grinned and looked back at Carter. "Be right back."

Carter blinked at Henry as Jo moved off after Zane. "I believe that several of the machines you people came up with did that. But our minds?"

"Never mind." Henry waved in the air. "The point is, we want him to connect to his subconscious, but Fargo's conscious mind—like everyone else's—is going to want to help fill in the blank. The conscious is id. It's ego. And the ego always wants to be helpful. It's going to *give* him nouns. Items. But these nouns aren't going to be right."

Carter looked from Henry to Julia, then back to Henry. "You don't want to listen to the nouns."

"Okay, fine, leave it at that," Henry said. "But instead of ignoring those nouns, we write them down in order to appease the conscious so it will allow the subconscious to speak."

"So you're saying"—Carter rubbed at his chin—"that our conscious mind gets jealous if we ignore it and try to talk to our subconscious."

"Right."

"Uh-huh. Riiiiiight. Well . . . you all have fun with that."

Henry shrugged. "You'd be surprised at the results, Carter. This procedure and others like it had quite a success rate—though it's not something that was ever reported in numbers. All we know is that SRI managed its own stable of psychics for U.S. intelligence agencies, garnering information for them for years. Most notable was a description of a big crane at the Soviet nuclear research facility—an area we weren't able to penetrate with any camera back in the late seventies."

Julia chimed in. "And a description of a new class of Soviet missile submarine before it even became known. They also found the location of a downed American bomber in Africa. By the eighties, the whole intelligence community was using the SRI group."

"So?" Carter held out his hands. "What happened to them? If it was so great, how come we don't use it now?"

Julia smiled. "Who says we don't?"

"Oh, now don't you go all conspiracy theory on me." Carter looked at Henry.

"Officially, when the Democrats lost the house in the midnineties, the Defense Intelligence Agency, or DIA, handed the project over to the CIA. They hired the American Institutes for Research, or AIR, to evaluate it. AIR decided that there wasn't enough documentation to prove the program was a viable asset to aid in the defense of the United States."

Carter grinned. "Bean counters."

"Exactly," Henry said. "It was declassified, the program shut down, and all research and notes sent here to GD. About four years ago one of the members of the Institute of Noetic Sciences—"

Carter shook his head, blinking. "The what?"

"The Institute of Parapsychology," Fargo interjected, his elbows on the table as he toyed with the pencil.

"Well, not the same thing," Henry said. "That institute still exists. Noetic science explores the inner cosmos of the mind: the consciousness, soul, the spirit, and its effects on the body and the world around it."

Carter looked from Fargo to Henry. "And that's different than parapsychology?"

"Well, yes." Henry frowned. "Anyway, Dr. Schmetzer started up his own study of Remote Viewing here at GD."

"He still here?"

"No, he died about two years ago."

"So was he successful at this?" Carter hesitated. "Or did he get shut down, too?"

"Dunno." Henry shrugged. "I mean, yes, it was cut off. Most of the rumor at the time was that Schmetzer was successful, but he was having trouble with his subjects."

"Trouble?"

"I wish I knew. Most of the research notes are still redacted. I'm working on getting them released to me."

"Was Schmetzer a nutcase?" Carter inhaled, smelling the fritters. His stomach growled again.

"Oh no, no." Henry shook his head. "Dr. Schmetzer wasn't like that at all. He was a dedicated man of science and believed in experimentation to achieve outcome. Like the SRI program."

"What we're doing here," Julia said quickly, "is taking Targ and Puthoff's training regime and applying it to a course in noetic science. Sort of an eye-opener for the graduating seniors at Tesla. Try to make them aware that science isn't always about concrete facts and chemicals and neutrons."

"And . . ." Carter tilted his head as he looked at her. "You're buying into all this new-agey stuff?"

She looked at Fargo. "I'm interested in whatever Douglas is interested in."

Carter sighed. "I see. Well, that's all nice and good but—"

"Want to see it in action?" Henry said. "Just stay right there and we'll give it a test run. I've already used this on twenty students and gotten interesting results."

Grinning at Henry, Carter said, "*Interesting* results. You mean it's not working like you thought it would."

"Just watch." He turned to Fargo. "Now, just like we talked about earlier, Fargo. You know it's an object. So just relax, take a few deep breaths."

Fargo nodded quickly, closed his eyes, and started deep breathing. Within seconds his breathing increased and he grabbed at his chest.

Henry sighed. "Don't hyperventilate."

Fargo held out his right hand, index finger up to indicate a second. He steadied his breathing, still keeping his eyes closed. "Okay. Sorry."

"Now let your mind go. Remember, if you get a noun, just write that word to the side."

"Got it." Fargo's breathing wasn't any calmer. When he put his pencil down it was on the table, but Julia guided his hand to the pad.

Once on the paper, Fargo paused, frowning. "Wet."

"That's an adjective. Write that down."

Fargo did, scribbling the word to the side as he wrote it sideways. He then wrote a series of words. *Drippy, moist, cold, hairy, red—*

"Is *red* a noun?" he asked with his eyes closed.

"No, it's an adjective." Julia patted his shoulder.

He continued to write, and Carter leaned over to watch. *Dank, fuzzy, yellow—*

"Yellow? It's yellow and red?"

"Carter." Henry frowned and put his finger to his lips.

Carter took a step back. *Sorry,* he mouthed.

Rough, rubbery—Fargo then frowned and moved his hand away and wrote *rug* on the other side of the paper. He moved his hand back, and over the word *red* he wrote *old*.

The adjectives continued for a few more seconds before Henry stopped him. Two more nouns had appeared. *Car* and *yard*.

"Car . . . and yard?" Carter frowned.

"Well, can he see what it is now?" Fargo looked over at Henry.

Jo rejoined the group, moving in next to Carter. He glanced back to see Zane leaving the café.

"So did Fargo give it a try?" she asked. Apparently she'd finished her coffee and fritter and was ready for work.

Henry nodded and pulled the manila envelope back out. He slowly opened it and pulled out a page from a color magazine, keeping the subject image hidden from everyone. "Ready?"

"Yes, please," Fargo said.

With a sigh, Henry laid it on top of his writing paper.

Zoe laughed softly. "It's Elmo."

"Taking a bath," Carter said. "Yeah, Fargo . . . that's one interesting . . . rug. No, wait. It's a car." He snapped his fingers. "Maybe a yard?"

"I don't understand." Fargo frowned at the page. "When Julia did it, she got it right."

"You did?" Carter asked.

"Yes. Mine was an airplane engine."

Henry grinned. "She actually started drawing her target." He started to say something else just as his pager went off.

Carter's pager went off as well.

"What is it?" Julia asked.

Fargo looked at them and then pulled his own pager out. "I'm not getting a page."

Jo looked over Carter's arm at the pager. "Ooooh. Allison, 911."

Henry looked up at Carter. "Mansfield?"

"I want to go," Jo said.

But Carter shook his head. "No . . . you head in to the office, see what's going on there."

Jo shrugged.

Carter replaced the pager into his pocket. "Oh, this can't be good. I'll give you a ride to GD, Henry." He turned and kissed Zoe. "Trust him and talk to him. Okay?"

"Sure, Dad. Have fun."

He straightened and looked down at her as Henry grabbed his jacket and headed to the door. "Have fun with Mansfield? I'm going to wish I'd had a fritter."

Zoe pointed to the paper and envelopes in front of Julia and Fargo. "Can I try?"

CHAPTER 2

To Carter, General Mansfield seemed more like an angry bulldog than a military hero. And being put in charge of a town full of geniuses? Never quite seemed to sit right with the man.

The general was tall and lean. His face was set with a permanent scowl, accented by graying hair. His uniform was pressed as always as he stood in Global's infirmary, accompanied by a very worried-looking Allison Blake, director of Global Dynamics.

As Carter and Henry entered, the room was in a flurry of activity, with more soldiers and medical personnel than Carter could remember seeing since taking over as sheriff. Zane was also there, talking quietly with a few of the medical personnel. Off to the right stood a young man in an expensive suit speaking in hushed tones to someone on a cell phone.

"Sheriff Carter," General Mansfield said.

"General."

"Dr. Deacon."

Henry nodded. "So, General, what brings you to GD today?"

Allison looked at the general and turned to Henry and Carter. "General Mansfield is here to ask our help in a very sensitive matter—concerning national security."

Carter looked from Allison to Mansfield. "National security?" He pointed to the floor with a surprised look. "And you came *here*?"

"Chilling, isn't it?" Mansfield said as he clasped his hands behind him. "As many times as this town's put the security of this nation at risk—it's the true meaning of the word *ironic*."

"What seems to be the problem, General?" Henry said in a lighter tone. "What can we do for you?"

"To be brief, Doctor, I need you to tell me the last thoughts of a dead man."

Carter blinked. He half turned to Henry, who also appeared to be having trouble grasping the request. He put his hands on his hips. "Ah . . . I'm sorry." He tilted his head to the side. "What?"

"What the general means"—Allison spoke up, her eyes locking with Carter's and then Henry's—"is that he has an agent who was working on something top secret but was killed before he could report what he'd discovered. He needs us to find out what that information was."

"Can—" Carter looked at Allison and repeated his question. "Can we do that? I mean . . . suck out the thoughts of a dead person?"

"Actually, we can," said a new voice behind them.

Henry and Carter turned and parted from each other as Zane and the man in the suit joined them.

Mansfield gestured to the young man. "Dr. Deacon, Sheriff Carter, this is Dr. Aircom Graves. Dr. Graves works for the National Academy of Medicine. Dr. Graves is my expert in brain research and the creator of the Brain Box."

Carter's eyebrows arched as he shook the young man's hand. "Brain Box?"

Graves's own expression looked sympathetic. "I know the name's not terribly scientific, but it's what I nicknamed it during its inception, and it stuck." He released Carter's hand and offered his own to Henry. "It's very nice to meet you, Dr. Deacon."

"Likewise," Henry said. "Care to elaborate on what your Brain Box does?"

Nodding, Graves motioned them to follow him to a table set up in the far corner of the infirmary, away from the main examination tables. Carter stood between Graves and Henry, looking down at a silver box. It looked maybe five by five inches in size, and the shape wasn't exactly square, but more like a three-dimensional stop sign. The sides were silver and smooth, with no distinctive marks, except for two small lights on the side facing them. The lights flashed red and green alternately. "It's a box."

"A Brain Box," Graves said. "What my team and I were able to do is take the matrix technology Dr. Fontana created with the storycatcher devices and apply it with a more refined parameter."

"Whoa, wait right there. Stop." Carter held up his hands. "You're using the storycatcher technology on this thing? You do know those things made everyone lose their memories."

"Carter." Henry looked at him. "We fixed that problem."

"Yes, I'm aware of what happened," Graves said with a nod. "And I've built every precaution thinkable into this new device. Nothing like that will happen again."

"Famous last words around here." Carter still looked skeptical and nodded to the box. "Just . . . don't let Fargo anywhere near that thing. And don't show him any buttons."

"Dr. Graves." Henry crossed his arms over his chest but rubbed at his chin with his right index finger. "You said you refined the parameters—can you elaborate on that?"

"Sure." Graves picked up a small, thin box the size of a deck of cards and pointed it at a wall screen in front of them. The screen displayed several diagrams that left Carter taking a step back as the scientists talked. "Whereas your storycatcher devices absorbed a specific memory directed by the holder, the Brain Box selects *all* memories remaining in the cortex at the point of death, washing over the entire brain to store and record the electrical impulses, just like the storycatcher devices. We call it harvesting."

"So you've actually broadened the *retrieval* system," Henry said, looking at Graves. "So this device simply gathers all the memories available in the central cortex? Temporary or permanent?"

"Both."

"Very well done, Dr. Graves."

"The brain is an amazing thing, Dr. Deacon—"

"Please, call me Henry."

"Henry. Um . . . just call me Graves. Aircom's kind of an odd name. Remind me to tell you about it one day— when you're really bored."

Carter said, "And you can call me Sheriff." He hooked his thumbs into the belt of his uniform pants. "Dead people don't talk, last time I checked—so how do they tell you their memories?"

"They can't tell you," Graves said. "By any standard EKG, death can be defined by the lack of any brain activity, or firing synapses, which is the way the previous incarnation worked. But that's with a standard device. It only skims the top." He pressed the button on the device in his hand again and the image changed to an outline of a brain with tiny charges flickering randomly. "I took the base delivery system, which at its heart is those synaptic impulses, and fine-tuned the sensor and connection to bypass the speech component. In truth, the brain is still working after death, just not on a level any medical devices can detect. The Brain Box can see those faint pulses and harvest them. They're then reassembled in the box and, in theory, we can see a visual of the memories still floating about after death."

"Oh." Carter pursed his lips. "Sure. Yeah. I got that." He looked at Allison as he set his hands on his hips. "You get that?"

Allison smiled. "He means his box doesn't have to be told the memories, Carter. It records the brain's impulses."

Carter pursed his lips. "Ah." And then he frowned. "Sure."

"Interesting." Henry pursed his lips. "How do you *know* you're recording the last thoughts?"

Graves said, "Just before death there is a surge of these synaptic impulses. I defined that instant as the synaptic cry—when the mind acts on the only base survival mechanism it has: identity. Who it is, where it is, what it is. And it repeats this cycle—much like the replay of one's life—over and over till the moment it knows death is no longer imminent, or it dies."

"Sounds a lot like a soldier repeating name, rank, and serial number," Carter said.

"Not sure that's the same thing, Sheriff." Dr. Graves gave him a genuine smile. "But we'll go with it for now."

Carter returned the smile, then snapped his fingers. "You said replaying one's life—you mean seeing their life flash before their eyes just before they die."

"Right again, Sheriff. And those images should be there, stored in the cortex where other memories reside."

"And you've seen this work?" Henry said.

Graves pursed his lips and looked at the general. "Theoretically."

"The box itself is still classified as experimental." Mansfield spoke up. "I authorized its use in this case."

Carter looked from Graves to Mansfield and then back again, grinning with satisfaction. "It's not working, is it?"

The general looked away from Carter. "No. It's not."

Carter sighed. "I knew it."

"Actually, it *is* working." Graves spoke up as everyone looked at him. "In the sense that it recorded *something*. It's the translation I need help with."

Henry looked at the general. "What you're saying is—this is a test of the unit itself. You've used this device already to collect a dead man's last thoughts?"

"Yes."

"Oh," Carter said, and took a step back, pointing at the box. "There's technically a dead guy's soul in the box?"

Allison half smiled at him. "What is it, Carter? You afraid of ghosts?"

"That"—he pointed at her—"is a whole other box of nasty I do not want to get into."

"His memories," Graves said as he looked at Carter. "We have them; we just need to see if what he can tell us helps in what he was investigating."

Carter looked from Graves to Mansfield and then at Allison. "But . . . it's not *working*, right?"

Mansfield snorted as Graves shook his head. "The impulses are there. We can register that the harvesting worked. The memory is nearly full. But reassembling them . . ." He shook his head. "That's out of my purview, and I'm hoping Dr. Deacon can lend a hand."

"Really," Henry said, keeping his index finger and thumb pressed against his lip. "I'm not going to lie—I don't like this. This whole idea. You're actually hoping to peer into a dead man's private thoughts. It's like the government's final thumbprint on someone's life."

"But you did this with the storynest—" Graves said.

"No." Henry held up a finger. "That was *voluntary*. Each resident in this town was given a device and told to *choose* a memory. It was given willingly by each participant—not harvested. I have a slight problem with this scenario."

"Deacon." Mansfield stepped closer and pointed to the box. "That agent's last thoughts could contain vital information that we need. Information that could save the security of this nation. Now, I can *order* you to help Dr. Graves decipher that data—"

"I'll do it," Zane piped up.

All eyes turned to him.

Carter pursed his lips and looked at the young man. "You?"

He nodded. "Hey, I love a good puzzle—and I worked on the time capsule project with Dr. Fontana. The concept is fascinating. And if you look at the future application of this technology—how it could be used in solving murders—"

"Exactly," Graves said, and pointed at Zane. "That was originally why I wanted to create the device. But if it can help in this instance—"

"I don't like the idea of peering into a dead man's memories," Henry stated.

"Hey, I don't like the idea that a dead man's memories are even stored in a box," Allison said. "Zane, you can work with Dr. Graves?"

"Yes. That is, if I can have access to Dr. Graves's research so far?" Zane said.

"Sure."

"Oh, I'll do it," Henry said as he lowered his arms and shoved his hands into his pockets. He looked at Mansfield. "I'd also like to use one of my students: Lucas. He's just come in from MIT, and I think he'll be perfect on this project. He can help me learn and document how the government's working to get into our heads even after death."

Carter's attention snapped back to Henry at the mention of Lucas's name. Zoe hadn't said anything about Lucas being home at the same time as she was. Was it possible she didn't know?

Mansfield gave Henry a stiff smile. "Your concern is noted, Dr. Deacon. Dr. Blake, I'll leave this project in your hands. We need answers in forty-eight hours."

Zane, Carter, Allison, and Henry all started to protest as Mansfield put up his hand. "I told you—what this agent had in his head could prevent imminent disaster later. The sooner we have that information, the sooner we can act. Delaying will only make things worse." He nodded to everyone. "And may I remind you to keep this project a secret. Tell no one but me." He left the infirmary.

Carter cleared his throat. "Well . . . that was foreboding."

Graves sighed. "I am sorry about this. The Brain Box wasn't scheduled for practical testing on a deceased case for another month. But apparently whatever it was this agent was working on is very important."

Henry sighed. "I'll say. I haven't seen the general this enthused about anything in a while."

"That's enthusiastic? I'd hate to see bored." Carter moved in closer to Henry. "You said Lucas was in town?"

"Yes. Just arrived this morning." He frowned at Carter. "Why? Something wrong?"

"No—it's just—Zoe didn't seem to know he was coming home."

"I doubt she did." Henry slipped his hands from his pockets. "He called me a few days ago. Seems he's having a few . . . issues at school. Wanted to talk. I doubt he's shared this with anyone."

"Ah," Carter said. "Then maybe he'll call her tonight."

Henry nodded as he reached out and patted Carter's shoulder, then moved to Zane when the young scientist motioned for his attention.

Carter reached up and grabbed the back of his neck. He smiled when he saw Allison watching him. "What?"

"You seem . . . a little frazzled." She gave him a half smile. "Got some time tonight? I need a favor."

"Sure."

"Thanks. Be at my place around seven." She sighed. "But for now, I have a general to reassure." And with that she left the infirmary.

Watching the new guy standing by the box, Carter took a step closer and smiled, but didn't get too close to the box. "So, you come up with this idea? Harvesting memories?"

"No, it was Dr. Fontana's idea," Graves said. "I just thought of a different application."

There was something almost vulnerable about this guy to Carter. The sheriff paid closer attention to him, noting that he was a lot younger than he looked at first glance. Behind his silver-framed glasses, Carter pegged him at around twenty-nine. Give or take a few months. His eyes were gray, sheltered by dark straight brows, and his hair was a light brown and cut in an average FBI coiffure.

He also looked preoccupied as he stared at the box, as if seeing something Carter never would. "What happened to him?"

"The agent?" Graves cleared his throat before he spoke and turned his gray eyes to Carter. "Official report says it was a car accident. Drove his car into an eighteen-wheeler on the way to the airport."

"Did he die instantly?"

Graves looked pale. "Oh, yeah."

"How can we ever be sure of that?"

Graves sighed and looked at the box. "Because he was decapitated."

Pursing his lips, Carter frowned. His stomach soured at the thought of a severed head. "Glad I didn't have that fritter."

CHAPTᵉR 3

"Now, wait a minute," Fargo said after Julia opened the envelope, revealing that Zoe's descriptives and conscious guess at what was in the envelope was right once again. It'd been a large yellow and red dog getting a bath in the yard. "That's what my first one was supposed to be."

"You thought it was a rug," Julia said with a soft look at Fargo.

"Well"—he crossed his arms over his chest—"maybe I was actually viewing the image several down in the stack."

"Maybe you were," Zoe said as she slipped the page back into the envelope.

Café Diem's clientele started shifting toward lunch and Zoe realized she'd been sitting with Julia and Fargo for nearly two hours. She'd identified three out of three of the targets using this method, amazing herself and Julia as well.

Fargo—not so much.

Zoe sighed and grabbed up her towel. "Sorry, guys—but I promised Vincent I'd help, and I've been sitting here the whole time."

"No, no, that's okay," came Vincent's voice from Zoe's left. All three of them leaned out to see the café owner adjusting the suspended screen near the back. He came to them. "It's actually been kind of slow, and what you're doing is like a carnival show. Keeps the customers entertained."

"Carnival show?" Julia bristled. "Vincent, the work of Puthoff and Swann was very important to the noetic science field in this country."

Vincent shrugged and nodded to the counter. "See that freezer? The day I can't find anything in there, I'll try this little method to search for it. But for now"—he pointed to his head—"I'll stick with this."

The bell over the door jingled, and Deputy Lupo stepped in. She waved at Vincent, caught sight of Fargo, Julia, and Zoe, and approached, her thumbs shoved into her utility belt. "Hey—you guys still at it?"

"Oh, yes," Julia said, and motioned Jo closer. "Will you come try it? I'm getting as many test subjects as possible for Dr. Deacon. And I think the wider the variance in subjects, the better."

"Not sure I like the wide variance part, but okay." Jo moved between Fargo and Julia and took up the seat Zoe had vacated.

"Okay, do you remember what we talked about doing this morning with the descriptives and nouns?"

"Yeah, I do." Jo looked at Zoe, frowning. "Hey, when did Lucas get into town?"

"Lucas isn't in town." Zoe sat down in one of the empty seats facing Jo.

"Yeah, he is. I just saw him about an hour ago at the

hardware store." Jo smiled as Vincent brought her a coffee. "He was with some brunette."

Zoe felt her heart plunge to the soles of her feet. She blinked at Jo, not sure she'd heard the deputy sheriff correctly. "You . . . He was with a brunette?"

"Yeah." Jo picked up her coffee and blew over the top but didn't try to drink it. The steam curled up in front of her dark eyes. "She looked familiar—like I'd seen her in town before. I said hi, and both of them waved back at me."

Swallowing, Zoe looked down at the blank sheet of paper Julia had set in front of Jo. She could almost see Lucas's face superimposed on it. Almost. It'd been a few months since they'd actually seen each other—in the flesh. Not images on the computer or voices through a headset. It was like his image was fading from her memory.

"Zoe?" Jo leaned forward across the table and touched her shoulder. "Hey . . . you okay?"

"Yeah . . . sure. . . . Why wouldn't I be?"

"Oh no." The deputy sheriff's eyebrows arched. "You didn't know he was in town? He didn't tell you?"

"He's been . . . busy. We both have." Zoe shook her head. "It's okay. Really. I'll give him a call later, or he'll give me one. You try the View. See how you do at it." She forced a smile and avoided Jo's and Julia's eyes.

"Okay," Jo said softly, and put her hands on the paper. "So how's it going so far?"

Julia answered. "Well, up until Zoe here tried it, we were getting a pretty low score on accuracy."

"Really?" Jo grinned, her rough voice cracking. "Well, my turn." She took up the pencil.

"Okay, Jo, your target is a place."

"A place." Jo looked at the paper. She didn't close her eyes . . . but instead started writing words in a column on the sheet of paper. A very neat column.

Dark.

Musty.
Damp.
Wet.
Earthy.
Brown.
Green.

Then she moved to the right and wrote down *Shovels* before going back to the column.

Dirty.
Eerie.

"I'm not sure that's right. I don't think *eerie* is an adjective."

"Douglas, shush," Julia said.

Old.

Again she moved her hand to the side and wrote *Webs* and moved it back to the column.

"Webs? Like in spider?"

"Douglas . . ." Julia said in a warning voice.

Zoe watched with wide eyes and seemed to get an image in her head before Jo even finished. She knew what it was. Could see it in her mind.

A shed.

Finally Jo looked up, her eyes unfocused, and said, "This is that old shed out near the Burns farm. Sits on top of what they say is an Indian burial mound—but I'm thinking it's really just a pile of debris they used when they built in the new plumbing."

Julia reached out and touched Jo's shoulder.

Jo blinked and sat back and shivered. "Wow . . . that was . . ." She grinned. "Can I look now?"

Julia nodded.

Jo grabbed at the envelope under the paper and carefully opened the top. When she pulled out what looked like a photo to Zoe, Jo's grin widened even more. "Not bad, huh?"

"She cheated," Fargo said as he sat back and crossed his arms over his chest. "There is no way she just waltzed in here and got that right."

"Let me see." Zoe reached for the picture.

There it was.

The same image Zoe had had in her head.

She'd *seen* this, before she even knew it existed. Just as Jo had seen it in *her* head.

Jo crossed her arms over her chest. "Well, Fargo, I did. And guess what—I'd almost guess I went *to* target." She smirked. "Top *that*."

Zoe lowered the photo. "*To* target?"

Julia said, "Phase three of the SRI project? Usually the more gifted psychics in the program were able to do what Puthoff believed was a type of biolocation. They actually found themselves at the target. Or what they called *to* target."

"You did *not* just biolocate," Fargo said.

"Did too."

"Did not."

"Did too."

"Did—"

"Stop it," Julia interjected, and took the photo from Zoe. "Douglas, please. You're sounding like a child."

"Well, how come Jo can not only get it right first time but claim going to target?"

"Psychic abilities do not discriminate against the person," Julia said. "They just are."

Jo nodded. "One of the things the teacher of that class mentioned afterward, when a few of us stayed behind to chat," she began in a low voice, "was that RV could be used in another way. Something pretty scary."

Julia smiled. "You mean RI?"

"Yeah . . . that was about the only time I ever heard of it."

"RI?" Zoe asked, her mind still thinking of the shed, and of Lucas.

"Remote Influencing," Julia said.

"Ah, allow me," Fargo said as he held his hand out. "Puthoff and the others always believed that if a psychic was trained properly and showed the aptitude to continually go to target—it was possible to train them to do it on command."

"Uh-huh." Jo nodded. "I noticed during the class they didn't really do targets as people. And the teacher explained that that had a serious side to it with the application of Remote Influencing."

"You mean"—Zoe frowned—"you can actually *remotely* influence someone? How is that possible? You mean like hypnotic suggestion?"

"In a way. In their sleep," Julia said. "There were groups in the CIA that claimed they'd learned to do this. Claimed they could stand beside the target and not be seen, or know what went on in their target's thoughts." She shook her head. "But nothing was ever proven."

"Were they training people to spy using this?" Zoe looked at Jo, then Fargo, then Julia. "For real?"

Julia shrugged. "I'm not sure if SRI was or the CIA. I'm sure it could be done in theory, but in practical use? I know Dr. Schmetzer ran a project called Helix that was pretty top secret—but then it was canceled. All the third-phase records were locked down in Section Five."

"Why did you take that class?" Zoe asked. "The one you mentioned this morning. I mean . . . doesn't seem like something you'd be interested in."

"I studied everything the military was involved in while I was in Special Forces. This was a military project, no matter how out there it seemed. Always helps to know what your government is doing. But"—she put her hands on the table—"I need to get going." Jo frowned, then motioned to Zoe to follow her. "Hey, come over here for a sec."

Zoe followed the deputy out of the café and into the slightly chilled day. It was fall and the leaves on the trees were orange and brown, littering the café's outdoor tables.

Jo turned and tilted her head to Zoe. "You okay? This isn't about me asking about that brunette, is it?"

Zoe opened her mouth, then closed it as she focused on passing cars, trying very hard not to let her frustrations show on her face. "Jo . . . it's just that ever since we went to different schools . . . it feels like a gap is widening. I mean, yeah, I was afraid the distance would be a factor, but not like this." She finally looked at Jo. "I didn't even know he was in Eureka."

"He didn't tell you?"

"No." Zoe shook her head, realizing she still had her apron on and a towel over her shoulder. "I've e-mailed, tried to get him on videoconference. But when he does answer my e-mail, it's too short or he's busy. I just want to know what's going on."

"Well." Jo reached out and put a firm hand on Zoe's shoulder. "The first thing you've got to work on is trust. You've got to trust that whatever's happening, there is a reason for it. And if he's been distant, you have to trust that he has a reason for that, too. Yeah, it seems unfair he's not telling you what that is right now, but he will. Have faith he's going to contact you."

Zoe shifted her position, a breeze moving her bangs into her eyes. "But what if he doesn't?"

A half smile pulled at the side of Jo's mouth. "Then we do what I'd do to Zane if he shut me out."

"What's that?"

"We shoot him."

Zoe's eyes widened, and Jo started laughing as she pulled away. "No. Just kidding. Talk to him. Give him a day or so 'cause he said he just got into town. See if he calls you. If not, call him. You have to have trust for a relationship to work." She waved and got into her police cruiser.

With a sigh, Zoe turned around and headed back into the café. Vincent was now in the chair and scribbling down descriptives. As Zoe approached, Julia looked up at her and grinned.

"Julia . . . can I help you guys with this? I'd like to learn all I can."

Julia smiled as Fargo shook his head. "No, no, Vincent, that's a noun."

"*Smiley* is not a noun, Fargo."

"Yes, it is."

"No, it's not."

"Is."

"Not."

Julia glanced at the two arguing males and then leaned in close to Zoe. "Oh, please help me. . . ."

CHAPT^eR 4

Carter decided to go by Café Diem before heading into the office. Henry and Allison said it'd be a few hours getting the Brain Box project under way. The twins sat outside on one of the park benches along Archimedes Street as a city worker used some floating-frog-looking gizmo to suck the dead leaves off the sidewalk.

Just as the bell jingled, he heard Fargo's voice. "This isn't possible. That's four out of four."

Midday sun filtered through the front windows of Café Diem's lunch crowd. He spotted Fargo, Julia, Zoe, and a few customers sitting in the back near the fireplace. They'd pulled a bunch of the armchairs together around a single table and chair.

Vincent waved at Carter as he moved past him with a tray full of drinks. "Hey, Sheriff—care for some lunch?"

"No. . . ." He thought about the decapitated head's last memories and touched his middle. "Not . . . really hungry right now." He took in a deep breath and meandered around the eating patrons to the back.

"I have to say, Zoe," Julia was saying as he neared. "You've pretty much set the curve on this. Have you been checked for any latent psychic ability before?"

"Oh, no." Zoe shook her head as she slipped her latest target picture back into its folder and then shuffled the stack around. "I don't really believe in this stuff."

"Hi, Sheriff Carter." Julia waved at him from her seat.

Zoe turned and gave him a wide smile. "Hey, Dad . . . need lunch?"

"Sheriff Carter." Fargo stood up suddenly. "Does the director need me at GD?"

"Ah." Carter shook his head. "No . . . not really, Fargo. Henry and Zane have it all under control."

"Zane?" Fargo's face flushed red. "She called in Zane?"

"Fargo." Carter pointed down. "Sit. Now."

Fargo sat.

"So, Zoe, you're doing pretty good at this mumbo-jumbo? Need to be tested for"—he swallowed—"telepathic ability?" It was really hard to say those words out loud in a serious context. And keep a straight face. Which he did not.

Vincent finished setting down the drinks. "Sheriff, Zoe's a natural at this. And she's not using mumbo-jumbo but a very rigid, scientifically proven regime set aside by experts in the field."

"It's a fluke. There is no way anyone can get all of them right," Fargo muttered.

Vincent straightened. "Right, Fargo. That's because you can't seem to get *any* of them right."

Fargo looked at his drink and pointed. "Hah! Talk about not getting anything right. That's not what I drink."

"That's mine, Fargo," Zoe said as she slid the one beside it closer to him. "That's yours."

He picked it up, sniffed it, and then nodded. "Oh. Yes."

"Aren't you supposed to be, like . . . working?" Vincent asked him.

"Ah, Vincent . . . no." Carter shook his head. "This is exactly where Fargo needs to be." He caught the café owner's eye. "Trust me."

Vincent nodded slowly. "Gotcha. Coffee?"

Carter winked. "Please."

Fargo huffed. "The director will call me if she needs me. She knows I'm helping Henry."

Vincent clasped his tray with both hands in front of his ample middle. "Henry got paged back to GD—but you didn't."

"Shouldn't you be serving someone?" Fargo waved the café owner away as he settled back into his seat.

The bell jingled again, and Carter turned to see Lucas step inside.

Uh-oh. He leaned in close to Zoe's ear and whispered, "Go talk to him."

Only Zoe wasn't listening to him. She was already on her feet, and Carter sighed as he stepped back, giving Julia a helpless expression.

Zoe felt her heart flutter against her chest as Lucas stepped in. She held her breath as she looked at him. The white T-shirt, blue overshirt, and jeans. He looked exactly the way he had the last time she'd seen him.

He stopped just inside and looked around. Seeing Zoe, his eyes widened and he waved and moved closer. "Hey . . . Zoe. I didn't expect to see you here. Didn't know you were home."

Zoe was barely aware that her father had stepped away, or that he was watching her and Lucas. "I told you I was taking a short break. It was in my last e-mail." She maneuvered out from the table and stood a few inches away—she wanted to hug him—but she felt as if he were pushing against her with an invisible wall.

So she stayed in front of the table, holding her towel.

Lucas didn't move, either. Instead he shoved his hands into his pockets and gave her a weak smile. "Oh. Sorry. I don't think I opened it." He looked behind her at everyone. When his eyes saw her dad, they widened. "Hi, Sheriff Carter."

"Hello, Lucas."

Zoe's thoughts replayed what he'd said. He didn't . . . open it? What was that all about? Zoe felt her hope crash down around her as she lowered her gaze. Didn't open her e-mail? How could he say that when she lived to read his e-mails. . . . That was, when he sent them.

Her expression must have given something away because he immediately pulled a hand from his pocket and held it out. "I didn't mean that the way it sounded. I've just been . . ." He shrugged and lowered it. "I've been really busy."

Zoe agreed but kept her gaze averted, very much aware that Vincent, Fargo, Julia, and her dad were intently watching the exchange.

Glancing behind her at them, she moved away, putting a hand on Lucas's arm and leading him from the table to the farthest spot by the counter. When she was sure they were out of hearing distance, she moved back and removed her hand. That brief touch reminded her how much she missed him.

Didn't he miss her, too?

"So . . ." she began. "What brings you into town? I didn't know you were coming, either."

"Oh." He nodded. "I have some things I need to discuss with Henry. Things about my . . . my work. So . . ." He looked around. At anything but her. "So . . ." Then he nodded past her to the table. "What's going on with them?"

"Remote Viewing."

"Really? I've heard about that. Some noetic thing."

"Noetic?"

Lucas grinned, and his demeanor seemed to ease. His shoulders lowered, and he looked a bit more relaxed. It was the old Lucas returning, the one she'd fallen in love with. "It's really kind of a new word on an old science. Noetic science deals with, like, the inner cosmos of the mind. Things like intuition, feeling, reason, and all the senses. Not just the five basic."

"Ah, right, right. Henry talked about that this morning. Wow. . . ." She searched his face. "You really do know this stuff."

His shoulders lowered even farther. "At least I know something. Anyway, Remote Viewing is kinda lumped into that. The Stargate Project back in the seventies."

"Seems everyone knows about it."

"Not a big deal, really. I read somewhere it was canned. Why are Julia and Fargo doing it?"

"Well." She glanced back at them, happy to have something to talk about that didn't seem to make him nervous. "Henry is going to be teaching courses in theoretical science, and after Dr. Blake gave him access to some of the files at GD, he pulled up the research and started looking at it. Figured it'd be a good first class to teach as an introduction."

"Cool." He shrugged, shoving hands in pockets again. "You try it?"

"Yep. Got pretty good at it."

"Really?"

"Uh-huh. Four out of four."

He nodded and then frowned. "I really don't know what

that means. I mean, I know what the theory is behind Remote Viewing, but I don't know how you do it."

"Oh, it's really pretty simple. You just—"

Lucas blinked and held up his hand at that moment before pulling his phone out of his pocket. He touched the screen, frowning. "That's interesting. I'm not scheduled to meet with Henry till tomorrow, but he wants me to come to GD now."

"Oh." Zoe nodded. "Well . . . maybe you should go, then."

"Yeah. . . ." His expression continued to reflect confusion and what Zoe would call apprehension. He smiled at her as he put his phone back in his pocket. "Well . . . you'll have to tell me about it. . . . I'll call you when I'm free. Okay?"

"Sure."

He hesitated as he moved closer to her. Zoe felt her heart sink again as he kissed her on the cheek, moved away, and then was gone with a wave to the others. Zoe stood in her spot a few minutes before turning around.

Julia and Fargo and Vincent had been watching her. But when she turned, they all quickly looked away. Everyone except her dad. He was watching her, his expression sad. Vincent took the tray back to the counter, Julia buried her face in her notes, and Fargo—

Fargo got up and moved straight to her. "Did he get a page to go to GD?"

Zoe blinked. "Well . . . yeah."

"The sheriff, Henry, and even Lucas got pages. Henry uses Zane on whatever it is they're doing. Zane. Not me." He pointed to himself. "I didn't get one. Something's happening and they're leaving me out."

She couldn't help herself as Vincent returned almost immediately with a to-go cup for her dad. Nothing could stop her from saying, "There's probably a button my dad doesn't want you to push." And with that, she turned and moved behind the counter.

Fargo spun around and glared at the sheriff. He smiled, saluted with his coffee, and left the café.

Carter schooled his expression into one of stoic neutrality. Or at least that was what he hoped he looked like as he entered the impressive front gates of Global Dynamics. After leaving Café Diem, he'd met briefly with Jo at the station to go over any other complaints or things that needed his attention. He also asked her to look up anything she could on one Aircom Graves.

Then he'd driven back to GD to check on this Brain Box, which had him more than a bit nervous.

The fact that it was at all related to the time capsule project couldn't be a good thing. Add the general into the mix and the situation had trouble written all over it. That and the fact that they were digging into a dead man's memories.

Allison looked radiant in her gray dress and perfectly combed hair. It shined beneath the lobby's overhead lights, and he found himself returning her smile. "You look happy."

Allison nodded to the back of the retreating general. "Of course I am. I finally convinced Mansfield to just let the boys work. His man's with them. But as long as he was hanging around, hovering, nothing was going to get done. Or at least done easy."

When she frowned, Carter leaned in closer. "There's a *but*?"

"More like a *well*." She shifted her dark gaze to his. "It's like he doesn't trust Graves. I mean, I know it pays to be paranoid as a military officer, but he already said this is Dr. Graves's baby. Let him make it work."

"I don't think Mansfield trusts anyone."

Allison sighed. "Oh well—we've got less than forty-eight hours now. Need to go tell them to hurry it up before he gets back."

She turned and headed to the elevators. Carter followed. "So . . . you're okay with this whole thing?"

"With what?" She pressed a button and moved her key card over a sensor. "The Brain Box?"

"Spying on a man's last memories?"

Allison sighed. "I'm not comfortable with it, no. But the general insists it's a matter of national security." The doors slid open, and she stepped inside as Carter joined her. "And who am I to stand in the way of national anything?" she said as the doors slid shut.

"Guess that's why you didn't page Fargo?"

Allison obviously suppressed a grin. "I thought . . . it was better that Fargo use his time on Henry's teaching project."

Carter smirked. "You didn't want him anywhere near that box, did you?"

"No," she said quickly. "It has buttons." And then she wiped the smile from her face.

Carter listened to the hum of the elevator as they descended.

"So," Allison began. "Why do you have that look on *your* face?"

"What look?"

"That worried-father expression?"

"Oh . . . it's Zoe. And Lucas," He assumed they were heading back to the infirmary, but they missed it by one level. When he followed her out, he realized with a panicked start that he was now in Section Five, and this was the floor with the— "Oh no. . . ." he said, shaking his head. "No, no, no. You moved the box to Tess's lab?"

Allison stopped and looked back at him. "Carter, don't start." She gave him a pained look. "Henry's right, you know. All of what happened before has been taken care of. Dr. Graves is a top-honors biomedical engineer. From Johns Hopkins. He'll be careful."

"Yeah, and how often have I heard that before the sky opens up and there's some quantum, town-eating . . . *thing* threatening to end the world as we know it?"

"Jack . . ."

Carter lowered his hands. "Come on, Allison. Jenna was born in there . . . and we all almost died in there. Hell, you nearly forgot you were having a baby."

"Carter." She arched her eyebrows.

He shoved his hands into his pockets. "What if they all suddenly forget why they're in there and shoot this guy's last memories out into everyone's brain waves?"

She sighed. "Carter, that's just ridiculous. Please? If it'll make you feel better, then come and see what they're doing. Watch them to make sure they don't make any mistakes." She turned and continued on.

"Yeah, like I can make heads or tails of anything they're doing," Carter muttered, and followed her into the lab.

Tall gray doors slid to the sides as Allison preceded him in. Henry was there, talking with Dr. Graves in the far corner. Zane sat near the box, which was now decorated in an array of wires. Carter was a little surprised to see Lucas in front of a monitor, his eyebrows knitted together in concentration.

He looked up, saw Carter, and smiled. "Hi, Sheriff Carter. Again."

"Hi, Lucas. Taking a break from school?" He wanted to say, *Why are you making my daughter upset? Because if she's upset, then I'm upset, and I can be a very difficult opponent.* But he didn't. Just wasn't . . . appropriate. Yet.

"Yeah."

"Don't bother him, Carter," Henry piped up. "He's busy."

Carter opened his mouth and then closed it. Well. Yeah. Everyone looked busy.

Allison approached Henry and Dr. Graves. The younger man's frown turned up at the sight of her. Graves's attention focused on her, making Carter feel like—garnish.

Carter looked at Allison.

She, too, kept looking at Graves with more than a scientist's curiosity.

"So how's the dead guy coming along?" Carter blurted out.

Henry glanced at him and looked back at his monitor. But Dr. Graves gave Carter a polite smile. "Dr. Deacon and Zane figured out what I was missing."

"Oh?" Allison said.

"Actually it was Lucas," Zane voiced as he stood and came over to them, a white, flat tablet in his hands. He set it on the side table as a screen was projected in front of them. None of the symbols made sense. Carter moved around to stand behind Henry to get a better look.

Nope. Still looked like Greek from that angle, too.

"Originally, the storycatchers worked on the wireless connection through the optic nerves," Zane said. "Voice was the trigger mechanism, and the device translated the synaptic impulses into data that could be downloaded into the story matrix."

Carter nodded. "Yeah, yeah, I got that. People talked, and those little globes recorded."

Dr. Graves moved forward and touched a few keys on Zane's pad. The images shifted to a split screen. The right side looked like a series of ones and zeroes. The other half looked like some weird jumble-up of the alphabet. "The one on the left is what the data looks like from the storycatchers, translated by the matrix. The one on the right is what we got from our subject's final synaptic signals. Because I didn't have direct access to the storynest created by Dr. Fontana, I wrote my own code, streamlining it to fit the parameters needed for the Brain Box."

Carter frowned and turned his head sideways.

"You got that, Carter?" Henry looked back at him.

He nodded. "Uh . . . well . . . Uh, no."

Allison smiled. "Basically Dr. Graves wrote his own proprietary software—saved the data in a format that was faster and easier for it to deliver. It's not working"—she looked at Henry and then at Graves—"because the translator built into the storynest can't read the data."

Henry spoke up. "It's like trying to translate Greek with a Spanish translator. The two can't communicate."

"Precisely," Graves said.

Lucas stood and moved quickly to them, excusing himself as he slipped between Allison and Dr. Graves. He pressed another button. "Binary is the basic code originally used."

"I know that," Carter said. "Ones and zeroes. Just like in the *Matrix* movie."

Everyone glanced at him and then looked back at the monitor as Lucas continued. "But Graves's code is a strange combination of Greek and some structure I'm not familiar with."

Graves narrowed his eyes as he looked at the data. "Maori."

Everyone looked at him. "What?" Henry said. "You mean like the Maori people?"

"I . . . Yeah. The syntax on the reinterpretation is based on the Maori dialect."

"You speak that language?" Zane asked as he looked at Graves.

"Yeah. . . . My mother was Maori."

"You're from New Zealand?" Allison asked.

"No, I'm from Connecticut." Graves smiled. "But my mom was from New Zealand. But now that we know the syntax error—which is something I did subconsciously and never really understood it till now—"

"I can rewrite the translator program," Lucas said. "I can do that!" And he hurried back to his station.

Graves started to join Lucas, but Henry put a hand on his shoulder. "Let him do it, Air," he said in a low voice. "He needs to."

Carter watched the conversation between the two, catching Henry's unspoken innuendo concerning Lucas. More going on there than Carter knew. But he also noticed the look on Graves's face. It wasn't one of elation . . . not the face of a scientist who was now closer to achieving his goal. That look said he'd seen enough in this place.

No, Graves looked . . . worried.

About what?

That the translator still wouldn't work?

Or that it would?

CHAPT^eR 5

Most of what Henry, Zane, Lucas, and Graves talked
about clearly moved over Carter's realm of understanding.
He got the basics—the box had a dead man's memories and
Lucas was nearly finished rewriting whatever it was that
would allow Mansfield to see what those memories were.

Which was just . . . *creepy.*

And just felt morally . . . wrong on some levels.

Not to mention, Carter was already on edge being back
in this room with the storynest matrix operated—the same
room where he, Allison, and Zoe might have died from Dr.
Kennison's sonic sterilization because everyone had lost
their memories on how to turn the system off.

Henry and Allison assured him what they were doing
now wouldn't affect the town. But still . . . this was Eureka . . . and even though Fargo wasn't involved this time—

Carter really didn't want to take chances.

The door to the lab slid open and Allison stepped in, her

expression filled with determination. She smiled at Carter and moved to stand beside him. "How's it going?"

He gave her a half smile. "You're asking me?" Carter shrugged. "Lucas is almost finished." He nodded to the young man sitting at the matrix station where the Brain Box had been connected. Lucas had donned a black headband with small amber lights that pulsed against his temples. Carter pointed to him and leaned in close to Allison. "Are you sure that's not gonna cause a problem?"

Allison put a hand on his upper arm. "Will you stop being so paranoid?"

"That's my job."

"Okay, well, then think of something else." She turned to face him. "Tell me what you were thinking about earlier—the thing that gave you that long face. It was about Zoe?"

Carter nodded randomly and shrugged. "She's going through . . . uh, emotional stuff." He pushed his hands into his pants pockets. "Oh, you know . . . girl things."

"You mean boys? As in Lucas?"

Carter turned his head slowly and looked at her. "Yeah. This whole thing with her at Harvard and him at MIT—"

"That's something *they* need to work out, Carter." Allison's smile widened, but he saw the concern in her dark eyes. "You can't fix that for them. They need to learn to trust each other—being separated like that. It's going to be hard. But if they succeed, then the relationship will be stronger." She paused and looked at her hands. "Kinda like you and Tess."

He started. "Me and Tess?"

"Yeah . . . you here and her in Australia? I'm sure the two of you have to trust each other, right?"

"Well . . . yeah . . . but . . ." He pursed his lips, stopped, shrugged, and frowned back at Allison. "What do Tess and I have to do with Zoe and Lucas?"

Allison almost answered, until she saw Dr. Graves

move away from his station. Carter watched him as well, studying his face, his body language. Graves moved past them and stepped out of the lab.

Allison put a hand on Carter's arm. "I'll be back. Think I might need to do a little of my job."

"Your job?"

"Mediating. I don't think Dr. Graves is really happy about all this."

"About what he's doing?"

"Not really sure."

Carter didn't quite agree with that assessment but nodded as she followed him out of the lab. He sighed and strolled, hands still in pockets, to Henry and Zane and stood behind them.

After a few minutes Henry spoke up. "You don't have to hover, Carter."

"Naw . . . I know. It's just that . . . the last time this machine was on . . ."

"I know," Henry said. "I already told you—nothing like that will happen again. We've got a whole new set of protocols in place."

"You keep saying that," Carter said. "But I still have this hinky feeling."

Zane grinned but kept his gaze on the screen. "Hinky? It's all good. I've been going over Dr. Graves's research. Good stuff here. I'm amazed at how he was able to convert the optic retrieval to a straight synaptic harvest. I had to adjust the headset to reinterpret that as well." He waved over at Lucas. "You getting the test feed?"

Lucas looked over at them, his eyes unfocused. He blinked a few times and then smiled. "Yeah . . . it's working great. What was that anyway?"

"That"—Zane smiled—"was a very fond memory of mine from my eighth-grade science fair—where I took home first place."

"Yeah . . ." Lucas agreed. "But your scientific method wasn't even close to sound—and when you actually used that—oh my God—you cheated!"

Zane glanced over at him. "No, I didn't."

Carter looked at Zane's face and grinned as he pointed at the younger man. "Oh yes, you did—look at your face."

Zane closed his mouth and frowned. "Well . . . that was a long time ago. And besides . . ." He looked back at Lucas. "How did you know I cheated?"

Lucas pulled the headset off. "Part of the memory had bits of you building it. I could see what you were doing—and I kinda knew what you were thinking."

Henry looked up. "What do you mean, you knew what he was *thinking*?"

"Random thoughts. Ones that weren't mine. I could sense or I kinda knew the project was important, and that he had to impress Melissa . . ." He frowned. "Brubaker?"

Zane cleared his throat. "Okay . . . that's enough. In fact, that's a total upset on the TMI. You weren't supposed to get that in-depth on the emotional level."

Henry stood and moved to look at Zane's screen. "Well, I'll be. . . . Graves really has put something together that's unique. If it's possible to not only see the memory, but to experience the emotion with it?"

"What does that mean?" Carter looked from Zane to Henry.

"The storycatcher's means of recording memories was based on words translated into images. Very superficial because it's hard to program a recorder to translate the nuances in human speech. The feelings and inflections from anger to sadness. So you get a straight one-dimensional visual playback." Henry grinned. "But what Graves was able to do was to make that two-dimensional. Zane took a memory he'd recorded previously on the storycatcher and fed it through Lucas's translator—and he got the emotion backing the experience."

"But . . ." Carter arched his eyebrows. "Wouldn't that be more of a kudo for Lucas since he created the translation?"

Henry blinked. "Carter . . . you're right. You're absolutely right." He turned and nodded to Lucas. "Good job. Very good job."

Lucas looked slightly embarrassed.

Carter leaned closer to Henry. "But really, this doesn't sound all that good."

"On the contrary, Carter, it's fascinating."

"Not if you're talking about experiencing the last emotional experiences of a dead guy. That's just . . ." He shivered. "Creepier than before."

"Perhaps." Henry straightened and looked at Lucas. "You ready to test the data from the Brain Box?"

Lucas put the headset back on.

"I suggest just a small piece of the data to test. Zane." He turned and leaned over the younger man's shoulder. "Take"—he pointed at the illuminated screen—"that section there. Copy that and apply it to Lucas's translator." He patted Zane's shoulder. "I'm going to go find Graves."

Carter watched as Henry left the lab. This was so important that Henry had to leave just before an experiment? What was going on?

Zane nodded. "You ready, Lucas?"

"Yep."

Carter winced. It suddenly felt like the quiet before the boom.

He was already upstairs near the edge of the rotunda, his cell pressed to his ear. He spoke in soft tones, and Allison realized it wasn't English. A little closer and she caught the slight rise in his voice. She didn't know Maori, but she was pretty sure that loud talking translated into anger no matter what language.

When he shut the phone and shoved it into his pocket, she approached. "Dr. Graves?"

He turned. His expression shifted from irritation to relief. "Ah . . . Dr. Blake."

She moved near him. "You okay?"

Graves nodded, though she could tell from the expression that *okay* wasn't how he was at all. "Family troubles. Nothing that important. Was there something you needed to see me about?"

"Hey!" Henry half jogged out of the elevator and approached.

Allison looked at him. "Everything okay, Henry?"

He caught his breath. "Yes . . . I just wanted to show Dr. Graves something." He handed the young man his white tablet. "Look at those lower readings."

She watched Graves read the information. His expression grew more conflicted. Darker. Sadder.

Graves handed the tablet back to Henry. "That's . . . amazing."

"Are you sure you're okay, Dr. Graves? You seem a bit tense." Allison leaned her head to the right, trying to get a better look at his face.

"I just need some air, that's all."

"What is it?" She turned to Henry.

"Dr. Graves's work on the harvesting collection apparently collects thoughts, as well as emotions."

"You're serious?" She took the tablet when he offered it to her. Allison glanced over the paragraphs, read the results. "This is . . ."

"It's terrible," Graves said in a small voice.

She looked at Henry before turning back to Graves. "We need to talk, Dr. Graves."

Henry and Graves followed her up the stairs to the second floor of the rotunda and into her office. A wide floor-to-ceiling window looked out over the rotunda below.

He seemed so much younger now. No lines on his smooth face. At first glance, Aircom Graves seemed average, a face and demeanor that would disappear into a crowd. An all-American look that spoke of block parties in rural suburbs.

But there was something else about him, something Allison sensed that was much older. Wiser. Something very . . . sad.

Henry sat on one of the nearby couches, the tablet in his lap.

Graves moved to the window and looked down. He removed his glasses and folded them, carefully tucking them into the left breast pocket of his shirt. Rubbing the bridge of his nose, he sighed as she moved to stand beside him. "With all the work you do here, Dr. Blake—are you ever afraid that what you accomplish . . . will be used for the wrong reasons?"

Henry sighed. "You have no idea, Dr. Graves. I almost quit for that very reason. Wanted to leave Eureka because we'd become a place for results and not for discoveries."

Graves glanced over at Henry. "But you stayed."

"Yes, I did."

Allison smiled and leaned on the waist-level banister. "Aircom, I don't think there's a scientist alive that doesn't wonder that periodically. And here . . . more than that." She watched him, again amazed at how different he looked when he seemed to let his Clark Kent persona drop. "This incident has you doubting yourself? Or is it doubting the validity of the project?"

"When I was nine," Dr. Graves said as he leaned his elbows on the railing, looking at the rotunda. "My sister and I were out. I was playing baseball, in the park in my hometown, near the house. My sister was nearby with her friends, talking. Dad was away, Mom was home. And we were late leaving the park. We didn't want to go home and eat Brussels sprouts." He smiled. "But then there was something gnawing at me. Something was wrong . . . and I suddenly *knew* it. I *knew* . . ."

Allison shifted as she watched him.

"You knew?" Henry prompted. "You mean you had a premonition?"

"I yelled at my sister and took off for the house. I . . . never did know what it was that told me to go home. But when we got there . . . the front door was busted down. The place had been trashed. TV gone, stereo, VCR, everything. And my mom was—"

She put a hand to her mouth as she realized what he was saying. "Oh God. . . . Air, I'm so sorry."

"My sister fell apart. She and Mom had argued that morning over what she'd been wearing. They'd yelled pretty . . . nasty things at each other. I sort of pushed it all aside and called 911. Let the cops and paramedics in. And at that point I became fascinated with lifesaving. With what they were doing—that even though I knew it was hopeless, *they* still held hope. But she'd been stabbed with a kitchen knife, and there was blood everywhere."

He took in a deep breath, and Allison waited patiently.

"They never caught whoever did it. And I watched my sister's depression worsen. I wanted to help her—and I always wanted justice for Mom. For Dad. They never really got over it. So I finished prep school at Phillips Andover, then went into medical school, took a part-time job as an EMT, and worked in biology. Got into Johns Hopkins, was fascinated with biomedical engineering, and was recruited into the CIA a few years ago. Family recommendation."

Allison felt her heart move as she listened to him, felt she now understood him a little bit better.

"This was one of the reasons you conceived the idea of the Brain Box," Henry said.

Graves nodded, staring at the lobby but not really seeing it. He reached up and ran his fingers through his thick hair. "I saw . . . what Dr. Fontana had done with the time capsule project . . . the catchers and harnessing the memories."

"And you thought of a more constructive purpose for them?"

Graves turned then, his dark eyes wide, and looked at Henry. "No . . . not more constructive. The idea of the storycatcher is incredible, and what Fontana accomplished shouldn't be trivialized. What I wanted to do was somehow apply it to helping mankind on another level."

"To find murderers," Allison said, remembering what he'd said before.

"I originally wanted to use the concept to find murderers, yes. To somehow let the victim speak from the grave. Eyewitness accounts?" He shook his head. "They're just not reliable. The only real witness to any crime or murder is the one committing the crime, and the victim." He sighed, and his eyes were no longer wide, but dark and sad. "I wanted to find a better way to justice."

Allison frowned. "What else is bothering you?"

"Pick one. . . ." He shrugged. "I'm not so sure. I guess this is how most scientists feel . . . when they create something. Anything good can be used for evil. Like when Shakespeare said there is nothing either good or bad in the world, but thinking makes it so."

"The fact that it may be possible to also know the emotions behind the victim's last memories," Henry said. "That bothers you."

"Wouldn't it bother you?" Graves arched his brows as he stared at Henry. "Have you ever lost someone precious to you, Dr. Deacon? So precious that the very thought of knowing what went through their mind, what they were thinking, how they were feeling, was something you did"—he paused—"and didn't want to know?"

Allison watched as Henry set the tablet on the couch and stood. He moved slowly to Graves and stood in front of him. "Yes. I have. So I can understand what you're feeling. I *would* want to know their emotions." He glanced over at Allison and she put her hands to her mouth, thinking of Kim, Henry's deceased wife. "But I'm not sure I'd want total strangers to know. Or see."

Graves hung his head. "Even if you were afraid the memory . . . could reveal things that shouldn't be shown in the light of day?" He sighed. "Sorry. I'm . . . conflicted. And I shouldn't let this interfere with my job."

Allison pursed her lips as she looked down at the people below, thinking about what they were each thinking. "Dr. Graves—"

"Please . . . call me Air."

"Air." She tilted her head to the side to look at him. She thought of Nathan and fondled the diamond around her neck, careful not to set off the holographic recording of himself Nathan had had set inside the jewel's matrix. She, too, had wondered what his last memories were, and his emotions. She wanted to believe they were about her. To know otherwise, or for others to see?

No. "Did your mother give you that name?"

He smiled, and for the first time she thought she saw him relax. "It's a smashup of my mom's Maori family name and my dad's Irish roots. Mixing up Eire from Ireland and Aotearoa, which is New Zealand. The *com* part comes from Cimbrius or the Compatriot, the Mercury-like god of speed. So you come up with *Air* and *Com*."

Allison nodded. "Land of the clouds. Yes . . . I know. I visited New Zealand with my—" And she faltered, her thoughts focusing hard on Nathan for that instant. The two of them touring the beautiful countryside of New Zealand, during their first marriage.

"Dr. Blake?" Graves was facing her now, his eyes wide again.

She shook her head and blinked rapidly, pushing back the emotion putting pressure behind her eyes. "Please . . . call me Allison. And it's okay." She glanced at Henry. "Henry and I both understand how you feel. . . . We do."

"You both lost someone, too."

"Yes." She took in a deep breath. "But . . . the situations are different. And for now, the use of your device is apparently paramount to security. So for the moment, maybe, we don't have to point out the emotional context of the results."

Graves made a snorting noise and looked away. "National security—what does that mean anymore? You can couch anything in that to justify poking your nose where it doesn't belong."

"You don't believe Mansfield?"

"Never believe the military, Allison," he said, and his expression turned hard. He suddenly looked older. "Things are never what they seem."

"You got that right," Henry mumbled.

Allison opened her mouth to answer but was stopped when her pager went off. She pulled it from her pocket and looked at the tiny screen. "They're ready for a test." She smiled as they turned and started back to the elevator. "I'm sure Carter's happy Fargo isn't near a button."

CHAPTER 6

"This thing's not going to broadcast a dead guy's memories all over the town, is it? And we're sure Fargo's a million miles away?"

Zane reached out and took up a tablet from the right of the console. He tapped the screen several times. "No buttons, Sheriff, and no broadcasting. I'm not sure how many times we have to say that."

"Until I stop waiting for the boom."

Zane looked up at Carter through furrowed brows.

But Carter held up a hand. "Ah . . . don't you look at me with that tone. Nothing ever goes the way it's planned in Eureka."

"Well, you're right about that. But understand, Sheriff. This is a closed system. And Henry's made sure Fargo is more than occupied." Zane frowned as he watched the screen on the tablet.

Carter crossed his arms over his chest.

When Zane stopped talking Carter looked over at him, then glanced down at the tablet Zane was holding. "What?"

Zane's frown deepened. "Well, there's a classified file waiting in the mail queue—and it looks like it's addressed to Henry. It's about the Remote Viewing stuff."

Carter lowered his arms and shoved his hands into his pockets as he leaned toward Zane. "And?"

Zane looked up at Carter, but the sheriff was pretty sure the scientist wasn't really seeing him. "Oh, it's nothing. I just didn't expect anything in Schmetzer's notes to be designated Priority Red."

"Priority Red?"

"Yeah." Zane sighed. "When files are redacted—or sometimes just sealed—they're usually given a priority label. Lets the archives know where to file it. Blue, Green, Yellow—and Red. The more serious ones or important ones are labeled Priority Red."

"Zane, if there's a problem with what they're doing in the café, I need to know."

Zane looked at Carter. "Oh, no . . . no. Nothing on what they're doing. This is something in Schmetzer's notes and his project. I'll forward this on to Henry. Might be better to give him a call on it." He reached into his pocket and pulled out his phone.

Carter pointed at it. "That's not gonna work down here, remember? Wanna try the pager?"

"Oh . . . you're right." Zane replaced his cell and then took out the small, flat, silver PDA.

Carter stood between Zane and Lucas when Graves, Henry, and Allison stepped back into lab 511. He noticed their expressions and wondered what the three had talked about. Graves looked even younger without his glasses— really no older than Lucas.

Graves moved around to stand beside Lucas as Zane

signaled Henry over, and the three of them talked in hushed voices.

Carter looked over at Allison. "You guys okay?" he said in a low voice.

"We're fine. Just needed to air out a few things," she said.

Carter glanced back at Graves. "*Air* out?"

"Drop it, Carter," Allison said sharply, though the half smile on her lips told him she wasn't all that irritated with him.

"Okay," Zane said as he moved from his station to the storynest terminal. "Lucas, you ready?"

Lucas nodded, the halo still in place.

"Ah . . . you're sure this is safe, right?" Carter said.

"Don't worry, Carter." Allison gave him a no-nonsense glance. "We've taken every precaution. What could go wrong?"

"Oh, I wish you hadn't said that." Carter winced.

Graves looked over at Carter. "Is it really that bad?"

Carter arched his eyebrows. "You don't know the half of it."

"That's enough, Carter," Allison said.

Zane spoke up. "Lucas's translation app will spool it through the halo so that Lucas will see the images from the subject's point of view."

Allison looked at Lucas. "Let's do this."

Zane reached out and tapped a key.

The lights went out.

"See?" Carter said in the dark.

"Zane?" Allison said. "That wasn't funny."

Zane laughed to himself and the lights came back on. "Sorry. . . . I really couldn't help myself."

"Zane," Henry said in a scolding voice.

"Not funny," Carter said as he shook his head at Zane.

Zane held up his hands. "Okay. Bad joke. Let's do this again. Ready, Lucas?"

"Just hit the switch," the young man said.

"Here we go." Zane hit the key again.

Carter watched as the numbers and symbols on the screen tumbled back and forth and then disappeared one by one. He looked over at Lucas. His eyes were closed, his brow furrowed in concentration.

"Spooling complete," Zane said.

Abruptly Carter heard a snapping noise from somewhere and the overheads went out.

Allison gave a very angry sigh. "Zane—"

"That wasn't me," Zane said in the dark. "I'm not doing it this time."

A brilliant arc of blue-white light illuminated Lucas. Carter yelled out for everyone to take cover as sparks lit up the dark from the console where Lucas had been sitting. Within seconds, GD's backup system kicked in and the lights came back on.

Lucas was sprawled several feet away from the desk, which was now sparking and smoking. Carter ran to the young man and pulled the halo from his head. The amber lights had left two burned marks on the flesh, and Lucas wasn't moving.

Leaning down as Allison came to the opposite side, Carter pressed his ear to Lucas's chest. "We need help over here!" He tilted Lucas's head back to clear the airway, leaned in and breathed air into the boy's lungs, then sat back and started compressions on his chest.

Carter expected Henry to appear beside Allison—being the town's leading medical doctor. Instead Dr. Graves appeared, his expression calm as he bent over Lucas. "Dr. Deacon, do you have—"

But Henry was already there as Allison moved out of the way. He handed Dr. Graves the patches of an automated external defibrillator. Carter yanked Lucas's shirt open, exposing his chest. Dr. Graves went up on his knees and pressed the sticky electrode patches on the two vital areas. He looked back at the portable's monitor, watching the readout. "Clear!"

Carter sat back as Graves pressed the switch that sent the charge to the patches. Lucas's body jumped, and abruptly he was gasping for air, flailing his arms, and blinking.

Graves reached out to grab Lucas's face. "Lucas, look at me. I need you to look at me. Who am I?"

Lucas blinked rapidly before answering. "You're Dr. Graves. . . ."

"Where are you?"

"Global . . . lab . . . five one one. . . ."

"And who are you?"

"Lu-lucas . . ." He stopped moving around and breathed in slower, watching Graves. "I . . . What happened?"

"That's what I'd like to know," Graves said as he sat back and glanced over at Henry. "It looked like a feedback concussion."

Henry nodded just as Zane spoke up from Lucas's sparking console. "That's not exactly what it was."

"Then what was it?"

Carter looked at Graves. "I told you. Boom."

Zane shook his head but kept his gaze fixed on the screen in front of him. "I'm not sure yet."

Henry moved closer to Lucas. "You were knocked backward—can you remember what happened? Did you see anything?"

Lucas pushed himself up on his elbows to look at everyone. "No . . . I was waiting for the images . . . There was a second of light, and then . . ." He looked at Graves. "I saw you."

"Me?" Graves put a hand on his chest.

"Yeah, only I felt angry at you. And you were yelling back."

Henry stood. "Lucas, I'm going to need you to come with me to the infirmary."

Graves stood as Carter moved up and offered Lucas his hand. Lucas took it and stood, albeit a bit shaky. "But I'm fine."

"I'll be the judge of that." Henry nodded to Carter. "I'll check him out while Zane and Dr. Graves figure out what the hell just happened."

"Oh God . . ." Lucas said as he saw the smoking console. "I'm so sorry, Dr. Deacon. I did it again. . . . Nothing I do works. . . ."

"Stop it, Lucas," Henry said as he put a hand on the boy's shoulder. "This wasn't anything *you* did. You have got to trust yourself. Let's go. They can take care of this."

Carter watched as the two left lab 511 and then turned to Allison, his mouth open.

She put a finger up in his face to shush him. "Not one word." Turning, she moved to Zane and Graves, who were huddling over Lucas's station.

Sighing, Carter joined them and stood to the side.

The monitor was up and working, with a stream of readouts moving at lightning speed—faster than Carter could keep up with. Not that he understood any of it, but it looked important.

Abruptly the screen stopped and the symbols looked . . . broken.

Zane pointed. "What the hell is that?"

Graves leaned in closer. "Was that there before?"

"Hey, this is your harvest data, dude. I don't remember seeing it."

"Can I drive?"

Zane slipped out of his seat. Graves sat down, pulled his glasses from his pocket, and put them on. His fingers flew

over the keys as he pulled up several windows, all of the
text written in a code. "Looks like the translator skipped
something here. . . ."

"Could that have caused the feedback?" Allison said.

"I'm not sure. . . ." He looked at her over his glasses.
"I'll need to go back over the data, analyze each piece."

"Good." She straightened. "You two do that. I'm going to finish up in my office, call the general to fill him
in." She held up her hand as both Graves and Zane opened
their mouths to speak. "I'm not going to fill him in on
everything—just that we're making progress . . . sort of."
She turned to Carter. "Want to come with me to check on
Lucas? I'm sure Zoe will be asking you questions when
you go by Café Diem to pick up dinner."

Carter watched her walk away, frowning. With a glance
at the two men who were now back at the console, he left
the lab with her. "Dinner?"

"My house? Tonight? I need a favor and since the kids
are at a sitter's, I'm not cooking."

Carter stopped a few feet from the elevator. "Kids . . .
are with a sitter?"

"Yes, Carter." She frowned at him as she ran her key
card over the door. "You afraid to be alone with me?"

"Well . . . I . . . uh . . ." He shoved his hands into his
pockets. "Yeah, let's go check on Lucas."

"That machine has never given me fits before,"
Vincent protested as Zoe and Julia examined his hands.
Only minutes before, one of the toasters had shorted out,
sending a blue arc in Vincent's direction and zapping him
to the floor.

A few lights had also sparked as the café lost power for
a few seconds and the backup generators kicked in, and
several patrons got minor if not uncomfortable jolts.

"Well . . . looks like it was just some sort of power surge," Zoe said as she grinned at him. "You'll be fine."

Vincent returned her smile. "You really will make a great doctor, Zoe."

She and Julia moved back to the table where Fargo sat on his knees looking out the front window at the stopped traffic. "Whatever it was took the smart asphalt offline, too."

"Wonder what happened," Julia said as she slid down next to Fargo.

Zoe did a quick check to make sure everyone was okay before she sat down facing Fargo and Julia to continue the conversation they'd been having before the surge.

"Zoe . . ." Julia pursed her lips. "What you're asking—that's not really why we're doing this. That's like several phases beyond what Dr. Deacon wants to do."

"Oh wow," Fargo said. "There's, like, a traffic jam out there."

Julia swatted at his leg and he turned around and sat facing out.

Zoe nodded as stranded passengers—unsure if and when their cars would start again—filtered into the café for a snack or dinner.

She'd offered to help Vincent while she was home—and she really wanted to and felt guilty for not getting up to greet them as they came in—but this Remote Viewing was so . . . fascinating. And she was apparently good at it. She didn't want to stop trying.

Luckily Pilar had stopped by and offered to help Vincent after failing twice at Remote Viewing.

"Look," Zoe said. "I just want to try it. How bad can it be if Jo knew about it?"

"Zoe . . ." Fargo said. "Jo knew about it because she was Special Forces. Even if I believed in it—Remote Influencing is on the border of mind control. It's just . . ." He shrugged. "Silly."

"Yeah," Julia said, and leaned in closer over the table. "Let's just stick to RV, okay? You've already got a perfect score. I've got a few more envelopes you haven't tried."

Zoe pursed her lips at Julia and nodded, though her mind was on something else. She took one of the closed envelopes and set it under her paper, then took up her pencil. Seriously . . . did she have to actually View what was in the envelope?

Would her mind just automatically go to it because now she'd trained it to?

Or could she actually choose her own target?

It seemed half the point of this exercise was to identify a hidden target—so what if she tried a nonhidden target?

She knew Lucas was at GD, working. She knew he was in town. And she knew . . . well . . . *him*.

Enough that she knew something was bothering him and she wanted to know what it was. Yeah, Jo had said Lucas would tell her when he was ready, but Zoe needed answers right away. She hated *not* knowing.

And if RV was a way of knowing a thing—then why not pick a target herself and look inside that?

Was that how RI worked?

"Zoe?"

She blinked, not realizing she'd been staring at the blank paper. "Sorry. . . . Started daydreaming."

"Well, your target is a thing," Julia said.

Zoe knew that was a trigger, so she closed her eye and gave herself a new trigger, saying silently to herself, *Your target is Lucas.*

Lucas.

Lucas is the target.

Lucas—

Something flashed through her mind—just like before when she'd seen the shed. It was clear, and then it was gone.

She wrote down *hairy* and *brown*.

The she waited.

Lucas.

Another flash—a smile?

Teeth. But that was a noun, so she wrote it to the side.

New images came. Blowing hair, a breeze, sunlight in her face, a woman smiling at her, and the words *I love you*.

"Who the hell is that?" she said out loud, and at a volume she didn't realize till she looked around and noticed others staring at her.

Zoe looked down at the paper and her jaw dropped.

There was a soft image of a woman's face, from the side, looking at her. Smiling. Her short list of adjectives to the right.

"I didn't know you could draw," Fargo said as he took the paper and looked at it.

Julia took it from him and then looked at it. "That's a nice image—but who is it?"

"I don't—" Zoe blinked several times. "I don't know who it is."

"Why did you write"—Julia frowned—"*I love you* down at the bottom?"

"I did?" She snatched the paper away and looked. And there it was . . . in her own handwriting.

I love you.

Fargo grabbed the envelope and opened it. He slid the image out, facing him, and then grinned. "Ha! Not a perfect record! You got hairy and brown right—but you didn't get what this was right."

He turned to show her the pictures of a little brown kitten.

She didn't smile, her mind still flashing back to the images. The wind, sunlight, her smile.

I love you.

"Zoe . . ." Julia said as she took the paper again.

"I—I need to go help Vincent." She snatched the paper from Julia and stood, grabbing up her towel and moving to the counter. She vanished into the pantry and stood just inside, trying to catch her breath.

What . . . what had just happened? The images she'd seen were nearly as clear as the one of the shed. She could almost smell the air. . . . It was crisp and cold. And she thought she'd seen snow.

North.

It could have been Boston.

It could have been . . . MIT.

Could I . . . She put a hand on the side of the door. She'd been thinking of him. Targeting him. Trying to see into her target. Trying to . . . *Could I have been seeing Lucas . . . with another woman?*

CHAPTER 7

Lucas was already looking better by the time Carter and Allison arrived in the infirmary. Henry had him on the main diagnostic table and was standing beside him. The two were talking quietly as Allison stepped up. Carter moved to the opposite side just as his phone beeped. He had six messages waiting and an incoming call from Jo. With a wave he moved to the side. "Carter."

"Well, hello there."

"Jo?" Carter sighed. "You knew I was down in Section Five—you could have just called through the main GD switchboard."

"Wasn't too bad of an emergency—and I figured you were having sooo much fun."

"Yeah, a blast. What's up?"

"There was some kind of glitch on the grid about a half hour ago—shut down the smart asphalt and left a lot of people stranded. There have been complaints coming in from all over. Traeger's automatic mowers took out the flower beds by the courthouse, and all the mimetic dogs are meowing like cats."

Carter made a noise. "The dogs are acting like cats?"

Henry and Allison gave him a strange look.

Jo continued. "A lot of people were zapped by their televisions or their phones."

"Zapped? What do you mean, zapped?"

"Like a little electric charge." Jo sighed. "I got one, too—not scrious but annoying. But because some of the areas are still getting the backup generators to work, Mansfield's little army is coming in and taking control."

"What? What're they doing?"

"They're coming in and taking control, Carter. It's a zoo out here and they're establishing order."

"Zoo? You said it wasn't an emergency."

"It's not. That's why Mansfield is here."

Carter glanced over at the others. Allison was watching him, frowning. "So . . . what exactly are they doing?"

"They're out there now getting cars started, giving rides to stranded people. . . . And they're in the café now working on Vincent's espresso machine."

He tried really hard not to laugh. "Jo . . . it sounds like they're helping—not taking over. Don't you think you sound a bit paranoid?"

"I'm serious. . . ."

"Okay, then I'll do what I can from here, okay? You keep an eye on them and call me back if you see anything suspicious."

"This whole town is suspicious."

"Jo . . ."

"Okay, okay."

Carter disconnected and rejoined the others as all eyes looked at him. He smiled. "Apparently the little whatever-that-was affected the town's power. Smart asphalt system is down and a few electric devices gave people some shocks . . . and the dogs are meowing."

"So I heard," Allison said, half smiling.

Henry nodded. "I'm not surprised. The town's power grid is directly linked to GD's generator. The whole town itself works like a neural network. Do you need to go?"

"Apparently Mansfield's people are . . ." Carter smiled. *"Helping."*

"Good."

"No, not good—that means he's going to be in my hair in about two minutes," Allison said. She nodded to Lucas. "How's he doing?"

"I'm fine."

"That's not a call for you to make, Lucas," Henry said.

Carter noticed that Henry had a tablet in his hand and was touching the screen. A similar image appeared on a projection hologram over Lucas's head. "Everything checks out—on a diagnostic level. Synaptic firing . . . all working. EKG, normal. Blood work, normal."

"But?"

Henry looked at Allison. "His temperature's just a little elevated."

"I told you, I'm fine . . . and I want to go back to work. Please? I need to . . ." Lucas looked down at his hands. "I need to fix it."

"Fix what?" Carter said with a shrug. "From what I know—" He put a hand to his chest. "And you know I don't know that much about it—you didn't do anything to cause that feedback."

"Feedback?" Lucas looked at Carter and then Henry and Allison. "That was feedback?"

"Maybe," Allison said. "That's what Zane and Graves are looking into." She frowned. "What is it, Lucas? You don't look like you believe that."

"Well . . . no, I don't," Lucas said, and straightened into

an upright position. "See—I said I cleared my head—to wait for the images I was supposed to get from the halo. Only—I got a flash of light. And I saw a few images—"

"Right. You said you saw Dr. Graves."

"Yeah. Real quick. But I've been on the receiving end of feedback before. That wasn't it. That was like . . ." He reached up and rubbed at his temple. Carter noticed that the burn mark left by the halo was nearly gone. "It felt more like a burst. . . ."

"Burst?" Carter looked at each of them. "Well, yeah—it exploded in your face. Knocked you against the wall." He cut a look over at Allison. "As well as half the town. You know, 'cause nothing could go wrong."

Lucas turned a confused expression to Carter as he reached up and touched the bump on the back of his head. "Yeah . . . it's just that . . ."

"What?" Henry said.

Lucas shrugged. "Nothing. Maybe I shouldn't even try to be a scientist."

Henry sighed. "Lucas—accidents happen in the lab all the time. We all make mistakes."

"Yeah," Carter said. "Look at Fargo."

"You're not helping." With a glaring glance at Carter, Henry continued. "Now, we've analyzed your translator program and there's nothing wrong with it. Dr. Graves has already sent me the preliminaries on that—and he feels the problem is in his scripts for the proprietary sorting."

Carter looked at Allison. "Graves thinks his software was at fault?"

"Yes." She looked at Henry. "I don't need to tell you that—"

"What the hell is going on around here?"

Carter closed his eyes, his shoulders hitching unconsciously at the sound of General Mansfield's voice. He turned to see the military man move purposefully into the infirmary, two uniformed men with *MP* on their upper arms behind him.

Allison gave a soft, short sigh that only Carter saw and heard and turned a pleasant face to the man. "General—yes—there's been a slight delay in translating the data—"

"Dr. Blake," Mansfield interrupted. "May I remind you that time is a crucial factor here. The longer your people continue to destroy data as well as destroy this town we so graciously sponsor—"

"*My* people"—Allison interrupted him, emphasizing the first word—"haven't destroyed anything. In fact, from what I can tell, *your* proprietary software for your harvesting project caused a power surge in my equipment that could have killed someone and briefly took out GD's grid. So, since *my* people are having to take a little bit of extra precaution, I think it's relative that time also be used for safety from now on."

Carter looked from Allison to Mansfield. She never ceased to amaze him. She was also the only one he'd ever seen actually make Mansfield listen. Like now.

"I have my people out helping the town to try to alleviate some of the tension I keep sensing."

"Tension?" Allison frowned, and Carter realized she had now moved to full-on Director of Sarcasm. "You don't realize the tension out there is *because* of *your* presence here? How many people in this town worry about their jobs daily when they look at the economy and see the military making cuts? Then you come blazing in here with trucks and soldiers—all to protect a dead man's memories—you disrupt my schedule and that of several of my top scientists, and then you have the nerve to be *angry* when an accident occurs due to *your* inability to finish your own gruesome experiment?"

The infirmary was so quiet a pin would have made the sound of an elephant stomp.

Finally, the general looked past her to Lucas and Henry. "You okay, son?"

Carter laughed. "Wow. Good avoidance there."

Mansfield ignored Carter and focused on Lucas. "Son?"

"Yes, sir."

"Good." He refocused on Allison. "I expect a full report on this as soon as possible. I can't express to you how important it is that we find out what this man knew before his death."

"General." Carter put his hands on his hips. "Don't you debrief your spies?"

Mansfield frowned. "Spies?"

"Well, that's what he was, wasn't he? A spy? You say he had important information that threatens national security. So—why didn't you debrief him?"

Mansfield's jaw tightened as he glared at Carter, who expected to explode at any moment with the intense power of that stare. "The subject wasn't a spy, Sheriff. And as I believe you were told along with everyone else, he died before he could give a full report."

"Well, maybe not a spy, but he was an investigator of some sort. I'm thinking an agent-in-charge of something."

The general's eyes narrowed. "Mind explaining to me who helped you come up with that? Because I know you're not intelligent enough to put all that together yourself."

Carter shrugged, nonplussed. "Just me, General. Doesn't take rocket science." And it didn't. The fact that the general had purposefully omitted telling them who this man was or giving them any information on his background didn't escape Carter. People seemed to forget he had been a U.S. Marshal at one time.

"General," Allison said, taking the attention back to herself. "My people are working around the clock. We'll translate the data. But for now, let them work."

Mansfield glared at Allison. "The only reason I brought

this here was because Dr. Graves was certain *you* could help." With that, he turned and left the infirmary.

Allison whirled on Carter. "What the hell are you doing?"

"What? What am I doing?" He couldn't stop the smile that pulled at the corners of his mouth. "Did you not notice your little speech earlier? And besides, it's no secret. I'm pretty sure all of us already suspected this guy was a spy. And the general thinks he found something out that's important."

Henry, who'd kept his attention focused on his tablet, finally looked up and nodded. "Lucas looks fine. Just the elevated temperature, but I suggest he go home and rest."

"But I want to keep working on the software—"

Allison shook her head. "Home, Lucas. Now." She glared at him. "No protests."

Lucas gave a short sigh and lay back down on the table.

Carter caught his eye. "Want me to . . . tell Zoe what's happened?" It wasn't really interfering. Just . . . a small suggestion. Because he knew Lucas was going to say—

"No, no," Lucas mumbled. "I'll give her a call myself."

"Good."

"It's really a telling thing when the military doesn't trust their own agents," Allison said in a tired voice. "All this just to get what this guy had. I think they're all paranoid by nature."

"First rule of being in the military," Carter said as he watched Henry tap on his tablet a few more times. "Trust no one. Though"—he grinned at Allison—"that sounds more like conspiracy theory, doesn't it?"

Henry abruptly looked up from his tablet. "Excuse me. . . . I need to get back to the lab." And with that he was gone.

Carter watched after him a few seconds before looking at Allison. "That seem a little abrupt to you?"

"Henry?" She nodded. "Yeah, but after today . . ." She put her fingers to her temples and rubbed. "Nothing surprises me." She brought up her left wrist. "You've got an hour and a half to get to my place."

"Yeah . . . about that . . ."

And a broad smile replaced her frown. "I need help hanging shelves, Jack. Just a little menial labor."

He gave her a lopsided grin. "Oh. I knew that."

The evening crowd at Café Diem was moderate. The sky was turning a slight pink as the sun sank behind the trees. Carter pulled up at the café and jumped out. He'd had no need to call in an order for himself and Allison—because he was sure Vincent already had something waiting.

The café owner was unique that way.

Inside, he spotted Jo at the counter, eating a bowl of . . . something . . . talking with Vincent. "Everyone okay now?" he said to no one in particular.

Several people nodded or smiled at him, and he was glad not to see any of Mansfield's soldiers around. The streets were clear as well. So the uniforms did have a good use after all.

Vincent turned and held up a finger before producing two white sacks from under the counter and set them on top. "Oh, and tell Dr. Blake I put extra cheese on hers."

Carter pursed his lips as he neared the counter and gave the bags a once-over. "Care to tell me exactly what has extra cheese?"

"Bacon burgers." Vincent beamed. "Blue cheese. And it's apple bacon and steak fries."

"Wow . . . isn't that loaded with cholesterol?" Jo piped up.

"Yeah, well." Vincent shrugged. "Dr. Blake's been doing so well keeping her diet even for the baby, I figured why not one night?" He then winked at Carter. "And we all want her to be happy, right?"

Carter opened his mouth, then closed it, then frowned. "I'm going over because she needs me to hang shelves." He sensed an innuendo.

Vincent and Jo exchanged looks. Jo nodded. "Oh . . . is that what they call it now? Might want to use that term with Zane."

"Jo—" Carter paused.

Vincent shook his head and waved his hand dismissively. "Never mind, Sheriff. Jo and I were talking about . . . you know . . . with all the military people in." He looked to his left and then his right and leaned in to look at Carter over the bags. "Right?"

Carter narrowed his eyes. "Right what?"

"General Mansfield, all the heightened security around the town . . ."

"Vincent . . ." Carter winced. "Are you fishing for information?"

"Always. Got any?"

"What exactly are you fishing . . . for?"

Vincent gave him a half grin. "You tell me."

Sighing—basically because he had no idea what the man was wanting—Carter spotted Fargo and Julia in the far corner, in close to the same position as that morning, only they had a new victim in the chair. "Where's Zoe?"

Vincent and Jo exchanged looks again.

"Now, will you cut that out?" Carter said. "What is it?"

"Zoe went home," Vincent said as he straightened up. "I think she and Lucas are on the outs."

"There's no proof of that," Jo said as she pushed her utensil into the bowl and looked at Carter. "Zoe was helping Fargo and Julia all day—and then she got one wrong. I think it just upset her."

"Got one wrong . . ." Carter said. "You say that like she only—" His eyes widened as he realized what Jo had said. "Are you serious? She only got *one* wrong out of that whole mind mumbo-jumbo? Out of how many?"

"Seven," Julia said as she approached the counter. "I had ten envelopes ready and she blew through most of them. Nearly a perfect score."

Carter looked back at the table, where Fargo was watching a young man drawing circles on a piece of paper—with his eyes closed. He refocused on Julia. "You mean my Zoe? Really? She guessed that many right?"

"It's not guessing, Sheriff," Julia said. "We already told you."

"Yeah . . . remote seeing or something." He grinned. "It's guessing. So Zoe did that good, huh? Surely if she did, she wouldn't have gotten that upset over just one wrong. I've seen her pretty happy when she's missed more than that on a test."

Julia pursed her lips. "Well, it wasn't that it was wrong. . . . I don't think. It's *what* she . . . drew. . . ."

Carter looked from Vincent to Jo and then back to Julia. He arched his eyebrows. "Drew? Come on, guys. . . . I got blue cheese wafting into my face from these bags. Fill me in?"

Julia answered. "A lot of remote Viewers . . . find they can't describe what they're seeing. Not in any limited language sense. So the more advanced ones start to draw what it is. This type of Viewing has come in handy when it comes to looking into a building that infrared can't penetrate."

"Oh . . . okay."

"Well, she started putting words down and then just started drawing. . . ." Julia appeared as if she were looking for the right word.

"A girl," Fargo finished as he joined them, a stack of

packets and papers, folders, and a binder in his arms. "Some girl with really big teeth."

Carter leaned in closer. "And? Was that not what was in the envelope?"

"No." Julia shook her head. "It was a kitten. Now, it could have been a girl cat—"

"Julia—"

"Now stop it, Douglas. You've been on Zoe's case since she out-Viewed you."

"I have not been—"

"Yes, you have. You didn't get a single one right—"

"That's because you're partial to the girls winning—"

"Guys." Carter held up his hands. "Guys . . . please. So . . . her drawing, this picture of a girl? Do you have it?"

"No, she took it with her," Julia answered. "She also wrote something odd at the bottom of the picture."

"Odd?"

Fargo nodded. "She wrote *I love you* . . . and she put it in quotes."

"Quotes?"

"You know—" Fargo held up the index finger and middle finger of both hands to imitate quotes. "In quotes. Like someone said—"

"I got it, I got it." Carter reached up and grabbed at the two bags to lift them and then paused. "And no one knew this girl's face? Someone at school?"

"Maybe at Harvard?" Julia said.

"Okay. I'll see if Zoe'll let me look at it. You said she went home?"

Jo blew on a spoonful of . . . something wet. . . . "Yeah, about an hour ago. Said something about talking to Henry later."

"Oh . . . Henry," Julia said. "I need to talk to him. I need to get over to GD."

"Yeah, you do that." Carter hoisted the bags up and then lowered them to his side to look at Jo. "Zane'll probably be late—Mansfield's in an uproar on this one. And—" He frowned as he looked in her bowl. "What *is* that?"

"I tried to out-order Vincent again."

"Yes." Vincent leaned on the counter next to Jo. "And I made her a bet. I could get it for her, but she'd have to eat it."

"So"—Carter looked again at the bowl and the contents—"what did you order?"

Vincent looked concerned as he clasped his hands in front of him. "Sheriff . . . do you *really* want to know?"

Carter backed up, shaking his head slowly. "No . . . no . . . not at all. Night." And with that he left the café, set the bags in his car, pulled out his phone, and dialed home.

"Hello?"

"Hey, you okay?"

There was a pause. "Yeah. . . ."

"I heard you got one wrong."

There was another pause. "Yeah . . . maybe. I wish I had."

Carter pulled himself into the car and held the phone mashed between his shoulder and cheek. "What was that?"

"Oh, nothing. You coming home for dinner?"

"No . . . I'm heading to Allison's. Said she needs some shelves hung."

"Shelves hung, huh?" Zoe said, her voice perking. "I heard Tallia Marsden is watching the kids—"

"It's . . . a *favor*, Zoe."

"So that's what the adults are calling it these days. . . ." She sighed.

He grinned with embarrassment as he started the car. "Get some rest, okay? Lucas—" And then he stopped himself. He'd been about to tell her that Lucas was fine. But since she hadn't asked him, it occurred to him that Lucas hadn't called her like he promised. Zoe didn't know what'd happened.

"Yeah, Dad?"

"Lucas is working late tonight. So"—he put the car in reverse—"just get some sleep, okay, hon?"

"Okay. Night, Dad."

As he hung up the phone, Carter eased the SUV out of the parking spot and turned the car toward Allison's house.

For a favor.

It really was a favor.

CHAPTᴇR 8

"Wow, that's really well hung," Allison said.

Carter nearly fell off the ladder. "What?"

"The shelf, Carter."

He smirked down at her as he placed the level on the shelf and watched the bubble of air center up between the two black hash marks. He grinned with satisfaction and held his hands out to his sides above his shoulders. "There. All done, and all perfectly level."

The shelves Allison wanted hung were in the baby's room. Apparently two of the shelves had fallen on top of the crib the afternoon before and terrified the babysitter. Luckily Jenna hadn't been in the crib but in the living room. Allison wanted them rehung and reinforced.

He and Allison shared the meal at thc kitchen table when he arrived, Allison squealing with delight when Carter gave her Vincent's message about extra cheese.

Grabbing plates, Allison set out each burger, fries, black beans, and Vincent's own blend of sweet tea.

She'd talked about the baby with a smile in her eyes, though at times Carter felt a slight ping in his own chest. These were memories she should be sharing with Nathan.

Not me.

And after the burgers were cleared away, it was time for shelves.

Allison had come to the nursery door holding two steaming mugs of coffee before her comment. Carter stepped off the small ladder and took one of the mugs from her. The two of them moved to stand in the center of the room and surveyed the newly mounted shelves.

Carter sipped his coffee. It was perfect. "Now, what I did was attach the actual shelf holder—those two silver parts—to a stud. Apparently they were hammered into the drywall the first time. This way they're more stable and won't fall." He smiled. "In theory."

"Thanks so much, Carter." Allison sipped her own coffee. "I hung the shelves the first time and it's obvious I'm not good at this." She sighed. "It terrifies me that she could have been in this crib and those shelves . . ."

Carter reached out and put a hand on her shoulder. "Well, she wasn't. And to be honest"—he looked at the crib where he'd moved it by the window to get to the shelves—"I don't know why you don't leave the crib there."

She looked from the window to him. "Near an open window? Oh no, Carter, I'm too afraid someone'll come in and just take her."

He frowned. "Well, I hate to sound really awful about this, but if someone's going to come in and take her, these few steps from the window to the shelf aren't going to stop them."

Allison sipped her coffee. "I know . . . it sounds silly. I just . . . I get so paranoid when I think of her. Jenna is really the only thing I have left of Nathan . . . and I want to protect her. Do you realize how hard it was for me to even put her in here to sleep and not keep her in the bedroom with me?"

"I was wondering why you hadn't done that."

"Because I know if I don't get her used to sleeping in this room, she never will." Allison sighed as she moved from the nursery to the kitchen.

With a last glance at the shelves, Carter put the mug on the lowest one, folded up the ladder, and took it back outside to the garage. After retrieving his mug, he found Allison in the living room on the couch, her cup clasped between her hands.

He sat down in one of the chairs facing her and sipped his own coffee. "You okay?"

Her expression shifted to a frown. "I was talking with Dr. Graves earlier. He's not happy about how the general's using his Brain Box."

"Well, I have to say"—Carter leaned forward and set his mug on a coaster on the coffee table—"the whole idea is a bit creepy."

"Creepy? It's sick. Thinking that this guy was a spy is even worse. Aircom's upset because he'd originally wanted the technology to be used to catch murderers—taking the last memories of the victim and catching who killed them. But to use it to gouge out information like this?"

Carter clasped his hands together in front of him. "I think there's a fine line in all this. If you're talking about rights—whose rights do we violate? In the case of catching a murderer, I think there's a justification—same as a search and seizure when it's issued if we suspect someone is guilty of committing a crime."

"Yeah, but, Carter"—she shifted her position, moving her mug to her thigh—"what happens if that person isn't guilty? Now their life has been violated. What if someone—like this dead guy—what rights does he have in this situation? My understanding is that he died in a car accident—a fluke. He wasn't murdered. He just didn't make it to the debriefing. What if his last memories of dying in that crash aren't something anyone else is supposed to see? And what if a loved one were to see? To relive that kind of agony and fear?"

Carter felt himself shiver at the thought . . . at the idea of Zoe ever dying in such a way and then him being able to see it and experience it firsthand.

"I don't think Mansfield understands the sort of precedent he's setting with this technology," Allison said. "But I think Aircom does. I think he's terrified of it being used for the wrong reasons. I mean"—she sat up—"what if this could be used to actually harvest someone's memories from them against their will? Not just after dying? Can you imagine if this were to be used in interrogations?"

"Wow." Carter blinked at her. "You know, sometimes your mind goes to really scary places."

She smiled at him. "Sorry, Carter. But I do think of these things. Look at GD. All those experiments going on, all those bits and pieces being created and invented. It's up to me to look at them, analyze them, and understand where their applications can be used, and should."

With a sigh she brought her coffee back to her lips and sipped before continuing. "You've seen for yourself the dangers a lot of these inventions can present."

Carter snorted. "Firsthand."

"Exactly. And it's up to me, and to Henry in a lot of ways, to filter through them. Section Five is really the only buffer I have."

"Graves's idea is a good one—on catching murderers. And like all technologies like guns and automatic weapons, we have laws that prohibit the use of them in a wrong fashion." He pursed his lips. "Okay, maybe that really wasn't the best example I could have come up with."

"Oh, Carter." She laughed. "I understand the sentiment. I just look at things differently. Like I look at Dr. Graves."

Carter picked up his mug and held it in front of his mouth. "You like him."

"I admire him."

"No . . . I mean you *really* like him. But I think he's a little young for you."

"Carter." She glared at him. "I do not like him in any other way than having admiration for what he's done. And he has the one thing I've found that a lot of the scientists I've met in my life don't have. And that's a conscience."

"He does seem a little worried about something."

"Like I said, he's worried about what Mansfield's going to do."

Carter sipped his coffee and nodded just as his phone went off. He pulled it out of his back pocket and read the message from Jo. The information on Alroom Graves had come back and she'd read it. Her assessment?

BORING.

But Jo hadn't included any of the boring information in with her text.

"Need to go?"

He set the phone on the coffee table and leaned back. "Not for a few more minutes. I do want to get home soon, though. Zoe was a little upset earlier today."

"Oh? Why?"

"Remember how I told you about her and Lucas? Apparently they're not talking—not, like, really communicating. And then she found out he was here and he hadn't told her. Then she was doing experiments with Julia and Fargo and got something wrong. I think it's just been a bad day."

"Well, on the Lucas front, what did you tell her?"

"I told her to trust him. And if it got so bad, then talk to him. What was it going to hurt?"

"Good dad advice, Carter. And what are Julia and Fargo working on?"

He rolled his eyes and sighed. "Remote Seeing or something like that. They were in the café all day doing preliminary work for Henry. Apparently he's going to use it to start off his poetry classes."

Allison's laughter took him by surprise, and he couldn't help but smile with her.

"What did I say?"

"It's Remote *Viewing*, Carter. And the science is referred to as noetic science." She sighed. "I hadn't realized Henry had settled on that as his opener for his alternative sciences course."

"You don't like it?"

"I don't know that much about it." She sat up and set her mug down again. "But it's something I can read up on tonight after I put stuff back on the shelves, though." She patted her stomach. "Looking back at the amount of food I ate, early bed isn't out of the question as well."

Carter was reminded of the tightness in his own waistband as he stood and walked his mug back to the kitchen. Allison followed him in and refilled her cup from the carafe.

"So what are the boys doing tonight?"

"Well." She leaned on the refrigerator. "Henry called earlier and let me know they were able to get the translator working on the piece of data."

Carter blinked. "They did? You mean they can see a memory?"

"No." She sighed. "Not really see a memory . . . but they were getting a string of data that repeated itself. Not really sure what that was, but they're going to keep working on it. I'll have the phone by my bed in case they break through or something."

Nodding, Carter found himself watching her, appreciating her smile. There was an awkward second or two before he set his mug in the sink and stood in front of Allison. "Ah . . . well . . . I should be going. Thanks for dinner and the company."

Allison moved closer and set her own mug in the sink beside his. She stared at them for a few seconds before she looked up at Carter. "Thank you, Jack—and not just for the shelves. It's nice, having someone I can depend on. Talk, too."

"You mean having a handyman around?" Carter found himself grinning a bit more broadly than he meant to.

"Not just a handyman, Jack." She crossed her arms over her chest and then dropped them to her sides. "You've been . . . so nice to me, and to Kevin and Jenna. Since Nathan—and now with Tess so far away—" She looked up at him. "I feel a lot safer when you're around. It's nice to have someone you trust nearby. Even when we're both a bit . . . on our own."

He reached out to put his hands on her shoulders—stopped—and then finally rested them there. "Allison—I just want you to know that you can count on me. That I'll be there for you and Kevin, and Jenna."

She smiled up at him. "I know, Jack. And that . . . that makes me feel . . ."

He arched his eyebrows. "Feel . . ." He leaned his head down.

". . . I feel . . ."

A sharp clatter invaded the silence, and Carter turned to see that one of the mugs had tipped over onto the other one, both of them now on their sides.

Allison pulled back quickly. Carter put his hands down

and patted his stomach. "Boy, that was good food . . . and a lot of it. . . ."

"Yes . . . yes, it was. Remind me to thank Vincent tomorrow," she said hurriedly. "Well . . . good night, Carter."

He paused as his gaze lingered a few seconds. "Good night, Allison." He gave her a friendly, hesitant pat on her shoulder before he let himself out the door.

After he cranked the SUV, Carter stared at the front of Allison's house, his right hand on the key, his left on the steering wheel. He could just see her shadow through the window before the front light went out.

Carter's stomach tightened as he looked down at the wheel, though not really seeing it. Working with Allison day to day—he'd realized something tonight. That no matter how things ended up with Tess, no matter what else went on in his personal life—Allison would always possess a part of him. And whether it was saving the town, or just hanging a shelf, all she ever need do was ask.

The lights in the kitchen went out, and he waited until a light upstairs turned on. With a short sigh he put the SUV in reverse and smiled.

"I *will* be there for you, Allison. I promise."

Carter looked up at the window before he turned to his right and backed out of the driveway.

Zoe listened to Henry's voice mail message for the third time, sighing. She'd already called him three times, leaving a message for him to call her the first time. Why did she keep calling?

She wasn't sure.

No, that wasn't true. She was sure. She needed to talk to someone besides Fargo and Julia about what she'd seen and drawn. The piece of paper lay on the kitchen counter, on the center island, the woman's face looking up at her with her smile.

Zoe had never considered herself an artist, but she'd seen the face; she felt in her heart that she'd known this woman for a long time.

Intimately.

But those weren't her emotions.

After hanging up, she moved slowly back to the counter and looked down at her face.

"Zoe, is there anything I can get for you? Diagnostics show elevated levels of cortisol in your body, indicating you are experiencing a higher-than-normal level of stress."

She sighed, nodding. "Yeah, S.A.R.A.H., I'm a little stressed."

"May I suggest a nap? Sleep has been known in many studies to—"

"No, no. That's fine. I'm not tired right now. But thanks." She sat on the stool, looking down at the picture. Was it possible this was an image of memory out of Lucas's head? Had she really been able to View inside his mind?

If she closed her eyes, she could still see the image, much like a loop of film, of a woman in front of him, of snow, and the wind blowing her hair. Just before the image repeated, she said the words *I love you*.

"Oh, Lucas," Zoe said, and rested her elbow on the table, her hand against her head.

"Perhaps I can contact Lucas for you? He is presently at home."

Zoe started at this revelation. Her dad had said Lucas was working late. "S.A.R.A.H., are you sure Lucas is at home?"

"Yes. Are you sure you don't want me to contact him?"

"Oh, no, no. Please don't." She paused. "When did he get home?"

S.A.R.A.H. gave her a time. Zoe looked at the clock.

Two hours ago. He'd been home for two hours—and no call. Nothing.

And why had her dad lied? Did he know something? Was he covering for Lucas?

Why was everyone lying to her?

Frustrated, and feeling her cortisol levels rising, Zoe grabbed up a few sheets of paper, a picture of Lucas, and a pencil and decided to do her own experiment. Sliding her work from earlier to the side, Zoe set his picture beneath the stack of blank paper, put her pencil's lead to the surface, and closed her eyes.

Two deep breaths.

Just do what you did before.

Think of Lucas. He's at home.

Lucas.

What is Lucas doing?

Another deep breath.

Her pencil began to move.

Angry.

Frustrated.

Guilty.

Warm.

Smell . . .

Her hand moved to the right and wrote *coffee.*

Moving it back again, she thought of him again—

And abruptly she was looking at the woman again. Only this time she wasn't smiling. She was angry, her eyes narrowed. Zoe was sure she was yelling at this woman, feeling anger, frustration, guilt—she was feeling all of it—and then the girl was turning away.

The smells of . . .

Jasmine.

Soap.

Sweat.

Fear.

"You betrayed me. . . . How could you?"

"Zoe? You haven't responded in ten minutes and four seconds. I'm afraid I'll have to call Sheriff Carter if you don't—"

Zoe blinked, S.A.R.A.H.'s voice bringing her back to the kitchen. She dropped the pencil on the counter and put her hands to her head. A dull ache pulsed behind her eyes. "No, S.A.R.A.H. I'm all right. I guess I just . . ." And then her gaze fell on the piece of paper.

It was a scene . . . like a still from a movie . . . but drawn in graphite. The girl was there again, her eyes burning with sheer hatred. Her hands were down at her sides, balled into fists.

And again at the bottom were the words *You would betray me—after everything I've done for you?*

What the hell?

"Zoe?"

"I'm fine, S.A.R.A.H. Just tired. Don't worry about me." Zoe held the paper up and studied it, compared it to the one from earlier. Definitely the same girl . . . and she knew if she were inside Lucas's head, she'd be seeing this from his point of view. There was an arm, reaching out from the right, as if she were gesturing to the girl.

But . . . who was saying this? Who had betrayed whom?

"Oh, Lucas," she said aloud, softly. "Are you caught up in a love triangle?"

CHAPTER 9

"Welcome home, Sheriff."

"Hi, S.A.R.A.H.," Carter said as he came through the habitat door. He yawned as he stepped into the living room. He was still full of burger, and right now sleep sounded like a very good idea.

"Pigs . . . they're all pigs."

Carter paused and looked around the living room. "S.A.R.A.H. . . . was . . . that you?"

"No, Sheriff. That was Zoe."

"Zoe?" he called out, and made his way to the kitchen.

The kitchen, like just about every other part of the habitat, was state-of-the-art, Eureka style. Polished tile floor, lacquered center island with stools, and an AI-controlled pantry.

Zoe was sitting at the table, papers littering the surface. She was dressed in a pair of loungers and a tank top, and her hair looked . . . uncombed. "Zoe . . . everything okay?" he said as he came around to the opposite side and looked at her.

She held up a pencil, No. 2, and pointed at him. "Men are pigs. And they lie. You can't trust them."

He straightened. "Uh, S.A.R.A.H. . . ."

"Black coffee, coming up."

"And *you* lied, too." She continued pointing the pencil at him.

A side panel slid up beside the pantry, revealing a coffeemaker and tray. Within a few seconds a black mug filled with steaming, hot black coffee. Carter moved to retrieve it, thinking he was going to need it for this.

After a sip, he sat down beside Zoe and looked at her. "Care to tell me why you think men are pigs? And . . . why you think I lied to you?"

She glared at him. "Lucas didn't work late. He went home."

"Oh, he called?"

"No. S.A.R.A.H. told me."

Oh. Uh-oh. "Honey, I just didn't want—"

"Dad," Zoe said, and her voice was full of anguish as she interrupted him. "He's having an affair."

Carter blinked. "Whoa, wait. . . . How did we get to an affair? You mean he's seeing another girl?"

Another glare.

"Ah, woman. Sorry."

"And no, it's an affair."

"Why do you say it's an affair?"

With a sigh, she pushed the scattered papers to him. "Because I think *she's* married."

Carter's mouth formed a perfect O before he reached out to take the papers. Arranging them into a readable stack, he started moving through them. "Zoe . . . did you draw these?"

She nodded as she propped both elbows on the table and

pushed her palms into the sides of her face. "Yeah. I was Remote Viewing and did all of these."

Carter paused and looked at her. "Wait. . . . Julia and Fargo said you'd drawn the face of a woman. But . . . these are a lot of women. No . . . woman. These are all the *same* woman."

Lowering her arms, Zoe reached over to the stack and lazily pushed through them until she found one in particular and put it on top. "That's the first one I did."

To say he was impressed wasn't enough. Carter smiled as he looked down at the woman's face looking back at him. It was a beautiful pencil rendering of a smiling female, her hair in motion, and behind her— "Are these trees?"

"With snow. It was snowing."

He nodded and looked down, seeing the words *I love you* in quotes. "And . . . you say you saw this when you did that guessing thing?"

"Dad." She sighed. "Don't patronize me. I was Remote Viewing."

"But Fargo said you got it wrong—that it was a cat."

"Look." She put her hands out and grabbed the papers and started shuffling them. "I wanted to View something else, okay? Not the little pictures. Henry had mentioned Remote Influencing and how a lot of Viewers can go to target. And then Jo did a View and I actually saw the shed before she got the descriptions right."

"You saw a shed?"

"Yeah . . . in my mind. And I didn't even know that shed was real. There was a picture of it in the envelope, and the image in my head was the same one."

Carter frowned at her.

"Dad . . . I didn't make it up."

"Hey, hey, I didn't say that you did. But . . . what has a shed got to do with these?" He pointed to the papers.

"When we started the RV on what was a cat, I decided

I wanted to look at something different. So I thought of Lucas instead."

Carter pursed his lips. "You just thought of Lucas and this is what came to your mind?" He held up the picture of the smiling woman again. "You saw her and you think she came out of his head?"

"Yes, I do." She pulled up three more and laid them out. "So when I got home I did it a few more times and I got a different image each time, but look." She pointed to one of them. "In this one she looks really angry, and in this one she's got her back turned."

As Carter gave the drawn pictures a good look, it was obviously the same girl in each. There it was just like Zoe described; her back was turned, but the hair was unmistakable. There was another man there, but his face wasn't clear. In a third picture she was sleeping, and the angle was such that Carter felt he was in the bed beside her. In the fourth picture she was facing him and there was something under her arm. "Zoe . . . is that a gun?"

"I think so. . . ."

"Honey . . ." He set each of the papers out on the table side by side and looked at them. "Are you sure these pictures aren't, like . . . from a movie you watched the other night?"

"Dad!"

"I'm sorry, but"—he shook his head—"yes, they're all the same woman. All well staged. But, to say this is someone that Lucas is having an affair with?" He pointed to the one with the weapon. "And . . . a gun?"

"But I was looking into his head when I saw them."

"There's no evidence of that." Carter shook his head. "You can't really believe one human being can look inside another and know what they're seeing, can you?"

And just as he said it, he wished he hadn't. He realized that was exactly what they were doing at GD at the mo-

ment, extracting and trying to View the last memories of
a dead man.

Aw, damn it.

Zoe stood up and started gathering the sheets of paper.
"I thought you'd understand."

"What I understand, from a cop's point of view, is that
this doesn't prove anything." He put his hands on two of
the sheets to get her to stop. "Now, please, hear me out."

She didn't look at him, but she did sit back down.

"Let's look at this like I would if I were reviewing a case.
And this is evidence of a crime. Your suspect is Lucas."

Zoe nodded.

"Say these are all photographs and not drawings—no
matter how they were taken—okay? Now . . . for a DA to
use these in court, they have to give solid, visible proof that
the defendant is guilty of something." He gestured to them.
"Do you see Lucas in any of these?"

"Well, no, Dad, they're all from his point of view—what
he sees."

"Meaning you'd have to prove he was the photographer
that took them."

She opened her mouth to protest something, but then
closed it. "Yeah."

"Okay, let's say for a second I believe this crap—and
I'm the judge—I'm going to need that evidence. Anyone
could have taken these shots, right? What if you weren't in
Lucas's head? What if you were in someone else's head and
they were watching a movie?"

His stomach turned at saying what he was saying, because he honestly didn't believe a word of the Remote
Viewing theory. But in hindsight, he felt pretty good about
how he was rearranging it for her.

Or at least it sounded impressive.

Her shoulders slumped, and he knew she was listening
to him.

"So, what would be the most logical step as an investigator to take?"

"Question the suspect? Show him the photographs?"

Carter grinned. "That's my girl. You're saying that Lucas is having an affair, based on what you think you saw in his mind. But . . . have you even talked to him? Asked him? Come on, Zoe. Innocent until proven guilty, right?"

She lowered her head. "I feel like an idiot."

"No, no. It's okay. You're having trust issues . . . and I can understand that. You're young, going to different schools, and you haven't really talked. I'd say, take these—" He scooped up all the pieces of paper and stacked them neatly together to put them in front of her. "And show him. Ask him if he's ever seen her before. But I don't think I'd, uh . . . tell him you were trying to snoop in his head, okay?"

Zoe grinned and nodded. "Okay, Dad . . . I'll go give him a call right now," and she started to get up.

"Oh, no, wait, I'd do that in the morning," Carter said, and held out his hand. "Henry said he needed a good rest."

She turned and gave him a narrowed look. "A good rest? Why? Does this have to do with why you lied and said he was still at GD?"

Uh-oh.

Carter visibly winced.

"Dad." She sat back down, her gaze searching his face. "What are you not telling me? What's happened? Is Lucas okay?"

"Just—it's fine." He held up his hands in an attempt to soothe her. "He's fine. Just a little accident in the lab today that sort gave him a good . . ." He pursed his lips. "Shock."

Zoe had her hands on the table. "That power outage? Was that it? Whatever they're working on? Dad . . . that affected the whole town."

"Yeah, I know, which is still bothering me a little . . .

but it's okay. Henry checked him out and Lucas is fine. He was a little groggy, though, okay? So Henry sent him home to rest."

He wasn't sure what kind of reaction he thought Zoe would give. Worry, perhaps anger at not being told about this sooner, but what he didn't expect was the look of pure joy on her face as she stood up, came around the corner of the table, and gave him a tight squeeze.

Carter hugged her back but then pulled back and narrowed his eyes. "Who are you and what did you do to Zoe?"

"Don't you see? He hasn't called me because he's been at home resting. I know Henry usually gives you something to help you sleep, so now I'm pretty sure he's been asleep. And if he's asleep, I'm not sure these could have come from his head at all."

It always amazed Carter the way a person's mind sought out logic when there wasn't any. The thought that these images came from anyone's head at all was so farfetched, but now to reconcile that with the fact that because Lucas was possibly sleeping, then it couldn't have happened at all?

Carter sometimes believed he needed an instruction manual.

"So . . . you don't still think men are pigs?"

"No." She released him and started gathering her papers. "At least not at the moment. I was upset because he hadn't called me at all. But now that I know he's been resting, I think that's a good excuse. I'll still show him these tomorrow—see if he'll meet me at Café Diem for breakfast."

"That's a good idea," Carter said, and remained sitting as she gave him a quick kiss on the cheek, said good night, and headed upstairs.

"That went very well, Sheriff," S.A.R.A.H. said.

He brought the coffee mug to his lips. "I think so,

too." He took several large swallows, since the liquid had cooled. "Now if I could just remember what it was I did."

Henry, Zane, and Graves were still in the lab when Carter arrived. After tossing in bed for half an hour, he'd showered, dressed, and driven back down to GD.

"Jack—why are you up?" Henry said.

"Too much coffee."

The three of them stood around a single monitor. Carter moved to the side, still not quite sure he'd done the right thing with Zoe, and completely unsure of what they were talking about.

Zane finally spoke up. "I'm not sure if this pattern is really part of what we were looking at before."

Henry sighed. "We've been looking at these symbols for hours, and the best we can come up with is that they're repetitive. Let's step back from this and go over what we know."

Zane straightened, and Graves turned the chair to face Henry. Carter stepped back and leaned against Henry's console.

"Lucas rescripted the translator to process the data. I chose a smaller section to test it on, loaded it into the buffer—" Zane began.

Henry held up his hand. "Why did you copy it into a buffer?"

Zane arched his eyebrows. "Because I wasn't sure how the translator was going to interact with the storynest."

Henry nodded. "So, you applied the translator in a RAM buffer, not a hard node?"

"RAM?" Carter said. "You mean like computer RAM? Read-only memory or something?"

Henry shook his head. "Random access memory. You

know about temporary memory, in a computer? The memory you lose when you shut a computer off?"

"Yeah, I try to autosave now."

"Well, Zane spooled—copied—the data into a buffer made of designated RAM. Which acts like any other RAM. It's temporary. He didn't save it to a hard node, or hard drive."

Carter shook his head. "So . . . because it's in this buffer, that's why you're getting a looping error message?"

"No." Henry shook his head. "It's not the RAM itself but the designated—" He blinked a few times before waving Graves out of the way.

The young man moved as quickly as he could as Henry sat in the chair and started hitting keys. Carter glanced at Graves, who shrugged.

He touched the screen rapidly, opening and closing windows, then moved one window into the next. Abruptly the snowy window with the data became several lines of text that repeated itself over and over.

"What did you do?" Graves said as he leaned in to look beside Zane.

"When Zane said he'd actually applied the translator in the RAM, I realized memory capacity would be an issue. Not just memory as in RAM-assigned space, but because memories themselves aren't designable to a specific allocation."

Carter shook his head. "Okay. I'll ask. What?"

"He means the buffer wasn't big enough," Zane said. "Memory files shrink and expand per file—it's something we've noticed since working with the time capsule. Though the section we pulled might looked like it's twenty gig, it won't stay twenty gig." Zane looked at Carter. "You make the buffer thirty gig just to give yourself space. But once the data runs through the application—it may or may not expand to or beyond that allocated memory."

Graves nodded slowly. "Causing it to crash and not finish the translation."

Henry pointed at Graves. "Right. Which may or may not have caused the short when the new app tried to grab for more space to complete the task. The Brain Box has a thousand terabytes of unused storage. So I simply transferred Lucas's app over there and applied it to the same sequence."

Carter leaned in to look at the screen. It was text now, a repeating sequence of a name, a rank— "That's a name, rank, and serial number. Why is it giving name, rank, and serial number in text and not in a memory?"

Graves spoke up. "To convert the data from text to sensory through the halo takes an immersive video card the Brain Box doesn't have. It's simply a harvester and storage. We'd need to actually run it through the storynest using Henry's parameters."

"Right," Henry said. "The immersive network of the storynest should then help in interpreting the data to its visual component."

"You mean the storynest will make it into pictures?" Carter looked at Henry.

"Yes."

Carter continued leaning into the screen. "Jonathan Caruso," he said, reading from the continuously repeating text. "Not sure Mansfield would want us to know this guy's name. But why is he repeating his name, rank, and serial number at the point of death?"

"Maybe he was forced to right before he died?" Zane said.

"He died hitting a truck," Carter said as he straightened up. "I don't know about you guys, but if I'm about to hit the side of an eighteen-wheeler, that's not the last thing I'm going to be thinking."

Zane shook his head. "No—it'd be more along the lines of *oh shit*."

Carter held out his hands. "Exactly."

"That is if what's recorded really *are* his last memories," Zane said.

"They are." Graves nodded. "Remember what I said about synaptic cry? The only issue I've ever worried about is sequence. If someone's life flashes before their eyes—do they remember the last events first? Or last? This"—he pointed to the screen—"could be something he thought about before the impact."

Carter shook his head. "But again . . . why repeat this? Unless he really was a spy."

"You see why I insisted to Mansfield this project wasn't even close to being completed." Graves looked dejected. "We won't know till we get all the data translated and viewed."

Henry said, "Keep working on creating a section large enough on the storynest to use the video card—and start translating the rest of the data. Maybe by morning we can actually see what it was this man saw."

Carter stared at the repeating lines of text. "Or didn't want to see," he muttered to himself.

CHAPTᵉR 10

"This . . . this can't be happening to me. I mean . . .
it's not possible. The only instance in the history of the
world where this can happen is the beginning of the end
of time."

Those were the words Carter heard as he stepped into
Café Diem the next morning. Zoe had gotten up early and
left him a note, thanking him.

It felt good to be able to make his daughter feel better.
But it didn't explain the overwhelming sense of foreboding
that woke him—like something was wrong but he couldn't
put a finger on it. Might be the less than four hours of sleep
he'd had. He'd left GD around three in the morning and
fallen asleep immediately. Morning came way too fast.

Jo was at the counter, along with Julia, Fargo, and a few
other townsfolk.

Zoe came from the back with a bag and a cup and
handed it to one of the people standing by the counter near

the espresso machine. "There you go, and so sorry about the mix-up."

The customer nodded, though she didn't look happy. "Ten years I've been coming in here . . . and not once has that boy messed up an order." She leaned toward Zoe and looked about conspiratorially as if she didn't want anyone to hear, yet spoke with a stage whisper Carter was sure they picked up over at GD. "They might be messing with his head, too. All these military folk about? They're getting in our heads." She took her bag and cup, and hurried past Carter and out the door.

Zoe had a frown on her face as she turned to Carter, and her expression brightened visibly. "Morning, Dad. Lucas hasn't come in yet, but I'm ready for him when he does."

He approached the counter. "What . . . ?" He glanced back at the door. "Did she just say that Vincent got an order . . . *wrong*?"

"It's a tragedy," the rotund café owner said as he put his hands to the sides of his face, covering his muttonchops. "This just can't be happening to me. Sheriff—it's the sign of the apocalypse. Look for the four horsemen."

"Are you serious?" Carter couldn't hide the surprise in his voice. Since his first unannounced arrival in Eureka, Carter had been told there wasn't an order that Vincent couldn't fill—he always had what any customer wanted.

Always.

And during that time, Vincent had always been right. Always.

Zoe faced her dad, frowning. *Twice,* she mouthed, then flipped a towel over her shoulder and moved to bus a table.

Carter frowned at Vincent. "Maybe you need to let Henry take a look at you?"

But Vincent was inconsolable. He continued to stare at

the freezer, as if the room of mystery had somehow turned on him.

"You missed the best part," Jo said from her perch at the counter. "He got *lost* in the pantry, too. Zoe had to go in and find him."

Carter looked from Jo to Julia and Fargo, and both were nodding. They looked sad. Well, everyone but Jo, who looked . . . Carter frowned at her. "Jo . . . since when do you bite your nails?"

"I'm not biting my nails," she said around the finger in her mouth. "That's a nervous habit. I don't have any nervous habits."

His eyes widened a moment as he looked at her. "Then why are you doing it?"

"I'm not—" And then she finally noticed her finger in her mouth. She pulled it out and spit to the side beside Carter's shoe. "Oh my God. . . . I haven't done that since before I joined the military." She looked at her hands, turning them over. "I've been chewing my nails?"

"Ever since you sat down," Fargo said, and went back to his breakfast. Julia sat beside him, with an open notebook and scattered papers replacing any identifiable breakfast item.

Vincent abruptly burst out, "They brought one Pinch, a hungry lean-faced villain, a mere anatomy, a mountebank, a threadbare juggler, and a fortune-teller, a needy, hollow-eyed, sharp-looking wretch, a living dead man."

Carter turned and looked at Vincent. "What?"

Vincent lowered his arms and turned to look at the sheriff, his face and voice calm. "Shakespeare, Sheriff. *Comedy of Errors.* Act five, verse one."

Looking around at the staring patrons, Carter nodded slowly. "That's nice, Vincent. Just . . . if you have to spout . . . that stuff, go into the freezer."

"That stuff?" Vincent looked hurt. "Shakespeare!" He covered his face and ran into the freezer, closing the door behind him.

"Oh, no." Carter sighed, and focused on Fargo. "Why are you two still here?" He wasn't really curious, but he also wasn't sure what to make of the scene playing out in front of him. His sense of foreboding—the one that had followed him from sleep—was now on full overdrive.

"Dr. Blake thought it would be a good idea if we continued researching for Henry," Fargo said. "She thinks we're doing good work. And since it's our day off, we can at least spend the time together."

"Oh, please," Julia said as she pushed papers around. "The director just wants you out of her hair while the general and the military are at GD—that way you can't blow anything up."

Carter's jaw nearly hit the floor at Julia's statement.

Fargo's mouth opened as well, and he looked at Carter. "Is . . . is this true?"

"Well." Carter opened his mouth, closed it, then shrugged and nodded a little. "Uh . . ."

"That is so not true," Fargo protested.

"Oh, yes, it is," Julia said, and rounded on him with a look that pierced over her glasses. "Douglas, you have no real interest in this experiment other than a very Cro-Magnon need to win, or to be the best. All you've even talked about since yesterday was how you were tricked, or there was no way Zoe could have done as good as she did. You have no expertise in this area, no training, and no real knowledge. So you tell me—why do *you* think Henry or Director Blake wants you to work with me?"

Fargo blinked. "I— Why are you so mad at me?"

"I'm not mad. I'd just like to know what you did with yesterday's preliminary data."

"I didn't *do* anything with it. You had it."

"Well"—she gestured to the pile—"it's not here. And I specifically asked you to make sure it was all bound together. Not here," she said, and looked at the binder.

"I didn't *do* anything."

She rolled her eyes. "That's for sure."

"What is *that* supposed to mean?"

"Face it, Douglas. You suck at this—at Remote Viewing. You didn't get any of the targets right. And now you've done something with the results so that my findings for Henry won't reflect that. I'm not sure I can even trust you to be objective on this project anymore."

Fargo's jaw dropped, much like Carter's a few seconds earlier. "That is so not true," he said, his voice cracking. "I haven't done anything with the results. And for your information, I did get one of them right." He held up his index finger.

"No, you got it half right. You said it was a mammal with udders." She pulled all her papers together into the binder and slammed it shut. "Just say one, Douglas, Zoe"—she refocused on Zoe, standing behind the counter—"can I borrow that View you did yesterday? Wanted to make a copy of it for my notes."

"Sure." Zoe moved under the counter and pulled the first sheet from her bag. She handed it to Julia, who took it, straightened her glasses, and left the café.

Fargo was right behind her. "How come you want copies of what Zoe does and not what I did?" he said as he ran out the door.

Carter pursed his lips and blinked, and then looked at Jo, who shrugged and looked back down at her hands. Zoe came up to him as she set a tray of cups and saucers on the counter. "Fargo and Julia have been at it ever since I got here," she said softly. "It was like a broken record. She accuses him of hiding her findings and he protests. Rinse and repeat."

Carter moved from where he'd been standing to the seat Fargo had just vacated beside Jo. Vincent cleaned away Fargo's breakfast and set a steaming mug down in front of him—and then stood staring at him.

Leaning forward, Carter gave Vincent a half smile. "Something wrong?"

"I want you to taste it—see if I got it right."

Carter looked at his own mug—it looked like coffee. "You're not gonna go off on Shakespeare again, are you?"

Vincent stood and stared.

Carter leaned in and sniffed—and pulled up quickly. He tried not to make a face, but—

"It's wrong. . . ." Vincent started.

"Well, it's not wrong as much as it's not really what I'd normally drink." Carter held out his hands. "It's more like something my sister would drink."

Zoe moved from setting the dishes back on the counter to where her dad sat. She picked up the mug and sniffed, then gave Vincent a sad look. "It's chai."

Vincent cried out again. "For slander lives upon succession, for ever housed where it gets possession. . . ." He straightened his face and looked at the sheriff. "Act three, scene one."

Carter held up his hand. "Don't . . . do that again. Okay?"

"But, Sheriff, don't you see?" Vincent put his hands to his face again. "Three times? I've done this three times?" He put up his hands. "Oh, no. I can't be here. I—I can't do this today. I'm going home sick. There is something wrong with me . . . or is it the world?" He pointed to the outside street as a Hummer moved by slowly, then leaned in close to Carter. "It's them. You know it's them. No one knows why they're here . . . but we all suspect it."

Carter glanced at Zoe, who shrugged and took the chai

away. He looked back at Vincent and noticed a strange look in the man's eyes. Kinda . . . wild. "Suspect what?"

"Budget cuts." He nodded quickly. "The economy? We all know it's coming. They're gonna shut us down—I mean—we're not stupid. We all know how often the scientists here cause chaos on a daily basis. I mean, how often can we almost blow up the world before they get tired of it? And how often do you think the government is gonna keep paying for it?"

"That's got to be it, right?" Jo chimed in. "I mean . . . why else have all these soldiers here?"

Carter looked from Vincent to Jo and finally sat back. "Okay—I give—what the hell is going on here?"

Vincent narrowed his eyes at Carter. "That's what we'd all like to ask you. You seem to be in tight with the military." He crossed his arms over his ample middle. "Care to let us know what's going on? What's the real reason Eureka's being invaded by the military? *Et tu, Brute?*"

It was about that moment that Carter realized the subtle murmur that usually filled the inside of Café Diem had stopped. He slowly turned on his stool and looked around, realizing with a sinking feeling that everyone had stopped eating, and they were all staring at him.

He got up from his stool, glancing at Zoe. She was looking around as well, her eyes wide. "What's . . . going on?"

"Tell us, Sheriff," came a voice from the back. "Are we going to lose our jobs?"

"Yeah," came another one. "Are they going to take it all away from us?"

The door opened and Carter turned to see Henry step in, his face buried in the tablet he'd been using in the past few days. He moved with practiced ease to the counter and sighed. "Carter," he said as he looked up.

Carter looked back at everyone else.

The murmur had returned. Everyone was eating and talking. He looked back at Vincent, who was loading the coffee machine. Turning around fully once, he looked at Zoe. "Did you—"

She arched her eyebrows. "What's wrong?"

Carter stared at her. "You didn't see that?"

"See what?" Henry said as he looked around. "Something wrong?"

"Vincent." Carter pointed to the coffee machine. "Got orders wrong this morning."

Henry shrugged. "We're all human, Carter. We all make mistakes."

"No." Carter shook his head. "Not Vincent. He *never* gets orders wrong."

"Here ya go, Sheriff," Vincent said. "One coffee, hot, black."

"Vincent." Carter held up his right hand. "Did you or did you not just get three orders wrong in a row?"

The café owner blinked at him, then pouted, putting his hand to his face. "Oh, Sheriff . . . do you have to keep rubbing my face in it?"

Carter looked at Zoe. "And didn't Julia and Fargo have an argument?"

"Yeah." She frowned. "What's wrong, Dad?"

"But you didn't see everyone just go all 'Café of the Damned' just then?"

She laughed softly at him. "No, Dad, I didn't. You okay?"

Carter sat down slowly. "No . . . I mean yeah. . . ."

Henry put a hand on the table. "If I can get you to focus, Jack?"

Nodding, the sheriff looked at Henry. "Sure . . . what do you need?"

Henry moved from the counter by the door and came

around to take the seat Julia had sat in minutes earlier. "Give me your pager."

Carter reached into his back pocket and handed Henry the small, flat device. "What're you doing?"

"I'm going to transfer the information we gathered in that loop last night. Caruso's name, rank, and serial number."

"Why? I thought you were going to look up his background from GD."

Henry shook his head. "If I look up this guy on the Global network, they'll see it. And Mansfield's been keeping his identity a secret. At this point, I don't want to get shut out of this. I think there's a lot more going on here than just national secrets."

Jo spoke up. "You want us to look him up on the national database? I can use the computer at the sheriff's office. Carter's still got access to U.S. Marshal information."

Carter twisted in his seat and handed her the pager. "Here—find out who he is and who he worked for. Or at least, who he's listed as working for."

Jo pocketed it. "Got it. I'll get back with you soon as I dig something up."

"Also—" Henry held out his hands to her, and she put the pen and pad in them. Henry added another name and handed it back. "Look them both up. I'd appreciate it."

Jo looked at the piece of paper. "But I already looked him up."

"Who?" Jack asked.

"Aircom Graves," Jo said. "He's just . . . boring. A complete geek."

"Do you have the file?" Henry asked.

"Yeah, it's on his desk." She nodded at Carter.

"Then keep it with any information you find on Caruso and get back with Jack and me."

With that, she finished her coffee and left the café.

Still a bit uneasy at what he thought he'd seen earlier, Carter looked at Henry. "What exactly are you thinking?"

"Me? Nothing much. I just know how Mansfield works. What he's told you isn't really what's happening. And . . ." His voice trailed off.

"And?"

"Dr. Graves." He shook his head. "I know he's a brilliant scientist. Well, what I know, I know through the records available to GD. But who is he? I mean . . . his background at Johns Hopkins is impeccable. Biomedical engineering. But how is he involved in this project? And I just get a feeling. . . ."

"You mean about Dr. Graves." Jack sipped his coffee. "He invented the Brain Box. I don't think there's anything else to it."

"Yeah. Maybe."

"You think he's not really here for the reasons we've been told he is?"

Henry smiled. "That's it precisely."

"You don't trust him."

"I don't know."

Jack was thinking that Henry was being a bit more suspicious of things than he usually was when the door opened, just as Henry's beeper went off. Lucas walked in and Carter stared at him. The kid looked pale and a bit rumpled, as if he'd just rolled out of bed and walked all the way to the café.

Carter stood and closed the distance between himself and the boy. "Lucas?"

Lucas looked at the sheriff eye to eye, but Carter was sure he wasn't really seeing. "Hi, Sheriff. I need to—"

Carter looked over at Zoe, who was now moving from a table to Lucas. Stepping aside, Carter let her come nearer. "Lucas? Are you okay?"

He looked down at her, and a smile cracked his otherwise dulled expression. "Katie . . ."

Zoe took a quick step back.

Carter's mouth opened as well. Did Lucas just call his daughter by another girl's name?

Lucas moved forward and pointed at Zoe. "I told you to leave me alone. I don't trust you and I'm not going to fall prey to your mind games this time. You can't make me lie—not like before. It stops here and now."

Zoe moved back, blinking rapidly as Lucas put his hands over his ears and started repeating his name, his address, and his student ID.

Carter started to intervene. Something wasn't right in Lucas's eyes.

Abruptly Lucas collapsed, and Carter caught him under the arms. Vincent exclaimed as several of the patrons moved in to try to help. Carter lowered Lucas to the ground just as Henry knelt beside him and started checking vitals.

"He's unconscious," Henry said quickly as he opened each eye and then pressed his fingers to Lucas's neck. "His pulse is fast and erratic."

"Is this from the blast yesterday?" Carter said in a whisper to Henry.

"I don't know. I need to get him to GD." He touched Carter's shoulder and held up his pager. "I need you to meet Allison there as soon as possible. I'll take care of Lucas."

"Meet Allison?"

Henry nodded. "That was Zane that just beeped me. Apparently John Caruso's memories are missing from the Brain Box."

CHAPTER 11

"What do you mean, they're missing?" Allison said as she stood beside Zane and Dr. Graves facing the Brain Box as Carter came into the lab.

"Sorry I'm late," he called out as he moved up to stand beside her and watched. "Had a little trouble getting in. Apparently the guy at the gate decided not to trust my ID this morning."

Allison turned and gave him a curious look. "He did that to me, too."

"And me," Zane said. "And all I did was run out for pizza."

She turned back to him. "You haven't answered my question yet."

Zane shook his head. "We mean, the data that was inside the box is missing. It was there yesterday, and when Graves and I started the process of copying the information to the new node"—he held up his hand—"zero data."

"Well, not completely zero," Graves said. "But enough of it's gone that what's left isn't usable."

"Please tell me you made backups of the data?"

"Of course," Graves said with a slight edge to his voice. "But I sent them to my lab in Washington once we got on the road here. They're locked away, so it'll take a day or more to get them released and sent over here."

"Not to mention Mansfield's already been in here once demanding an update," Zane said in a tired voice. "I'm not sure how much longer I can deal with that guy."

Carter snorted. "Me and you both."

"Mansfield," Allison muttered. "If he'd just stay out of our hair for two minutes." She sighed. "What steps have you taken to figure out what happened to it?"

"All of them," Zane said as he tapped Graves on the shoulder. "Let me drive so I can show her."

Graves nodded and stood, moving slowly.

Carter watched him, taking note of his clothing. It looked to him as if the young man hadn't left the lab, showered, or changed. Graves suddenly looked at Carter. He was amazed at the depth of emotion in that face behind the silver-framed glasses.

Anger, frustration, loathing, hatred, relief . . . all balled into one look . . . before Graves gave him a half smile and turned his attention to Zane.

"These are the time stamps here." Zane keyed a few things and a holographic image appeared in front of them, making it easier for everyone to see. A spreadsheet of data appeared, with file names and dates to the left, size readings, and the strange symbols Carter had seen yesterday. "Now here and here—" Two of the lines of information glowed. "This is yesterday before we tried to translate using Lucas's program."

Allison pursed her lips as she looked at the suspended image. "Everything looks like it's there."

"Uh-huh." He switched screens and another spreadsheet of data showed up, only now the list consisted of two items with zero KB. "This is what we're seeing this morning. But what's even weirder is that if you look at the box's hard drive from, say, this terminal—" He switched screens again and the spreadsheet looked full again. "This is what you see."

"Which is the right image?" Allison said.

"The empty one," Zane said with a smirk. "Neat trick."

"So how is that happening?" Carter asked.

"We don't know," Graves said as he pulled off his glasses and rubbed his eyes. "It wasn't until Zane got back after picking up pizza that we even noticed the Brain Box was technically empty. Everything else in the system says the data is there. But it's not copyable."

"Well, this doesn't make sense," Allison said. "Air . . . were you here the whole time?"

"Yes . . . well . . . I took a nap while Zane went out. In the office next door. But I locked the lab up just as Zane showed me."

In Carter's opinion, Graves hadn't had long enough of a nap. He looked . . . rumpled.

"And neither of you noticed this before you went for pizza?"

Both of them shook their heads.

"So this data could have been missing much earlier—at any point?"

Graves nodded. "That's what I'm afraid of. Before the accident, it wasn't on a secure line. I hadn't initiated any restricted permissions. I just wanted to get it done and translated so Mansfield would get off my back." He nearly blushed as he ducked his head. "I'm sorry. . . . The man drives me crazy."

Allison smiled. "You're not alone, Air."

Carter nodded vigorously at the young man behind her

back and then looked at the floating screen. He narrowed his eyes. "Zane, put up the first image."

Zane complied.

Carter moved from the terminal and walked closer to the image. "Okay, now throw up the second one."

He did.

"Now the third."

Again the image shifted.

"It's exactly the same as the first."

"How do you mean?" Allison said.

"Well, I don't know what most of this means." He looked back at them and then made a face. "Okay so I don't know what *any* of it means, but what I can look at is inconsistencies. Or, in this case—" He turned back. "First image again."

The first image appeared. Carter pointed to the third line down, and the eleventh line down. "What are these?"

Graves shrugged. "Those are actually just redundant file—RAM images that represent scripts inside of the application. They work like a gather network."

Carter turned and looked at him. "So . . . all that talk means they're not part of the data, right?"

"Right."

"Well, then say that," Carter muttered. "Zane, next image."

The next image appeared. "Okay, the only remaining information is those two same files."

Everyone agreed.

"With different time stamps."

Allison moved to stand beside Carter. "Zane, the third image."

The third image returned, only this time where every other file had a newer time stamp, those two files still held the same time stamp as the first image. "Well, I'll be. . . ." Allison said.

"See—" Carter pointed at the image. "A lot of the criminals I dealt with were thieves of some kind. And they always used this trick to make it out to appear there was no one in the building. You know . . . hack in and run a loop of say an empty office for a security camera, but while in truth they're in there. I don't understand the data, but it sure looks to me as if there's a gap here."

Allison turned and moved back to the terminal. "Zane, I want you and Graves to go over the lab's logs minute by minute from the point the box became part of the internal network. Then let me know the first time there is a discrepancy." She looked at Carter. "I need to go check on Lucas—and then we need to have a little talk with Mansfield."

Carter hurried after Allison as she left the lab. "Do we have to?"

"Sorry, Carter, but it looks to me like someone's been tampering with the lab's computer. To hide the memories of a dead guy." She stopped at the elevator and faced him. "And before I put any more of Global's files or systems in danger from outside tampering, I want to know exactly who and what I'm dealing with here."

Carter wasn't surprised to see Zoe in the infirmary with Lucas and Henry. Julia was there as well, and Carter stopped and looked around. "Where's Fargo? He's not here, is he?"

Julia smiled and blushed. "Oh . . . no. I put him to work organizing my preliminary work on the Remote Viewing project."

"Here?" Carter pointed to the floor.

"No, at my place."

"That'll keep him busy for a while?"

"Carter," Allison admonished him. "Get off Fargo's case," she said as she passed him.

"Hey, you didn't want him around, either," he muttered, and moved to the bed.

Lucas lay flat on the examination table, the same one Carter had found himself on and seen Zoe on too many times for comfort. Lucas was paler than before, and Henry was looking at the monitor above the boy's head.

"What's wrong with him?" Allison said in a concerned voice.

Carter moved up behind Zoe, and she leaned back against him. He could feel how tense she was . . . and worried.

"Well." Henry sighed. "I honestly don't know."

Carter looked at Allison and then at Henry. "There haven't been too many times you've said that, Henry."

"True, but this is one of them." He reached to the back of his neck and rubbed at it. "He has a low-grade fever, but we can't find any sign of infection. He has elevated cholesterol levels—high for someone as young as he is. His serotonin is low . . . extremely low."

"He's depressed?" Allison said.

Henry nodded. He glanced at Zoe and then at Carter. "I'm not sure he'd want me to say this, especially around Zoe. . . ."

"What?" Zoe said. "He's seeing another woman, isn't he?"

Henry frowned as Allison said, "Zoe? What do you mean?"

Carter held up a hand. "Oh . . . nothing. Go on with what you were going to say." He didn't really want to draw attention to Zoe's drawings just yet, or her insane belief that they were out of Lucas's head.

"Lucas has been having a hard time at MIT. Several of the projects he's been working on—didn't go so well. He blamed himself. I spoke with his adviser and he's assured me that Lucas wasn't at fault, but of course"—he looked at

Zoe—"Lucas still blamed himself. He was afraid he was failing and he didn't want to admit that to you."

"Me?" She shook her head. "But how does that give him a reason to cheat?"

"Oh, he's not cheating." Henry shook his head. "Lucas isn't capable of cheating. And his professors all agree he's one of the brightest minds in their classes."

"I think what she means is"—Allison smiled at Zoe—"he was cheating with another woman. Right?"

Zoe sighed. "He called me Katie . . . and accused me of something, right before he passed out." Her eyes teared up. "Who is Katie?" She turned and half ran, half walked from the room.

Carter started after her, but Allison stopped him. "No, let her go."

He sighed and shoved his hands into his pockets. "Yeah . . . you're right."

Allison smiled. "Henry, what *can* you say is wrong with him?"

"Not much. He's sleeping for now. And like I said, elevated temperature, low serotonin—which, if he hasn't been getting sleep, could lead to depression. We'll just have to wait and see for the moment. I'll set up a monitoring bot on his vitals. I need to get back to the lab and see how Graves and Zane are doing."

"Oh, did you talk to—"

"Graves called and let me know what you need them to do. Good idea." He looked at Carter. "And you let me know as soon as you know." With that, he glanced at Allison and left the infirmary.

Allison looked at the door and then to Carter. "Let him know when you know? You going to fill me in?"

Having known Henry now for a while, Carter had been able to read the man's gestures as a way of nonverbally saying, *Fill her in.* "Yeah . . . but let's take a walk, okay?"

The two of them took the elevator to the roof arboretum. There he strolled to the edge overlooking the parking lot. It was a nice place, where many of the employees brought their lunch and ate, read books during break, or came to socialize.

Because of the early hour there was no one else on the roof. And it was Saturday.

"Now you care to tell me why you're so paranoid about going to my office to talk?"

"They were able to translate a text version of the data from the Brain Box," he said as he watched her. "It was a man's name, rank, and serial number."

"We know his identity?" Her eyes widened. "If General Mansfield found out—"

"He'd probably . . . blow a fuse." Carter smiled. "Henry gave me the name and asked me to look him up. Didn't want to use Global's system. He seemed a bit paranoid about it."

"Seems everyone's on edge with the military here," Allison said as a breeze blew her hair. She moved it from her face and frowned up at him. "What was the name?"

"Jonathan Caruso. Jo's running it for me. She already ran Dr. Graves's history as well."

"Why Graves? We know everything about him."

"We know what's on his record." He smiled. "But my time as a marshal proved to me that what's there in black and white isn't always the truth."

"But why investigate him? He's working with us on this."

"Wasn't me that wanted to know. It was Henry." He shrugged. "Jo had already looked him up and said he was boring. She's got the file in the office."

"What are you not telling me, Carter?"

He paused for a few seconds. "Ever since yesterday— something's been wrong. I can't pinpoint it. I can't say what it is. But it's like this feeling of doom. That something's going to happen. And when I walked into Café Diem this morning, Vincent had messed up two orders, and then he messed up mine."

Her eyes widened. "But Vincent *never* misses an order."

"Exactly. Vincent started spouting Shakespeare—"

"He only does that when he's really stressed," she said.

"—and then Julia and Fargo had it out, and Jo was biting her nails."

"Carter . . . Julia and Fargo often argue—it's what makes their relationship so dynamic. And—what's so special about biting nails?"

"I never see Jo do that—it's a nervous habit. She always watches for suspects who do that. And the argument between Fargo and Julia? She was accusing Fargo of sabotaging her work."

Allison laughed. "Well . . . I'm sure Fargo didn't do it on purpose, but I *can* see it happening by accident."

Carter felt as if he were striking out on all fronts with Allison. "There was a second . . . in the café . . . where everyone's eyes were on me, Allison. Everyone was watching me and wanting to know why the military was here. Were we being shut down? Was the government going to pull the plug on Eureka?"

"Did they? I mean—did everyone ask you that?"

He put up his hands. "No. I blinked and it was all normal, Allison. The whole place went *Twilight Zone* and then"—he snapped his fingers—"normal again."

"Sounds like you were hallucinating, and the town *is* a bit paranoid with the military in here, too," Allison said. "But things are fine. We'll get this situation sorted out and then Mansfield can leave."

Her pager went off and she removed it from her pocket and looked at it. "Oh . . . gotta get back to the office. Sitter's gotta go to the bathroom."

Carter frowned. "In your office?"

"Yeah." She moved her hair from her face as she reposi-tioned the pager in her pocket. "I brought Jenna in to work with me."

"Why? The sitter couldn't come to your house?"

"Yes . . . but I felt a little paranoid myself leaving them in the house. I mean . . . what if another shelf fell?" She blinked and put a hand on his arm. "Oh, it's not a reflection on you or your hanging skills with the shelf. It's just—what if the house caught fire? Or something happened to the sit-ter and then Jenna was all alone?" She started to the eleva-tor. "I just don't trust leaving them in that house anymore."

Carter rubbed at his face. Vincent misses orders, Julia accuses Fargo of sabotage, Jo bites her nails, Henry doesn't trust Graves, and now Allison doesn't trust her own house.

What was going on?

CHAPTᵉR 12

While Allison checked on Jenna, Carter made his way back down to lab 511 to watch them work on the box, after stopping in to check on Lucas. Zoe was still there and intended to stay there until Lucas woke up—or one of the doctors there made headway on what was wrong with him.

Zane and Graves were deep in conversation by the Brain Box. Carter smiled at them as he walked by and went straight to Henry, who was busy at the storynest terminal. He looked up at Carter, glanced over at Graves and Zane, and then said in a low voice, "You heard back from Jo?"

Carter pursed his lips as he shook his head, keeping his own voice low. "Nah . . . she'll get back to me soon as she's got something." He nodded at the storynest. "Anything concrete? Someone tamper with it?"

"Yes, someone did." Henry pointed to the screen. It went from a display of storynest inventory, which Carter remembered looking at with Allison a while back, to a split screen of the three images he'd seen earlier. "But not at the time the information went missing."

"I—don't follow you."

"Everything you or I or anyone else does on a computer system leaves an electronic footprint of some kind. Whether it's a date and time stamp like you saw, or your IP address when you hit Web sites. There's always some sign that someone's been there. And in the case of the storynest versus the Brain Box"—he nodded to the two men—"someone had already set up that box to feed false information."

Carter frowned. "Why?"

"My guess is because they knew it would go missing once they got here, or they were planning on failure."

"What exactly are you suggesting, Henry?"

"I'm suggesting that we're not being given all the information here. Mansfield's got this whole facility spooked because we're supposedly dealing with something that smacks of national security. And the town's in an uproar and for some reason they're all spreading rumors that they're going to shut Eureka down because of budget cuts."

"Yeah . . ." Carter thought of his waking nightmare that morning. "I can see that."

"But Jack—what's the real story?"

"Well, I'd assume it's the one Mansfield's been giving."

Henry arched his eyebrows. "Is it? Carter . . ." He handed Carter the halo. "Put this on and tell me if this is national security."

Carter took the small, slim unit—having worn it before to review memories when Tess had worked on the archiving project—and started to slip it on. He paused and looked at Henry. "I'm not gonna get shocked, am I? You know . . . sailing across the room?" He looked at the device. "Or have my memories erased?"

"Just put it on."

Carter complied and closed his eyes. There was a flash against his eyelids and abruptly he saw clear images of a woman in front of him. She was angry and pacing back and forth, her hair obscuring her face. She was ranting, her voice clear in his head. ". . . all of my life for this. I've devoted everything to this project, and with a sustainable singularity within our reach, Juicebox can finally be realized. And I will not let you throw it away just because of your stupid moral code. . . ."

The scene shifted again to boots crunching in the snow. He was looking down as he walked, and she was talking again. ". . . not what you think. He killed my mother. He deserved what happened to him. . . ."

"But you abuse what you can do—you use it for the worst kind of evil—"

The scene shifted to a room full of men and women in suits, some in lab coats, all of them glaring at him as he spoke. ". . . here to interrupt or to interfere with your daily routine. I'm just here to get to the truth. There is a lot of money at stake here, as well as the future of a sustainable singularity. . . ."

Darkness, and then her voice again, but there was nothing to see. ". . . can't let Juicebox die, John. I'm sorry, but you can't interfere. If you see a large truck . . . you will drive into it. . . ."

Abruptly Carter *could* see. He was behind the wheel of a car, his foot on the gas pedal, as he accelerated into the path of an eighteen-wheeler, head-on, just before—

Carter snatched the halo off and jumped out of his seat. He was breathing heavy, blinking, and running his hands through his hair. "What . . . ? How . . . ? Who the . . . ?" He looked at Henry as he started pacing. "What the hell was that? And what has a juice box got to do with any of it?"

Henry bent over and retrieved the halo from the floor. "I don't know—but Allison and I were more interested in this sustainable singularity. What you just saw was visually behind the name, rank, and serial number."

"Uh . . ." He winced at Henry. "What?"

"I ran the data through Lucas's translator, and what showed up as name, rank, and serial number as text gave me those visuals."

"But . . . none of that made sense."

"No . . . it didn't. But this is all we have saved from what was harvested. Luckily it was in the storynest and untouched. Someone physically moved those files, Jack."

Carter looked at the two men. "You think it's Graves?"

"Possibly—but why? What purpose would it serve to go in and delete or tamper with the data? If whatever it is this person saw or knows is a matter of national security, I would assume General Mansfield would have vetted anyone involved in this project."

"But," Carter said, "Mansfield's already said he didn't have a choice. Graves was already on the project and is the only one qualified. What if Graves is afraid there's more in those memories that somehow implicates him?"

"In what?" Henry arched his eyebrows in question.

Carter touched the back of his neck. "Haven't figured that part out yet." He lowered his hand and sighed. "Has Graves seen this? Did you ask him about Juicebox?"

"Yes, he saw it; no, he didn't know what Juicebox was. His reaction was a lot like yours. But since he saw it, he's been a little more tight-lipped around me. I think he doesn't trust me."

"The whole town seems to have taken a paranoia pill." Carter thought of Allison and her bringing the baby in and decided his head hurt too much to really get into it all at the moment.

Carter nodded. "Right. So what we've got is missing data. And you haven't found it anywhere on GD's systems?"

"Searched the entire network. It's not here."

"And we have a piece of those memories that show . . . nothing that makes sense." Carter made a face. "Henry . . ." He straightened. "I thought . . . when Graves first came in . . . he said he made a copy of the data from the Brain Box to the Global computer system."

"If he did, I can't find it."

"Well, a search is all about keywords, right? Strings—did I say that right?"

Henry grinned. "I know what you mean."

"Maybe you have to change the parameters of the search?" He shrugged. "I know that Zoe's had to show me that a few times when I Googled. Like, never Google 'hot rods' if you want Mustang parts, 'cause"—he shook his head and whistled—"you'd be amazed what that'll bring up in a search engine."

"Ah . . ." Henry gave the sheriff a half grin. "I see. But you're right. I'd not thought of that. I'll start a search—see if I can find it. Did Graves *say* he copied it?"

"He says he has a copy back in Washington." Carter shook his head. "But that doesn't really hold a lot of water with me. And I swear I heard him say he was making a backup copy."

"I'll look." Henry turned to the two men. "Hey, Zane? Can you come here and check something for me?"

Zane straightened and approached. Carter moved back and watched as Graves went to stand by the Brain Box. After a few seconds he moved his thumb under his chin, and Carter took a few hesitant steps closer to notice that Graves was staring intently, but not at anything in particular. Carter recognized the look of someone deep in his own memories.

Carefully he moved into what he hoped was the young man's peripheral vision.

Graves looked over at him blankly and then gave a shallow smile. "Hi, Sheriff Carter. Back again?"

"Yeah," he said, shoving his hands into his pockets. "I just can't get enough of this place."

Sighing, the younger man also pushed his hands into the pockets of his trousers. "There was a time when I wanted to work at Global. Years ago, before I started doing research in Washington. I'd put in time at a few of the other facilities—but never here."

"Other facilities?"

Graves nodded to him. "Yeah—you didn't know there were others?"

"Must've . . . uh, slipped my mind."

"Eureka might be the biggest and the best, but it's not the only high-powered research lab, Sheriff. I've visited most of them. But in the end, the best work comes out of Eureka."

Carter stared at him, "Are you saying there are other—"

"—government-chartered research labs?" Graves said. "I'm part of a team that looks over the data from each and then sees how the advancements can be applied. So when I saw the storynest—" He shrugged. "I had such high hopes for it."

"But you don't anymore?"

"Sheriff—" Graves ran a hand through his thick brown hair. The motion made several sections of his hair stick up at odd angles. "Let's say your last thoughts, before you died, were of someone other than your spouse? Or they were about something bad you did—or about something bad someone else did. Or maybe even a family secret you were taking to the grave. Do you think the government has the right to go in and expose those memories?"

Carter pulled out his hand and pointed at the ground in a slight gesture. "Well, no . . . except that family secret one.

Especially if it was about the inheritance." When Graves didn't crack a smile, Carter straightened his expression and sniffed. "Sorry. It's just that—I find the whole concept a bit on the spooky side."

"I agree with that," Graves said. "Having anyone look inside of your head." He shrugged. "Wasn't what I had in mind."

"Yeah." Carter nodded. "Allison told me how you intended this thing to be used. And—being in law enforcement and a former U.S. Marshal, I commend you on that."

"Thanks, Sheriff." He looked at the box. "Sometimes I'm not sure if we should be messing with the mind at all. Theories of conscious thought, the universe, the effect of the mind on the body and its surroundings—it's all been lumped into noetic science for now."

"Noetic . . ." Carter snapped his fingers. "I just heard about that. Remote Viewing?"

Graves's eyes widened as he looked at the sheriff. "You know about that? About Stargate, Ingo Swann?"

The names were all familiar, and Carter was sure he'd gotten them from Julia or Fargo, but as to who did what? Nope. "I just know my daughter's been playing with it."

"Sheriff." Graves looked very serious behind his glasses. "Remote Viewing isn't something anyone should *play* with. It's very dangerous in the wrong hands." He looked at the Brain Box. "Just like this."

"Well, yeah, maybe," Carter said, feeling completely out of his element and trying to figure out why he'd started the conversation to begin with, other than to get to know the suspect. "But this"—he gestured to the box—"this is real. This is"—he then brought his other hand up and gestured to the box—"tangible. The idea of using your mind to see something far away?"

"It isn't an old idea, Sheriff. You can look through history and see where out-of-body travel was considered the norm. The paranormal—though often thought of as a neat reality TV show—does have valid points to it."

"Yeah, but how do you explain seeing scenes in your head?"

"I don't follow."

"Well, take my daughter, Zoe, who's been doing these experiments with Fargo and Julia—" He paused. "You don't know them. And it's better not to get into Fargo's chaos field. Never mind." He waved it away. "She did about five of these Views and got them all right. And then she got one wrong—saw something totally different. And then she tried it again last night and kept seeing the same woman over and over again but in different scenes." He shook his head. "I didn't know she could draw."

"She . . ." Graves looked surprisingly interested. "Your daughter drew from a RV session. With no other training? That's . . . that's incredible, Sheriff. Has she shown these abilities before?"

"Like this? No. Just started yesterday, and then last night. You should see the pictures."

Zoe's voice came over the intercom. "Henry?"

"Zoe?"

"Can you come to the infirmary? It's Lucas. Something's wrong."

CHAPTER 13

Carter, Allison, and Zoe stood around the infirmary, along with various medical personnel, as Henry and Julia examined Lucas. According to Zoe, Lucas's blood pressure had dropped, causing the monitoring alarms to go off. She checked the vitals herself, seeing another decrease in his serotonin levels as well as his glucose levels.

And then Lucas had a seizure.

Allison pulled Zoe aside and Carter followed, his attention snapping between his daughter and Henry. He was hoping to get some kind of idea of what was happening.

"Zoe . . . tell me again what were you doing when this happened?"

Carter looked at his daughter, and his heart went out to her. He hated to see his little girl in pain—any kind of pain—whether physical or emotional. And with her growing up and becoming a woman, he was uncertain most of the time where his boundaries were as a dad. When to comfort her and when not to.

Sometimes it just sucked being a parent.

Zoe's eyes were red-rimmed, and her nose was red as well. Her face looked flushed and swollen from crying, and he reached out to her, unable to stop. To his comfort, she moved into his embrace and held on tight as she spoke with Allison.

"I was sitting with him, and reading the charts. Testing what I knew and what I didn't." She sniffed and wiped her eyes. "He took a deep breath and opened his eyes. He started talking to me, about school. It didn't make any sense at first—sort of disjointed—and I wasn't sure he was fully awake. And then he called me Katie again, and started talking about bureaucracy and how I was never going to control his mind again, and said he wasn't a scientist at all but a failure."

Allison frowned. "Why does he keep calling you Katie?"

"I don't know." Zoe sniffed again. "What bureaucracy? School? The fact he's not doing good? It's not anything he's told me about. . . . That is, when we used to call each other all the time."

Carter nodded. "Yeah . . . I remember the bill."

She pinched him and he jumped, but she held him tighter and he leaned down and kissed the top of her head. "And then his eyes rolled back into his head. . . ."

Allison looked up at Carter. "But what could cause a seizure? I don't know of anything in Lucas's medical history that could cause anything like that."

"Maybe Henry can find something," Carter said.

As if on cue, Henry moved away from Lucas and approached them. Carter did not like the look on his face. "I only wish it were that easy," he said.

"What is it?" Allison asked.

Henry motioned for them to follow him over to one of the monitor stations and sat down. He pulled up several images, none of which Carter recognized as anything familiar. "Working for me, Lucas had regular checkups. Fine, healthy young man. Now, earlier I did say his serotonin levels were low, which can be caused by lack of sleep, and stress, and given his experience in the past two months, I wasn't surprised to see that."

Zoe sniffed. "But I would never see him like that—not as a failure. That's what you're saying, isn't it? He was depressed. Those readings were normal for someone depressed."

Henry nodded. "Yes. But convincing him he was doing just fine was going to take time. So I put him to work on this project because I felt it was one where he could have a success that would maybe boost his own self-confidence. He just doesn't trust himself anymore."

"And he doesn't trust me," Zoe said as she pushed a strand of hair from her face. "If he trusted me . . . he'd have confided in me . . . and he wouldn't have cheated on me."

"You don't know that," Allison said.

"I have no idea why he's calling you Katie. Unless there's brain damage of some fashion."

"I doubt it," Zoe said. "He called me Katie before he had the seizure."

"Henry, about that." Allison crossed her arms. "Other than the serotonin levels and added stress—those things just aren't enough to make him seize like that. What else is happening in there?"

"That"—Henry held up a finger—"was something puzzling me. I'd looked at his medical records a hundred times. So I sent a message to the attending physician at MIT and we both reexamined his scans. Odd that no one saw this."

"This?" Allison and Carter glanced at each other.

Carter pursed his lips. "You found something?"

Henry pressed a few keys. "Yes. And it makes sense given his current state."

The image magnified and Carter narrowed his eyes, still unsure what it was he was looking at.

"The image on the left is a shot of Lucas's brain from three months ago, when I gave him the physical. The one on the right is of the same area, but taken five minutes ago."

Carter pursed his lips again and looked from one to the other. "Is it me . . . or is there a big, blobby shadow on that right one?"

Allison shook her head. "Oh my God, Henry, how could any of us have missed this?"

"Because it wasn't there three months ago," Henry said. "It explains a lot of what he's been describing on the phone. The headaches, the inability to think clearly. Shaking in his extremities. Yes, those are also symptoms of stress and lack of sleep, but this . . ."

"What? So this isn't stress?" Carter asked.

Zoe turned and pressed her face into his chest. "It's a tumor, Dad. Lucas has a brain tumor."

Carter's response was drowned out when a loud, brain-numbing voice bellowed, "Dr. Blake, a word with you."

Carter sighed as he looked up to see General Mansfield moving fast into the infirmary. And he didn't look too happy.

"General." Allison held up her hand. "This is not the time—"

"This is *exactly* the time," he said as he moved to stand in front of her, towering over Henry, who remained seated. Even Zoe clung to Carter harder as the general neared. Mansfield looked around before motioning to her. "Come with me. You, too, Dr. Deacon."

"I have a patient—"

"Now."

Carter frowned at the general's behavior. The man had never been one of Carter's favorite people, but they'd gotten along fairly well, even after Mansfield fired him because of Thorn. Of course, being hired back again because Henry as mayor had never approved it was poetic justice, and Carter always felt Mansfield hated it.

He put his hands on Zoe's upper arms and kissed her forehead. "Stay here with Lucas. I'm going to go see what this is about." And he followed Henry, Allison, and Mansfield out of the room.

A hand on his shoulder caused him to turn, and Julia was there. "Sheriff, there's something about this tumor that's odd—"

"Julia, any tumor is odd."

"I know, Sheriff—but this one isn't real."

He put a hand on her hand. "Not now, Julia. Let's see about calming the general first, okay?"

She nodded and reluctantly returned to the infirmary.

Allison took the lead and steered them to her office, where she gestured for the general to take a seat. When he didn't, she moved behind her desk.

Mansfield pointed at Carter. "I didn't ask you in here."

"No, I did," Allison said.

Carter didn't look at her even though he was fully aware she'd just lied.

She continued. "Now . . . let's start this again as adults, General." She laced her fingers together and put them on her desk. "What seems to be the problem?"

He rounded on her and set his hat on the desk. "Don't patronize me, Director. I just went and checked on what's supposed to be top priority in this facility and find only Dr. Graves and Mr. Donovan working on it—" He pointed to Henry. "I hear that Dr. Deacon is in the infirmary looking after some sick kid while time is ticking away on what we need to find in that box."

"That sick kid happens to be working on your little pet project," Allison said in a sharp tone. "Or have you already forgotten what I told you yesterday?"

Carter moved to the back of the room beside the floor-to-ceiling window overlooking the rotunda. He glanced down to watch a few people as Allison attempted to put the general in his place.

"Zane is one of our top scientists, and you said it yourself—Aircom Graves is the top expert in his field as well. No one stopped work on your little project, General, but the lives and well-being of everyone in this building are *my* responsibility. So when I have an employee suddenly become ill, no matter who it is, I take care of them. And neither you nor the United States government is going to tell me what's more important in my own building. Do I make myself clear?"

"You're playing with fire, Director. What's in that box is a matter of—"

"I know, I know. National security. You know"—she sat back—"you people toss those words around so much now, they've lost their meaning. You bring a piece of technology in here that you insist has a dead man's thoughts in it and tell me to decipher what's inside without even a hint of why. Was this guy a spy, Mansfield? Was he doing something illegal? Why the secrecy?" She crossed her arms in front of her. "I have a high level of security myself, and I made a few inquiries about why you would be here. And you know what answer I received?"

Carter looked from the rotunda back to Mansfield. The sheriff was positioned so that he could see the general's face and was positive the man had just flinched. Just a little bit. But it was there. Yes! He glanced over at Henry, who was busy looking at the white tablet in his hand, pressing the screen, and frowning.

When the general didn't answer, she leaned forward and put her hands on her desk. "No one at the DoD knew *why* you were here. In fact, a few of them were a little surprised you were in Eureka. Last they knew you were at PNNL."

Carter opened his mouth, but Henry said, "Pacific Northwest National Laboratory. It's not far from here, in Washington state."

The general moved from Allison's desk and clasped his hands behind his back. "Why I'm here is none of your or anyone else's business. When I say it's a matter of national security, that's exactly what it is."

"Then perhaps you can tell me," Henry spoke up as he looked at Mansfield, "why the images we've been able to translate so far from that box mention a sustainable singularity?"

Mansfield snapped his head around to look at Henry. He took several steps toward him. "You were able to decipher the memories? You can see them? How much have you been able to see? How long before we can see the rest?"

Carter looked from Henry to Allison. He started to say something about the rest of the memories disappearing like Casper, but the warning look in Allison's eyes was enough for him to hesitate. He looked back through the window to see Graves and Fargo disappear into the elevator.

Instead he looked at Allison and said, "Who let Fargo back in the building?"

No one answered, but it still worried him. They were all locked in a game of stare-down. The last place he wanted Fargo to go was lab 511, and Graves didn't know about Fargo's history for finding buttons to push.

"General," Allison said. "They're working on the rest of it—but I'd like to know exactly what it is this deceased person either saw or witnessed. And what if these memories aren't what you're so sure they are? What about private ones? I daresay the harvesting program Dr. Graves created is not able to weed the military memories from the personal ones. Who are we to invade this man's—"

The general shook his head. "He got to you, didn't he?"

Allison stopped talking and looked at Henry. Henry leaned his head toward the general. "Who got to us?"

"Graves."

That caught Carter's attention, and he refocused on the conversation in the office, though he still kept a running reminder to go find Fargo. "What do you mean by 'he got to us'?"

"Exactly how it sounds, Sheriff." Mansfield sneered as he shot Carter a glare. "Oh, the man's brilliant. One of you eggheads. Well"—he sneered at Carter—"not you."

Carter smiled. "Likewise."

"Top in his class at Johns Hopkins. Worked in government labs for several years now, a lot of it looking over the discoveries made by Eureka as well as the other labs. When I read what he'd done with the technology Dr. Fontana had created with the storynest, I was amazed. I understand what practical applications he had in store for it—and I believe it does have its use there. But when this situation came up, his Brain Box was the first thing that came to mind to solve the problem." He sighed. "Who knew the guy was going to get all wishy-washy?"

Henry clasped his hands in front of him, cradling the tablet against his chest. "You mean Dr. Graves is having an ethical issue with how you're applying his science. Gee. Wow. And no other scientist on the planet has ever had issues with the DoD."

"Nice sarcasm, Dr. Deacon. I'm aware there's no love lost between us and them. And if the damn technology had been finished when this happened, his ass would have been the last one I'd have brought along with me. Hell—if it were finished—I'd already have the information I needed and wouldn't be here." Mansfield looked at Allison. "There wasn't enough time once we were able to take possession of the body—Graves flew to PNNL with his device and used it to harvest what he could."

Carter glanced at Allison. That was the first piece of information the general had given them on the dead guy, Jonathan Caruso. "So he was already at PNNL," Carter said. "Where you were last reported."

The general didn't look at Carter, but continued to speak directly to Allison. Carter smirked at Henry, who returned the glance.

"Graves told me the translation would need work once he harvested the memories, and it was his idea to come here. Insisted he needed to get a firsthand look at Dr. Fontana's time capsule project in hopes of converting the memories to images or viable thoughts. He was enthusiastic on the phone—until he arrived and saw the body. Not sure if it was realizing he was staring at siphoning the memories of a real corpse or something else that turned his stomach. Either way—he's been subtly fighting me ever since."

"Subtly fighting you?" Henry said. "In what way?"

"Insisting we come here, for starters," Mansfield quipped, giving Henry a look. "Insisting the data may not reveal what I want it to reveal. Constantly reminding me of the precedent this sort of thing will create. Letting me know he intends to make a full report and disclosure of my unethical practices to his superiors."

"I don't see where how he feels would be any different than any normal person would."

"I don't trust his findings, Dr. Deacon. And I don't always trust yours or this facility."

"Sounds a bit paranoid."

"There's a lot of that going around," Carter muttered. "General, from what I've seen of Dr. Graves, he's been more than willing to help Dr. Blake's people. The only person who's not been helpful is you."

"You're stepping on dangerous ground, Sheriff. You have no idea what it is you're dealing with."

"That's because you won't tell us," Allison said. "General, as I said before, once we have a clear and coherent image of Graves's harvest from the Brain Box, I will call you. Now . . . if we can get back to work? And please"—she stood—"make sure to keep your people out of my people's hair?"

The general retrieved his hat from her desk and strode to the door. With a glance back he said, "You are all ordered not to talk about singularities or anything you may or may not have seen from that box. Do I make myself clear? There's not much time left, Dr. Blake. Please don't force my hand with the higher-ups."

With that, he left.

Allison turned her intense stare on Carter. "Carter, why did you—

But he held up his finger. "Uh . . . can we hold that very angry look and tone for a sec? One little emergency at a time? I just saw"—he pointed at the window—"Fargo go down the elevator with Graves."

All three of them left the director's office and made a direct line for the elevator door.

CHAPTᵉR 14

In the elevator, Carter leaned in to whisper to Allison. "Where was the baby? She wasn't in your office."

Allison glanced at Henry and whispered, "Sitter took her for a walk."

"I can hear both of you, you know," Henry said. "And Allison, you know bringing a baby into GD like that is strictly against company policy."

"Yes, I know, Henry. But I was feeling distrustful of my house," she said, and she told him how the shelf collapsed almost on top of the crib.

Henry asked the same question Carter had—why not move the bed beside the window?

"Because anyone can come through the window and grab her."

"Allison," Henry said gently as they stepped out of the elevator. "If someone is going to come in through your window, those few steps from the window to the—"

Carter turned and caught Henry's attention and gave him a shake of his head, as if to say, *I already pointed that out.*

Entering the lab, Carter felt his heart sink to his feet when he saw Fargo sitting at the storynest with Graves beside him. "Hey, hey, hey," he said in a loud voice, as if scolding a child. "You know you're not allowed near that machine."

Fargo looked up and gave the sheriff a pained expression. "That was an accident—and I successfully fixed it, if you recall."

"Oh, I recall, all right."

"Fargo," Allison said as she motioned for him to move away from the storynest.

Graves straightened. "Did I miss something?"

"How much of the report on the storynest project did you read?" Allison said. "You did read the report on the events that occurred when the catchers triggered memory loss? And how we"—she pointed at herself and Carter—"almost died by being turned into goo?"

"Well, yes, I did, but that was fixed, problem solved. No harm was done. But why do you keep bringing it up?"

"Did you miss the goo explanation?" Carter muttered. "Just a word of warning—Fargo has a tendency to push the wrong button."

"Fine, fine," Fargo said, crossing his arms over his chest. "All Dr. Graves wanted was for me to show him how the remote halo works. I'm going to find a place where I'm wanted." He faced the ceiling and left the room.

Allison looked at Graves. "Why the remote halo?"

The young man smiled at Dr. Blake as he took the seat Fargo had just vacated. "Streamlining purposes. As the harvester works now, the actual neural synaptic retriever isn't very portable. I wanted to use the design for the halo so that, say"—he shrugged—"in the future if detectives or MEs do use it for memory retrieval, it's easier to manipulate."

Carter nodded. "You wanna make it more attractive." Made sense to him. But why right now?

"I understand your curiosity, Air." She put a hand on the storynest's surface. "But right now, we need to find the missing data before the general explodes."

"He came to see you, too?" Zane asked.

"Was he in here?" Allison said, moving from the storynest to Zane and Henry.

"Oh, yeah, he was." The young scientist kept his eyes focused on the monitor before him. "All bluster and menacing anger. But we didn't say anything."

"We know," Carter said, smiling. "Any luck finding it?"

Zane shook his head. "No—and I've done a full Global neural network sweep."

"Oh, come on—you guys can pinpoint unpronounceable isotopic . . . stuff." He looked around as words failed him. "But you can't pinpoint data?"

"Not if it's just not here." Zane ran his fingers through his hair. "And that's what's not making sense. It was on the Brain Box when Dr. Graves and I connected the unit to the Global network. There isn't any other access into it."

"Not to mention," Graves said as he left the storynest and joined them, "I built a series of security protocols into the hard drive. You'd have to know six different numeric passwords to even access it."

"So what about the copy of it you made when you first got here?" Carter said, looking directly at Dr. Graves, Mansfield's words ringing in his head. He didn't care for the general, not even a little bit. But the man hadn't gotten to where he was on hunches and guesses. He read people, and Carter had to admit, when he tried to read Dr. Graves, it was hard.

Graves nodded. "I did make a copy. I simply transmitted it high-speed to my server there. Faster and more secure. Not many technologies out there exist that can intercept that data speed."

"Is there someone you can call there?" Carter tilted his head to the side. "Like a lab assistant? Just to check to make sure there *is* a backup copy. I mean—" He used his left hand to gesture at the young man and then smiled. "You've probably already talked to them, right? To see about getting that copy here? If this high speed is really . . . that high speed?" Carter put his hands together. "I mean . . . why waste any more time if you have a copy you can send?"

Graves's expression faltered only for a second before he nodded, and then he smiled. "That's an excellent idea, Sheriff. I've been so worried about actually translating the data, it never occurred to me to simply have the backup copy sent to Global in the same manner."

"Right." This kid was lying . . . but about what?

What was going on?

He looked at Henry, Zane, and Allison. Hadn't they all noticed?

"Dr. Graves," Henry said as he checked his Global PDA, "go ahead and have that done. Carter's right. No need wasting any more time trying to find something that doesn't want to be found. If you'll excuse me, I'm going to go check on Lucas." He gave Carter an odd glance before leaving the room.

"I hope Lucas is going to be okay," Allison said.

Carter pursed his lips. "Don't you find it odd . . . that Lucas suddenly develops a brain tumor right after getting shocked by that thing?" He pointed to the storynest.

She frowned at him. "Carter—will you drop it? That machine did not give him a brain tumor. Henry said Lucas had been complaining of headaches for a while. Fatigue.

He had all the classic symptoms before he came home from MIT."

Shoving his hands into his pockets, he watched Graves pull his cell phone out and make a call, talking softly into the device. Zane sighed behind them, and the two turned toward the young scientist.

"Something?" Allison said.

"Oh, on finding the missing information? No . . ." He crossed his arms over his shirt. "But I started putting a lot of what we learned into the mainframe, did some searches on a few government sites, and found something interesting," He looked at each of them. "About a recent discovery from CERN. A sustainable microsingularity."

Allison's eyes widened. "Are you serious?" She moved around the desk to look at his monitor.

Carter followed. "That was named in those memories— but what exactly is that?"

The director scanned the article before responding. "It's a small, managed black hole," she said, her gaze focused on the screen. "If something like that were possible, and sustainable, such a phenomenon could power ten states, fuel a manned space program—"

"Or atomize a metropolis like New York with greater ease than any current technology," Graves said as he joined them. He put his cell phone back in his pocket. "It's dangerous."

Allison nodded. "I agree—but the positive applications are so much more."

"Director Blake," Graves said in a soft voice, "It doesn't matter how many good things you can get out of it. It only takes one bad one to obliterate millions."

"Wait. . . ." Carter held up his hand. "Didn't Tess and you guys try to do that a while back? It blew up during the test because of something Lucas did?"

"That was looking into proving the existence of dark

matter," Zane said as he sat back. "Not the same thing. And we sort of put that one on hold." He smiled. "Haven't finished rebuilding our collider yet."

"You have one here?" Graves's eyes widened.

"Yeah, you wanna see it?" Zane stood up.

"Absolutely."

"Guys." Allison held up her hand. "We can't be taking sightseeing tours. We need to get this done and get Mansfield out of here."

"But we can't really do anything until we get the backup files from Air's lab in Washington," Zane said as he pushed his chair away. "And I need a break to stretch my legs."

"He's right," Graves agreed. "I called my assistant. It'll take about an hour to get through the security and get the proper filing—but we'll get it here in about two hours."

Allison sighed. "Well, if that's the best you can do, then I guess we'll just have to keep the general busy," she said, looking at Carter.

"Okay, let's go," Zane said, and the two men headed out the door.

"This is going to be the longest day of my life," she said as she took Zane's chair and started looking at the article again. "But at least I can look into this and see what there is of it. I mean, Carter, this is a huge thing here. I can't believe we haven't heard about it yet. Do you realize what kind of positive impact this kind of find could have on the economy right now? Limitless energy—cheaper in the long run." She shook her head. "I only wish we'd come up with it here. I wonder if it was the guys at CERN or an affiliate."

Carter nodded absently. "Yeah . . . but . . . how does it involve the dead guy? This John Caruso. Is this thing a matter of national security? 'Cause if it is"—he pointed to the computer—"they really need to crack down on the bloggers."

Allison gave him a withering look. "No, Carter. But we'll find out soon as we get the new data. You've seen how well Lucas's translator works, and then Mansfield can see what he needs to see and he can leave." She looked up over the monitor at Carter. "What?"

He arched his eyebrows as he refocused his gaze on her. "What?"

"That face."

"What face?"

"The one you were just making. I know that face."

He pointed to his face. "This face?" He grinned.

"Carter . . . spill it. What is it?"

Sighing, he moved to the storynest and looked at the split monitors. "Remember when we were trapped down here and about to be turned to goo?"

"Yes, very vividly." She arched an eyebrow at him.

Carter smiled. "Do you also remember why we couldn't call for help?"

"Well, yeah, because you can't. Section Five blocks standard cell signals."

"Right, security issues."

She looked at him. "What?"

"Then how was it Dr. Graves was able to make a call on his cell phone just now?"

Allison blinked, then sat back. "Oh God. . . . I didn't even notice. He lied. Why would he lie about that?"

"Because I think—and God, don't ever tell Mansfield this because I'd shoot myself—but I think the general might be right about Graves. On some level."

"You think Air's trying to sabotage this whole operation?"

"That"—he rubbed at the back of his neck—"I don't know. I don't get the sense that he's, like . . . a bad guy. It's more of a feeling of we're not getting the whole picture."

Allison pulled out her Global PDA. "Well, I want to have him brought back here so he can explain himself."

"No," Carter said. "Not yet. Let him do what he's doing. We need the pieces of the puzzle. We assumed this dead guy was a spy, because he's got something in his head that involves national security. And we've both seen the argument about the synchronic thing."

"Singularity."

"Yeah, that." He pointed at her. "And this Juicebox reference—which makes no sense at all. But what if Caruso knew something Mansfield needs, and Graves doesn't want him to know?"

"But, Carter, that makes no sense. I looked up Dr. Graves's background. There's nothing in his dossier to suggest anything this . . ." She shrugged. "Underhanded. I mean, he created this whole thing to catch criminals."

"Right, right. And you said yourself that he wasn't happy about what the general was doing. What if that same sensitivity is now being called into question—" His eyes widened. "What if he saw what was in that guy's mind— saw that whole argument—and deleted it?" He held up his hand. "Makes sense. Can't see the memories. Mission's a failure. Mansfield scrubs the whole idea of using the Brain Box this way."

"No, no . . . I don't buy it, Carter." She pointed at him. "And neither do you."

He sighed. "You're right. I don't. Which sucks, 'cause it sounded *really* good. Look, don't say anything yet, but keep an eye on him, okay?" He turned to the door, then looked back. "And see if you can find anything on there about juice boxes."

"Why?"

"I don't know—I think because it's the one word that just makes no sense to me."

Her eyes widened. "You mean other than stable micro-singularity?"

"Okay—three words."

"Where are you going?" she called out.

He turned before hitting the door release. "Gonna head to the office and find Jo. See if she's found anything out on our Mr. Caruso."

CHAPTᵉR 15

Carter had just exited the elevators into Global's rotunda when Henry approached him, pad in hand, and a serious expression on his face. "Carter . . . I need to talk to you."

"Henry—what is it? Is it Lucas?"

The look on his friend's face set off alarms in Carter's head. The two men moved to the side away from the main flux of traffic, Carter with his cell phone in hand. It beeped before Henry could say a word. Carter looked at the screen. "Good God. . . . Seventeen messages?"

Henry's eyes widened. "From?"

Carter started thumbing through them. "Calls from a lot of different people . . . I wonder what's going on." He held up a finger as he speed-dialed Jo. Henry held his electronic pad to his chest.

"Well, nice of you to emerge from Section Five," came Jo's clipped response.

"Jo—why don't you just use the GD switchboard? I told you that already."

"Well, that's if it's something I can't handle. And there's nothing—I can't handle."

"Jo—I got seventeen messages from different people on my phone. What is it you're handling—that's *not* being handled?"

"All right." She sounded more frustrated than he could ever remember hearing her. "The whole town's going crazy. More than usual, I might add. I had twenty-five people in the office less than an hour ago, all accusing Sam Heart of being a spy for the military and singlehandedly responsible for the general and his men being here."

Carter blinked. "Why would they think that?" He looked at Henry.

"How the hell should I know? Half these people make no sense to me—especially when they start spouting crap like Sam was out with special spy gear, tapping their phones, listening to the conversations in town, going through their financial records. Now, say, if Taggart was around, I could understand them accusing him. But Sam? The guy's a sheep farmer."

"Jo, Sam's also one of the janitors at GD—where in the hell would he get this special sneaky . . . snooper . . ." How come it sounded even dumber when he said it out loud? ". . . spy stuff? What did you do?"

"I shot them."

"Jo—"

"What do you think I did? I kicked 'em out of the office and told them that if they touched Sam, I'd arrest all of them. Oh . . . but that's not even the good stuff."

Carter put a hand to his head. "Do I want to know?"

"Oh . . . let's see. . . ." He heard papers shuffling. "Vincent closed Café Diem because he thought the military was using some mind ray on him to make him mess up orders.

Then he turned right around and opened it back up because he wasn't going to let them get away with it. The Finesteins near the edge of town? They've led a gang from their neighborhood to set up a roadblock in and out of town to check IDs, insisting no one is really who they seem. The Rowans started cutting down trees on Euripides, which of course set off the Parks Department employees who planted them over thirty years ago—"

"What the hell is wrong with everyone?"

"Beats me—but I'm ready to really shoot someone."

Carter held up a hand. "No, Jo, no end-of-the-world guns. I'll be there shortly and hopefully help you handle some of this. Ah . . . is there anyone not paranoid you can deputize?"

There was a pause. "Fargo?"

Silence.

"On second thought—hold the fort down, Jo. Oh . . . did you have time to look up Caruso?"

"Yeah, I did. Reports on your desk."

"Spy?"

Jo sighed. "Not like you think. Okay—I gotta go—another little group just pushed their way in here." And he heard her saying, "All right, people," and the sound of a round being loaded into a chamber before she hung up.

Carter stared at the cell in his hand and looked at Henry. "Are you sure Fargo hasn't pressed a button or pulled a lever or maybe even thrown a switch?"

"Let me guess—increased paranoia? Inability to trust people they've known for years?"

Nodding, Carter put his phone back in his pocket. "That about covers it. How do you know?"

"Because Allison's getting similar complaints in here. Scientists who've worked together for years are suddenly not talking—reporting suspicious activity about their fellow lab mates."

"Henry—suspicious doesn't even begin to describe some of the stuff that happens in here."

He gave Carter a half smile. "I'm just letting you know I am seeing a lot of this behavior. Even in myself. Just now I found myself mistrusting Julia's findings with Lucas. And it wasn't that her methods were wrong—on the contrary, Julia is very meticulous and astute."

"So why would you mistrust her?"

"I had to ask myself that. Couldn't really find a reason, other than an overwhelming feeling of dread—as if I'm being watched. I think a lot of it has to do with the general's men being all over the town. The state of the economy— and the rumors that they're going to shut Eureka down." He held up his hand. "All I'm saying is—I think a lot of the heightened paranoia is just being aggravated by the situation. And not by anything we're doing here."

"Yeah, well, tell that to Jo before she takes someone's head off." He nodded to the tablet. "You wanted to show me something?"

Henry's expression turned grave. "It's Lucas. The shadow we saw earlier—it's no longer a shadow, Carter. It's thickening in size."   .

"You mean the tumor's growing—like in the past few hours?" He frowned. "Do tumors do that? Wait. . . . I mean *normal* tumors?"

"No, Jack, they don't. That's why I was double-checking Julia's findings. We've done three or four scans now on Lucas's brain and we can't find anything physically there."

"You mean you can't touch it?" Carter winced. "I mean—it's not physically in his brain?"

"Exactly," Henry said. "Tumors have mass—they're physical. But this shadow has no mass measurement."

Carter frowned and held up his right index finger. "Julia told me the tumor wasn't real. . . ."

"Which I mistrusted. But she's right."

A few people brushed past the two of them. Carter reached behind his neck. "So how can you have a tumor that's not real?"

"No one knows, and I've checked the equipment twice. I thought before when we did the preliminaries that it was just a fluke that we hadn't caught any of the telltale signs of brain cancer in Lucas's blood. But now after running a whole battery of tests"—he shook his head—"it's like a ghost."

"A ghost tumor?" Carter blinked. "Henry, do you realize how weird that sounds? I mean, like, weirder than normal?"

"We did an MRI on Lucas an hour ago to pinpoint where the tumor was located. Nothing showed up. Not on any of the normal-range scans. But when we applied different light frequencies known to show us the synaptic pathways inside the brain, that's when the shadow became visible."

"Say that again?"

"It means the tumor only shows up on specific types of scans. Specifically, scans using light." Henry turned the tablet around so that Carter could see it.

The image was nearly the same as the one he'd seen earlier in the infirmary, only now the shadow was much darker and it looked as if it was covering a larger area of Lucas's brain. "That's kinda scary looking."

"Yes, it is." Henry nodded. "Especially since I don't know how to get rid of it."

"What?"

"Carter—a tumor is something substantial. Something I can physically touch. But this? This is something that deals with Lucas's neural pathways. His thoughts. Something in that part of the brain we haven't even been able to tap into yet."

"So . . . what do we do now? What's going to happen to Lucas?"

Straightening, Henry rubbed his forehead. "At the rate the shadow's growing? It's having a physical effect on him in that it's causing the severe headaches and complete lapses in coherence. Twice he's called me by another name. He thinks Zoe is someone named Katie, and he spit on Julia."

"He spit on her?"

"I know . . . none of this is making sense. I'm afraid, though, if I don't do something within the next five hours—" He sighed. "The pressure this thing is exuding on his mental state—Carter, it's going to kill him."

Carter honked the horn of his SUV as he eased it down Main Street. People slowly moved out of the way, over half of them holding up picket signs. Only the signs weren't the usual. He saw a few that said *Down with Global* and another one that said *The Military Wants Your Babies*. There was even a sign that said *Don't Eat the Lettuce*.

"Come on, people," Carter said over the SUV's speaker. "Stop blocking the road."

He parked in front of the station and got out. He was immediately accosted by a dozen or so sign-holding residents, all of them shouting at once.

Pinned against the car door, Carter held up his hands to gain a bit of distance. "Everybody move back! Please!"

They did as he said, and Carter quickly moved around the vehicle into the building—which was clogged by more people. Most of them were orderly. Most.

Some were shouting.

The loudest was Jo.

"Please! People! If you don't form a single-file line, I am going to start shooting!"

Once they saw Carter trying to make his way through the crowd, all attention turned from getting in the door to see Jo to trying to get his attention. Holding his hand on his weapon—to make sure it didn't suddenly go missing in the crowd—Carter tried to placate people on his way through until he could make it inside to stand by Jo.

"I see you've got them under control," he said to her as he turned and sized them up.

"Oh, yeah? Well, now they're all sure there are mind experiments going on in Eureka and we're trying to read their thoughts."

"Say what?"

"It's true, Sheriff!" one of the crowd shouted at him. This guy held a sign that said *My Cat Can Read Your Thoughts* and had what looked like a skullcap on.

Carter frowned as he pointed to the man's head. "Is that . . . is that tinfoil?"

"It sure is, Sheriff. It blocks their psychic rays. But the deputy's right. I saw them doing it in Café Diem. Those mind experiments."

"Mind experiments in Café—" And then he remembered what Julia and Fargo had been doing. He sighed and put his hands up, waiting for everyone to calm down. "Please . . . just settle down. Please. Okay, good. First off, the experiment you saw at Café Diem was simply research that was being done to teach a class over at Tesla—"

"What? You mean they're going to teach our children how to read minds?" came another voice in the crowd.

Abruptly half of the crowd pulled out tinfoil caps and put them on.

"Oh, jeez," Carter muttered before he raised his hands to get their attention again. "That's not what I said. Nor what I meant. The experiment was harmless. And no one is teaching your children to read minds." He paused. "Now, the military are not here to shut down the town, take your jobs, or your homes. They're simply here to oversee something that's being worked on over at Global."

"What kind of something?"

"Is it dangerous? Are they afraid of it?"

"What kind of stuff are they trying to do to us at that crazy place?"

Carter recognized that last voice. He spotted Dr. Anderson from Section Five in the crowd, his arms crossed, his middle-aged pasty face set into a frown. Sighing, Carter pointed at him. "Dr. Anderson—that crazy place is where you get to work on your own experiments."

"Oh. Right."

"And for the rest of you—Global Dynamics is subsidized by the government. If they want the people there to work on something and monitor it, then they have that right. But they are not here for anything . . . nefarious." He put his hands together. "I want all of you to go back to your day, please? Back to your jobs, and don't worry. Once they've finished at Global, the military will leave."

No one moved for a second. Jo pulled out her weapon and chambered a round.

People turned in a hurry and filed out of the office.

Not until everyone was out did Carter turn and point to the weapon. "Jo—put that back."

Looking disappointed, she sighed, powered it down, and returned it to her wall safe of weapons. Carter relaxed a little and moved to his desk. He sat down in his chair and rubbed at his eyes. "This day . . ."

"Can't get any better," Jo finished for him. "No. I agree. But that"—she pointed to the closed door—"is what I've been dealing with all day. It's like . . . everyone took an extra dose of 'paranoid and stupid' this morning."

"No one's trusting anyone. Kinda like Mansfield and

this whole idea of looking into someone's thoughts to get information."

Jo made a face. "Creepy. How's Lucas?"

"Not good." He leaned back. "Henry tried to explain it me—what was wrong. He has a tumor but he doesn't have a tumor. And the tumor he doesn't have is killing him."

"Say that again?"

"Yeah. Tell me about it." He sat forward and looked at the folder on his desk. "This it?"

Jo nodded. "What I could find on your Jonathan Caruso. Interesting stuff—but the guy wasn't an international spy. He was a homegrown cop for the Department of Energy." She pointed at him as she returned to her desk. "Just like you. And this Dr. Graves—he's just what he says he is. A nerd from D.C."

Carter opened the file and started reading.

Special Agent Jonathan Caruso, twenty-eight, married, no children. Graduated from the Midwest, attended MIT, recruited into Quantico before graduating, and was assigned in Washington, D.C., inside the Department of Energy. Present assignment at PNNL. Status: Deceased. "Wow . . . you're right. Not much in the way of a spy."

He looked at Aircom Graves's file. It read pretty much the same. School at Phillips Andover, originally from Connecticut. Johns Hopkins, recruited out of college. Biomedical engineering. One sister.

"You try contacting the widow?" Carter said.

"No contact information."

"Nothing?" Carter looked back at the file and flipped up the page. Nothing at all on the wife. Just a name. Kathryn Caruso. He looked at the picture of John Caruso.

Young looking, medium build. Not the nerdy type at all. Flipping through all of it, he looked at Jo. "You get any photos of her?"

"Nope." She shook her head. "Not a lot on her."

He turned to his computer and paused. "Crap." Pulling out his phone, he hit speed dial. When Allison answered, he said, "Are you in your office?"

"Yes."

"Still looking at that stuff on the single—well, that thing?"

She laughed in his ear. "You mean the sustainable microsingularity? Yes, I am."

"Was it something they were doing at PNNL? I mean, would PNNL have anything to do with it?"

"Actually, they did. I learned the information was sent there from CERN. How did you know?"

Carter looked back at Caruso's files. "What would the Department of Energy have to do with it?"

"With PNNL? Nothing, really—but they would definitely be interested in the information on this singularity. Remember what I told you about it being a limitless source of energy?"

"Yeah . . ."

"That would fall under their purview of funding costs. Now, from what I've been reading on a few scientists' blogs—"

"Scientists blog?"

"Yes, Carter. They do. There seems to be some sort of argument between the DoD scientists and the DoE researchers about the applications for the find. Huh . . ." She paused.

"What is it?"

"Well . . . one scientist says on his blog that the office of the inspector general sent an investigator in to review . . ." She paused again, and then it sounded as if she was reading straight from the blog. ". . . inappropriate behaviors of prejudicial mishandling when submitting funding requests."

"And that means . . . ?"

"I have no idea. To me, it says someone got their hand slapped when they cheated on something. Um . . . oh, wow. That investigator was killed in a car wreck just a few days ago. Carter, why are you asking about this?"

But he was looking at Caruso's file again. Under employment, he'd missed the second line, giving Caruso's title. He'd seen Department of Energy, just not the Inspector General part.

Special Agent, Director of Western Operations.

"Allison . . . I think the memories missing from the Brain Box belong to that investigator."

CHAPTᵉR 16

After listening to Henry and Julia discuss what could be done for Lucas's brain—and hearing the words *brain* and *surgery* thrown into the mix—Fargo decided he could find somewhere else to be. He knew the director was in— and he'd already told Julia he wasn't working on the Remote Viewing with her anymore, especially after she made those ridiculous accusations about him sabotaging her work—so why not see about anything new on the schedule?

After all, his title was Assistant to the Director.

When the elevator opened so he could take it to the rotunda, Fargo was surprised to see Dr. Graves and Zane inside. "Oh, sorry. I—I was heading up."

"Hey, Fargo," Graves said in a cheery voice. "Where are you off to?"

"Director's office."

Graves's eyes widened for a second. "Oh well . . . Zane was going to show me Global's collider. Wanna come?"

Zane opened his mouth, but Fargo pointed at him. "That was not my fault. That was Lucas."

Graves smiled as Fargo stepped into the elevator. "It's okay. I read the report. I know why the collider blew up."

"Yeah, well . . ." Zane said. "That's not saying that Fargo here hasn't developed a reputation."

Fargo crossed his arms over his chest and faced the door. "Yeah, and thanks to that capsule of Dr. Fontana's, I'm going to be reminded of it over and over and over." He glanced back to his right at Graves. "So do you read all the reports from Eureka?"

"Yes. It's my job to sift through them, pick out the juicy parts, and collate the rest into *interesting*, *absurd*, or *useful*."

"I'm sure a lot of the stuff you get out of here fills the absurd pile," Zane said.

"Not as much as some of the ridiculous stuff I get from Area 51."

Fargo snapped around and faced Graves at the mention of an opportunity to ridicule Area 51. "Oh? Really? So when you say *absurd*, it's really bad science?"

Graves nodded slowly at Fargo. "Bad science, disproven theories. We have our own vetters that look through the experiments and verify their outcomes. Fifty-one has a lot of"—he winced and lifted his right hand, wiggling it in the air—"meh."

"Meh?" Zane grinned. "Technical term?"

"Always."

The doors opened and Zane led the way down the hall, which moved into a slow bow before they turned right into a door. Fargo jumped in after Zane to see for himself how the work on repairing the collider was going. Before, when it had exploded because of the magnetic fields generated by Lucas's device, the entire window overlooking the collider had blown in on them. It'd been a miracle no one was seriously injured.

He ran to the replaced glass and looked at the half-repaired collider. Even now Eureka engineers were crawling over it, using hover-enhanced mechanical arms to wield objects and perform smaller tasks as puppeteers with large monitors guided their progress.

Ah . . . it was beautiful.

"Don't touch anything, Fargo," Zane said as he moved up beside him.

"And this is what exploded?" Graves asked as he leaned forward, his hands on the replaced railing. "God . . . it's got to be great to work here."

Zane nodded as he watched them as well. "It has its moments." He looked at Graves. "But your job has got to be pretty interesting itself."

"Maybe," he said. "I pilfer through new science and adapt it. Find uses for it—the small stuff, I mean. Not the larger-scope discoveries. More like the storynest. I look at it, see its potential and its danger. And if I'm lucky, I can get funding and work on practical applications myself."

"Who exactly do you work for?"

Graves shrugged. "Does it matter? Unofficially I'm with the DoD. Branch office. Research and development. When I first had the idea for the Brain Box, my initial report was refused. But when I resubmitted it as an idea to catch murderers"—he shrugged—"it was approved."

Zane turned and leaned back on the bar. Fargo was now fascinated with what Graves was saying and moved in closer as well, walking to the front of the workstation Zane had been seated at during that explosive experiment, and leaned on it.

"So," Zane said. "Then you're given the time to develop?"

"No," he said, turning to face them. "I'm supposed to assign it to a developer scientist. We have a steady revolving door of science majors, grad students, research fellowships—those wanting specialized projects. I take their names, education, and specialties and pair them with the project, setting a deadline, and then I check their results. But this one"—he shrugged—"I took this one myself. Which means I was working on it outside my regular job, spending my off-hours and vacation in the lab. The work was going slower that way, but this is more along my field and I felt I was the best qualified."

"But it wasn't completely finished when Herr General called to use the machine?"

"The only thing I knew it could do was harvest the last memories—those imprinted on the dying brain's synaptic cry."

"Synaptic cry?" Fargo said.

Zane answered this one, having already heard the explanation before. "That's what Dr. Graves calls those last throes of life, when the mind is telling itself who it is—it's a survival mechanism." He crossed his arms over his chest.

Fargo looked from Zane to Graves. "That's incredible."

Graves nodded. "Sheriff Carter said it best—likening it to that moment when your life flashes before your eyes. It's very real, and those images are all there the same way they're there when Dr. Fontana's storycatchers interface with the optical nerve to create the video diary."

"So, literally, you're catching the last thoughts of a dying man or woman."

"Yes. It's all up here." Graves reached up and tapped his temple. "Recorded on impulses that can be downloaded and viewed. Welcome to the future."

"Wow," Fargo said.

"Yeah."

"But—" Zane said. "Dr. Blake mentioned you were having personal issues with using it. And I have to admit, I'm a little creeped out by the idea. I mean . . . if something happened to me and my life flashed before my eyes—I'm not sure there are a lot of things in that movie I'd want anybody—especially Jo—to see."

Fargo's attention snapped from Graves to Zane. "Oh? Like what? What wouldn't you like her to know?"

"Oh, like I'm going to tell you so you can run and tell her? No way, Fargo. And besides, aren't there things in *your* brain you'd prefer Julia not know about?"

"Well . . ." Fargo opened his mouth and then shut it. He was silent for a few seconds before saying, "Well, thanks to Dr. Fontana's memory capsule, most everybody else has already exposed all my faults."

"Other people's perceptions," Graves said.

Zane rubbed at his chin. "That does bring something up, though—something I was thinking about when we were working on the project. Sometimes—or really most of the time—memories are subjective. Like in an accident there are always three sides to a story. My side, their side, and the truth."

"Yes." Graves nodded. "But the synaptic imprints viewed by the optic nerve and heard by tympanic muscles are from the side that tells the truth. Our id interprets them in the way that will"—he shrugged—"make us feel better."

"So what's recorded—"

"Is what really occurred." He grinned. "Now try to explain that to the military—they don't believe anything anyone says. And even if we get these memories sorted and viewed—and the general doesn't like what he sees—he still won't believe it. Because it's not what he wants it to be."

"Kinda makes all this moot," Fargo said.

Zane frowned as he looked at Graves. "Did you know the guy? The one whose memories are in the box?"

Graves hesitated before answering, chewing on his lower lip for a few seconds. "I can't tell you anything officially— I signed a thousand NDAs when I took this job. But I can say this." He didn't look at Zane as he spoke, and his voice took on a faraway quality. "We don't really know anyone as well as we think we do."

Zane and Fargo exchanged glances. Fargo arched his eyebrows, looking uncertain. "Spoken like a true employee for the government," he said, and laughed nervously. "Well . . . this"—he patted the new shiny console—"this looks good in here. So . . . do you think what's happening to Lucas has anything to do with the explosion yesterday? This brain tumor?"

"At first I didn't think so. But a brain tumor can't happen overnight. Though the shock might have triggered something. But in the end, you can't just manifest one." He stopped, blinked, and looked at Fargo. "How did you know about that? You weren't even here yesterday."

Fargo opened his mouth and then closed it before adjusting his glasses.

"You read the director's files again."

"I did not," Fargo protested. "Well, only a little. Okay, so . . . I read what I could find. But I wasn't here because I was doing important work."

"Uh-huh. All that mind mumbo-jumbo that Henry wants to teach." Zane shook his head. "Noetic science. What a joke."

Graves looked up. "You don't believe in mind sciences?"

"Oh . . . I didn't say that. I just tend to like hard science. Something tangible, not esoteric."

Fargo snorted. "You? The man who was in the grip of some prehistoric parasite not long ago?"

"We're not going to talk about that, Fargo," Zane said. "But from what Julia tells me"—he smirked—"you didn't get a single View right the whole day."

"That is so not true," Fargo protested. "Well . . . part of one."

"Don't worry, Fargo." Graves spoke up. "I did a bit of Remote Viewing myself once, and found I didn't have the knack for it. But . . . I did hear from the sheriff that Zoe was able to draw her View? I'd like to hear more about that. Might help pass the time while the backup is sent from Washington."

Fargo shot both of them a harsh look. "Zoe. Got all but one right. And I told you what she did on that last one." He looked at Graves. "She's never even tried to View before."

"Neither have you," Zane said. "And you failed."

"It's not about succeeding or failing," Fargo said. "It's just about seeing who has more of a psychic connection than others."

Zane made a rude noise.

"No, no," Graves said as he pushed his glasses up on his nose. "Theories in noetic science have been proven time and again, Zane. The Stargate Project itself did produce positive results for years, and the military did benefit from many of their findings. Secret, well-hidden bases could be seen from the inside, mapped out accurately. Several rescue operations, as well as black ops missions, credit their success to Remote Viewers' accuracy in finding targets or describing never-before-seen places."

"Really?" Zane tilted his head to the side. "Then how come we've never heard of this?"

"Didn't you learn what the word *secret* meant, Zane?" Fargo said.

Zane started to reply, but Graves held up a hand. "Fargo's right. There is a lot of Stargate material that has been released, but there's a lot that hasn't. And won't. For example, Remote Viewing did transcend into Remote Influencing in some levels of the project, as Viewers got better and were able to fine-tune and hone their skills. But in the end, even those able to touch the minds of other people lost themselves to madness and paranoia. And if this science exists"—Graves looked at Zane over his glasses—"is it something you really want out there in the public?"

"Well, no, but no one would believe it anyway."

"Exactly, because the whole idea has been painted in the media to be nothing more than an idea for bad movies. No one will ever take it seriously—sanctioned by the government or not." He smiled, but the expression did not reach his eyes. "I for one am happy there are those out there with the ability to use RI who won't because they don't believe. Sometimes it's best to protect the world with lies. Produce failures so attention shifts elsewhere."

"Well," Fargo said finally. "I just didn't get the whole big deal with what we were doing. So what if Zoe got all those manila folders right? The drawing was totally off. I wish she'd left it with Julia as evidence she got it wrong."

Zane glared at Fargo. "Don't you think what Zoe's going through right now with Lucas is enough misery, Fargo? I hate that she's having to go through anything at all."

Suddenly feeling awful about what he'd said, Fargo slumped his shoulders, then brightened, pointing with his right index finger. "You know, she tried it again this morning while in the infirmary. Said she was getting a headache that wouldn't stop, and she drew this." He reached into his back pocket and pulled out a half-folded, half-wadded sheet of paper. He started unfolding it.

"Fargo—you stole that from Zoe?"

"I did not steal it," he said. "I borrowed it. I'm gonna give it back. But it's the same girl she drew yesterday—the one that said *I love you* under it. Only this time she put a name to it." And he held out the paper.

Graves took it quickly before Zane could see it. The young man's eyes widened as he stared at the drawing. He removed his glasses and looked again.

"Aircom? You okay?" Zane said as he watched him.

"I—" Graves said softly. "I just—has she ever seen this woman?"

Zane shrugged as Fargo shook his head. "She said she

hasn't. But she says she keeps seeing her, over and over. And she'd drawn this series of pictures of her. All very good. I think she's become obsessed with her."

Graves continued to stare at the likeness, and then his gaze focused down on the word written below the smiling woman. "Kathryn."

"I'm assuming that's her name," Fargo said. "Or maybe it's a character in a book Zoe's read or seen in a movie. Henry thinks she's just tired and stressed and needs to rest as he looks for a way to fix Lucas's brain."

Fargo reached out to take the paper, but Graves pulled it back. "Sorry—but did you say Zoe was in the infirmary?"

"Yeah, she's there with Lucas. Though she might be taking a nap."

"And she just started drawing this girl—yesterday afternoon?"

"Uh-huh." Fargo glanced at Zane, who was watching Graves. "You okay?"

"I'm fine. I'm better than fine." He folded the paper. "Can I keep this? I'll go and get it back to her right now, okay?"

"Sure," Fargo said as he watched Graves move past them and then out the door. He turned back to Zane. "How rude."

"Maybe." Zane rubbed at his stubbled chin. "Or maybe not. I need to go make a phone call." He moved past Fargo to leave the room as well.

Fargo stood in the collider observatory room for a few more minutes, watching the workers through the heavy glass, deciding he should go find the director or find something to do.

CHAPTER 17

Zoe continued to sit by Lucas's side, dazed by every-thing that had happened. Just last night she was worried that Lucas had been seeing another woman—the brunette she'd seen in her Viewing. And now she wasn't even sure if Lucas had a future himself—besides one with her.

Henry had tried to be positive before he'd left, just moments ago. He and Julia were working on ways to relieve whatever pressure appeared to be weighing down on Lucas's mind—but it was hard to try to cure a phantom illness. A tumor that wasn't really there. It was like trying to exorcise a ghost.

Impossible.

Zoe talked to his parents, assuring them she'd stay with Lucas until they could find a way to help. The doctors at Global were the best, and she trusted Henry implicitly.

Julia stepped into the room, a tablet nestled in the crook of her arm. She walked up to Lucas, checked the vitals on the board to the left, and then gave Zoe a smile. "I'd tell you there's been no change—but I think by now you know how to read all of this."

Zoe nodded. "I haven't been at Harvard long, but my experience here has sort of introduced me to a lot of it." She reached out and took Lucas's hand. His skin was still warm to the touch, his eyes closed. He was very still, only now and then frowning as if having a nightmare. "I just wish there were some way I could see in and tell you what's wrong. I even tried Viewing again last night. But nothing happened."

"You were trying to look inside his head?" Julia paused and watched her. "I told you how dangerous that can be."

"Why is it dangerous?" But Zoe was pretty sure she already knew that answer. It was dangerous because sometimes it was better not to know what others were thinking. It was wrong to look inside another's thoughts and spy, to come in and invade his privacy.

Julia set the tablet to the side. "It's dangerous—but not really in the way you're thinking, Zoe. I did a bit more reading on the projects Dr. Schmetzer put together. And apparently every test subject he used to move to Remote Influencing"—she shrugged—"suffered a mental breakdown of some sort. They insisted they were looking into other people's minds and seeing terrible things. A cheating wife or husband, a murder plot. But in the end, all they suffered was a lot of heartache and paranoia and no substantial proof that what they saw was the truth."

She heard Julia and understood the warning. But Zoe couldn't bring herself to believe that what she'd seen—the images of that woman and that man—wasn't real. She'd seen them, heard them speak. It was always the same.

The same woman looking at Lucas.

"I'm sorry—I didn't mean to interrupt."

A young man approached Lucas's bed. He was of average height, with brown hair, dark eyes, and glasses, and dressed in a nice if not rumpled shirt and slacks. His sneakers seemed incongruous with the rest of him, but also added a bit of what Zoe thought would be his own personality. She hadn't seen him around GD. "Hi—I'm Zoe."

Julia moved to him and gestured for him to come closer. "Aircom, this is Zoe Carter, Sheriff Carter's daughter. Zoe, this is Dr. Aircom Graves. He's here with General Mansfield."

Zoe released Lucas's hand and slid off the stool to offer him her hand. "Nice to meet you—Aircom?"

"Call me Air." He smiled and his grip was firm, and not too overpowering. His hand was warm and soft. No calluses. "It's nice to meet you, Zoe."

"Air was showing me his Brain Box." Julia frowned. "Though I'm not sure we're supposed to talk about that."

"Brain Box?" Zoe gave the two of them a half smile. "What is that?"

Graves glanced at Julia and said, "I—work for the government, picking apart a lot of the super research labs' breakthroughs. I took Dr. Fontana's storynest idea and sort of"—he frowned—"tweaked it."

"Wait." Zoe narrowed her eyes. "Are you the one that's supposed to be working on a dead guy?"

"Well," Julia said hurriedly. "Not really a dead guy."

Graves moved closer and looked at Lucas. "Lucas was working with us yesterday—he helped rewrite the translator application that allowed your storynest matrix to interpolate the synaptic impulses recorded there into a visual diary to actually do the same to the harvested memories of the deceased."

Zoe felt a chill run up her back at what the young man had just said. "You mean . . . you're looking at a dead guy's memories?"

"His last memories," Graves said. "The last things recorded in his brain, those final images before death—" He held up a hand. "I know it sounds terrible. But it could have positive applications."

Even though Zoe felt a bit creeped out, she found herself nodding as her own brain began thinking of the ramifications. "No, no—I can see it. I mean, if you could actually record a dying person's memories, then you could, like—find out if someone killed them. See who the murderer was. Or if they witnessed something."

Graves smiled. "That was exactly my thought when I started putting it together."

Zoe took Lucas's hand again. "So Lucas was helping you—when the explosion happened?"

"Yes." Graves's eyes widened. "Oh, but that couldn't have caused this. At least I don't think so."

"No," Julia agreed. "I read the attending physicians' report on Lucas. He received a pretty good shock to his system, but nothing that would cause a brain tumor."

"I felt bad when that happened," Graves said. "But Zane was able to correct the errors and the translator works."

"So you were able to look at the memories?" She watched him, a bit fascinated with him. And something else. He looked . . . familiar?

"Some of them. But not all. Someone stole the data out of the Brain Box."

"Oh no," Julia said in a shocked voice. "Have you told Henry or the sheriff?"

"Yes. And I've called my office in Washington to send the backup copy." He reached out with his left arm, his shirt-sleeve riding up to expose a watch. "Which should be here by now." He lowered his arm. "But once we get those, we should be able to interpret the memories and get out of your hair."

"But what about the stolen ones?" Julia asked. "I mean . . . why would anyone steal a dead person's memories?"

Zoe shook her head, shrugging. She really didn't know much about whatever this was, but her own mind—the one she was honing at Harvard—began running scenarios. "Could be this guy was a spy? And the thief doesn't want anyone to see what he remembers? Or if this guy was murdered, he could identify his killer." She looked at Graves. "Was he murdered?"

"No. Car crash."

Zoe noticed a slight hesitation before Dr. Graves answered.

"Okay, then maybe he got the license plate?"

Julia laughed lightly. "Don't think that would work—because that would mean the guy that hit him would know about Eureka, be able to break into Global's security, and know exactly how to get stuff off the Brain Box." She looked at Graves. "Right?"

"Right." He nodded. "The spy theory seems to be running rampant, though. All over the town."

"Well, having the general here doesn't help things," Zoe said, and looked back at Lucas. He was frowning again, and she wondered what the nightmares were. "Is he in pain like that?" she asked Julia.

"I don't know," she said. "I don't think so. Nothing registering on the EKG." She moved to the side table and looked around, then made a small gasp and reached out for a notebook. "Oh, no."

"What?" Zoe said.

Julia held up the notebook. "Here it is—the notes I accused Fargo of taking out of the Remote Viewing log from yesterday. Oh . . . I must have left them here and then accused him." She thumbed through them. "Now I feel terrible. I need to tell him."

"Remote Viewing." Graves looked at both of them but then focused on Zoe. "Fargo was telling me about that earlier. He and Sheriff Carter. You've both been Viewing?"

"Yes," Julia said. "Well, no, not me. Zoe here did. And she got all but one right."

"Can we not talk about this right now?" Zoe said under her breath.

"You did?" Graves said. "That's wonderful. Your dad told me you actually started drawing in a View?"

Zoe nodded.

"Yes, she did. She drew an incredible likeness to some woman I'd never seen before. I didn't know she could draw."

"Neither did I," Zoe said. "But yeah . . . I drew." She looked at Graves. "You know about Remote Viewing."

He grinned. "I look through government labs' secret projects. Yeah, I've heard of Remote Viewing. Though a lot of what they did was later proven to be trace memory."

"You don't believe it taps into the hive mind theory?" Julia said.

"Ah." He winced. "I'm afraid I don't. I do enjoy the theories, but not so much the practicality. The means of the experiments—the number of fails versus successes—just weren't enough to prove it to be a valid means of extricating information in unknown areas. In theory, it all works."

"Then how do you explain Zoe getting all but one right?"

"Out of how many?"

Zoe spoke up. "Six. I got six right. Then the seventh went all kinds of strange."

"I'd say lucky guess?"

"You sound like my dad," Zoe said.

"I like your dad. He's a no-nonsense kind of guy."

Julia sighed and took up her tablet. "Well, you two can debate the validity of Remote Viewing versus the fact that you, Dr. Graves, record the memories of dead people. I need to go find Douglas and apologize."

"Last I saw him he was in the area with the collider."

She gave him a bright look and left the infirmary.

Zoe slumped in her stool, still clasping Lucas's hand. "You know, she's right. Your skepticism is a little odd, given what you're doing."

"No, not really." He moved to stand where Julia had stood, opposite Zoe. "I don't doubt the theories, and I have a healthy respect for noetic science. But"—he smiled at her—"I also like things tangible. And though memories are in a sense esoteric by nature, I can bring them down to their base premise and make them accessible to everyone."

She noticed his smile vanish almost immediately and leaned forward. "But?"

"But?"

"You didn't believe half of what you just said."

His eyes widened. "You read minds, too?"

"No, but I do read faces. What's got you bothered?"

Turning, he crossed his arms over his chest. "Not really taking into account 'can we,' but *should* we? I mean, should we really be able to look into a person's mind? Steal their thoughts or their memories?"

"Well, when it comes to dying memories—" She looked at Lucas and sort of wished this conversation weren't happening right now, not with the threat of his own death looming. "I can't say. I just know . . . that a widow or a girlfriend left behind might want to know what it was they were thinking. Want to know . . . if maybe their last thoughts were of them?"

"I can understand that," Graves said, and his voice was soft. "But . . . should anyone else see them? A government official? A stranger? No. I don't think those memories belong to anyone else."

Zoe looked at him and was sure she'd caught real emotion in his voice. "You don't think this man's memories should be looked at?"

He shrugged. "What does it really matter what I think

or believe? I work for the government, Zoe. But"—he sighed—"I am curious about this View that caused you to draw."

"Oh. That." She started to tell him that it wasn't the envelope she'd been aiming for, but wanting to see inside Lucas's mind. That she was sure she'd seen what was there. She changed her mind, though—it was bad enough that Julia and Fargo thought she was losing it. But a total stranger? "Yeah. Really strange. It's the same girl. Brunette. Very pretty. There's snow. And in some of the different scenes I drew there were other people."

"Different scenes? How much did you draw?" He leaned his head to the side. "Or did you try several different Views?"

"Different Views." She would admit that much. "After I saw the first one, I kept trying, and I kept seeing the same girl, only different places. And then on one I wrote the name *Kathryn*."

Graves nodded but didn't really seem surprised. "Why Kathryn?"

"I'm not sure. I just knew it was her name. Weird, huh?" She squeezed Lucas's hand. "I wrote *I love you* on the first one." She still didn't want to tell him that Lucas had also called her Katie. She'd already talked to Julia about it, and Julia had said it could have been a school friend of Lucas's in Boston.

Maybe. But she didn't want to expose her own insecurities to Dr. Graves.

"Zoe . . . is it possible I could see these drawings?"

"Well—" She looked at Lucas. The drawings were at home, and she wasn't sure she wanted to leave Lucas.

"Please? I'm sure the staff here can take care of him. If only for a little while?" He looked at his watch again. "Maybe for lunch? You've got to eat."

Zoe grinned. She *was* hungry, and one of Vincent's bean

soups sounded good. "Okay. I'll meet you at Café Diem in an hour? Oh, wait. . . . Let me make sure he opened it back up. I know he was threatening to close it for the day because he kept getting orders wrong. If it is closed, I know of a couple places. I'll meet you there and bring the drawings and you bring an appetite. You eaten there yet?"

"No, I haven't."

"Well, you'll love it." She decided she might want to call ahead and see if the stout café owner was okay, or if things had settled down. She hadn't left the infirmary since Lucas collapsed. Leaving him now seemed wrong—but Zoe wasn't sure she could sit here for another hour. She needed a distraction. Something.

"Okay, in an hour." He nodded to her. "It's been nice to meet you, Zoe. And I truly hope Lucas gets better. He seemed like a good kid."

She watched him leave and then looked back to Lucas. Yes, he was a good kid, wasn't he? And again she remembered everything that Henry had told her—about Lucas having trouble in school and feeling like a failure.

She, too, had had some rough classes at Harvard and had a lot of things go wrong. But she'd never shared that with anyone. Just as Lucas hadn't. And here he'd told Henry that he was afraid she'd see him as someone who couldn't cut it outside Eureka.

But . . . even knowing all that . . . it didn't explain away that woman. Or the scenes she now had in her head, the ones from the Views.

No. Something was up. And she wanted him to survive so that she could find out what, and make it better. Perhaps Dr. Graves could help.

With a kiss to Lucas's forehead, she slipped off the stool, told the nurse she'd be back, and left Global for home.

CHAPTᵉR 18

Fargo continued to talk to himself as he stalked down the hallway to the storage room for Section Five. In truth, this section had more than twenty storage rooms just on this floor, but the director had wanted him to check out the smaller one, double-checking inventory with the latest reports.

He knew it was busywork. Had to be. His talents were wasted doing this kind of manual labor. He should be right in the middle of whatever it was they were doing. It wasn't like he didn't already know what was happening. Sorta.

Well, kinda.

He'd gotten to know Dr. Graves. And he knew it all had something to do with that box in the lab. He used his key card and opened the storage room. Taking out his PDA, he started scanning the contents of each shelf and checking them against the inventory list.

"Hey, Fargo."

Yelling out, Fargo turned to see Dr. Graves standing behind him. The scientist had changed clothes, replacing his white shirt with a blue one and a sports jacket. It looked as if he'd showered as well. "Oh, God . . . don't do that."

"Oh, I'm sorry—I was on my way to grab a late lunch when I saw the door open. What's all in here?"

"Oh . . . this is where we keep a lot of the smaller devices or things used for experiments in Section Five."

Graves stood in the center of the room, hands on his hips. "This is pretty impressive, Fargo. Hey, did you keep the storycatcher devices in here?"

"Yeah." He frowned. "But I'm not allowed to touch those."

"Oh, I didn't ask you to touch them." Graves shrugged. "I just wanted to see one for myself. I mean, after all, it was that technology I used for the Brain Box. Kinda nostalgic for me, you know?"

Yeah, Fargo did kind of know. And he liked Graves so far. He went to the door and looked to his right, and then his left, and then with a smile closed the door. Moving back in, he grabbed the wheeled ladder and moved it to one of the shelves on the far right. After climbing, he grabbed the top briefcase off a stack of them and then eased his way down.

In the center of the room was an empty table. Fargo set the briefcase on the table and, with a dramatic pause, looked at Graves. "You ready?"

Graves nodded.

Fargo then unhitched the two latches and opened the lid. Inside sat two dozen deactivated story globes, all of which resembled milky white plastic balls, but when Graves reached in to pick one up, it was revealed to have a flat bottom.

Graves held up the device and looked at it. "So this is it."

"I'm surprised you weren't given a bunch of these to work from," Fargo said.

"Most of the time I only get the science on paper, not in practical use. And to be honest—this was one of the department's lowest-priority calls. I'd actually started to file it away when I began imagining its potential to catch criminals."

Fargo's eyes widened. "Is that what that box is for?"

"Yes, Fargo, it is." He set the storycatcher back into the briefcase. "I do thank you for letting me see them. And I suspect this area is highly restricted?"

As Fargo shut the briefcase and took it back to the ladder, he spoke. "No. Actually I think as long as your key card has access down here, you can get into this room. These are all low priority. But there are other rooms that actually require blood DNA to get into." He set the briefcase back and half climbed, half jumped down.

When he turned to Graves, the man looked pale. "What?"

"Fargo, are you serious?"

Fargo nodded. "No, I'm not." He grinned.

Graves made a grunt and waved at Fargo. "Okay . . . thanks again, Fargo."

"Zane, have you even moved from that spot?" Henry said as he, Allison, and Carter entered lab 511. The three of them had met up in Allison's office and traveled down together.

"Actually . . . I have," the young man said as he glanced up at Henry. "And I think I may have found the missing files from the Brain Box."

Henry grinned as he moved to lean in beside Zane. "The storynest."

A sideways grin pulled at Zane's lips. "So you were thinking what I was thinking."

Carter blinked and looked at the two of them. "Then why didn't the searches pick it up before?"

"Because we were looking for Dr. Graves's proprietary code, not the converted one. And"—Henry nodded to the storynest—"this machine was taken offline from the rest of Global, remember? As part of the added security."

"Oh, yeah," Carter said. "So we didn't do that memory-suck thing again. But I still don't get how you two figured out where the memories were."

Henry straightened. "Something I thought of while looking at the scans of Lucas's brain. That and what we'd seen of the tampering earlier on the Brain Box itself. He had a normal-looking scan a few months ago. He had a normal-looking scan a few days ago during his checkup. But now he's got a phantom tumor."

Henry held up his tablet. "Diagnostic records on the lab's systems from a month ago. From a week ago. And from before Dr. Graves copied the test files into the storynest to use the immersive video card."

"Henry," Carter began. "Let's pretend I have no idea what you're talking about—"

"Jack," Henry grinned. "The storynest has an unbelievable storage capacity, but it's offline from the rest of GD." He gestured toward Carter with his hand. "To prevent that mind-suck thing. Which means the files on the storynest are backed up separately. The searches we've been doing wouldn't have noticed anything on the storynest because it wasn't looking there. It doesn't have access to it."

Allison smiled. "So they're there?"

Zane pulled up two screens on each of the dual monitors of the storynest. The images looked identical except for the difference in file sizes. "The information was stuffed down and then sent in a burst. The storynest did what it normally does—it assigned them a catalog number and parked them in the largest available space." He pointed to the right panel where there was one more file than on the left. "Which just happens to be in Fargo's memory files."

"I didn't do it!" Fargo said as he entered the lab. "I heard my name, but I haven't touched that machine."

"Relax," Henry said. "What are you doing in here?"

"I was just helping Dr. Graves next door and thought I'd come in here and see if you needed anything."

Carter shrugged. "So the only reason they're stored under Fargo is because he has more empty space . . . in his memories . . . than anyone else?" He couldn't suppress a grin.

"Ha ha ha, Sheriff." Fargo sighed. "If you'll remember, I deleted several of the storynest memories other people had of me."

"Which emptied up a good deal of space," Henry said. "Zane . . . see if you can extract them so we can take a look."

"I thought you'd never ask," Zane said.

Carter looked down at the folders in his hand. "Fargo, where is Dr. Graves?"

"Oh, he ran out to grab some lunch."

"We," Zane said abruptly, "might have a problem."

Henry stood and went back to the storynest. "What is it?"

"Well . . ." Zane said. "This is just screwy."

"Define *screwy.*"

Zane said hurriedly, "This isn't making any sense. The files read substantial memory—you see that? But when I feed it into the translator, it's coming up with zero space. It's like that earlier problem."

Carter sighed. "Ah, great. Did someone tamper with the images, like before?"

"No." Zane shook his head. "Not this time. I double-checked. But you can see it right there." He pointed with his index finger. "The file itself is broken down into four separate pieces, and each piece is reading close to twenty terabytes. This thing is massive. But look what happens when I transfer it into the translator."

Henry knelt down as Allison came around to look as well. Carter trailed behind.

The left file reading changed when Zane dropped it on top of the translator application. The outcome was indeed zero.

Empty.

"Did the application delete it?" Allison asked.

"No . . ." Zane shook his head.

"Check the translator log. See what it did."

Zane nodded and pulled the log up, all pages of command lines and reports. Henry put his finger to the monitor and followed one of them across the page. "Nothing. See where it kicked it out? Says the file contained no serviceable data."

"Well, hell." Zane sat back in his chair. "What the hell is going on? Is it a ghost file?"

"And you're sure these are the ones from the Brain Box?" Allison said.

"Well, we'd be more sure if we could open them up and view them," Zane said. "I found them hidden in the storynest, which made them practically invisible to the sweep we did using GD's search. But when I try to translate them—"

"They show up empty." She sighed. "We keep hitting these walls."

"Or whoever it is that doesn't want us to see the rest of these memories is one step ahead of us," Henry said.

She looked at Henry. "How's Lucas?"

"Not any better, but only a small bit worse. He's slipped

into a coma, which I think is better. His EKG has quieted, which means he's finally resting. Whatever that tumor is doing? It's really messing with his REM state. His serotonin levels are almost nil."

"He needs to have it removed," Allison said. "And we need to get this whole thing out of this facility. Now."

Henry nodded to the folders in Carter's hands. "What are those?"

"Oh, uh, information on Aircom Graves and Jonathan Caruso."

"So we know more about Mr. Name, Rank, and Serial Number now?" Zane asked.

"Yeah, a good bit," Allison said. "I also added printouts of articles I found concerning information that arrived at PNNL from CERN. And about a dead investigator."

Carter handed the folder over to Henry. "Somehow this keeps leading back to PNNL. I don't know how, or why. But I've got a feeling."

"PNNL?" Zane said.

"It's the Pacific Northwest National Laboratory. In Richland, Washington," Henry said as he looked through the files. "Ah, the sustainable microsingularity I keep hearing about. Are they serious about these findings?"

"Apparently, and they're very hush-hush about them," Allison said. "I had to use my clearance to get even this much on the project."

"And this dead guy," Zane said as he stood and looked over Henry's shoulders at the file, "has something to do with it? How does General Mansfield have anything to do with a scientific find?"

"National security," Henry said, looking up and focusing on Allison and Carter. "This kind of technology could sustain energy or destroy. I'm sure it's the *destroy* part that has him more concerned."

"So did this guy, like, steal secrets or something?" Zane said as he read. "There's not a lot here."

"Mr. Caruso actually worked for the Department of Energy. And we suspect he was the investigator sent by the attorney general's office to investigate bad things." Allison sighed. "What the hell has Mansfield gotten us into?"

"So he's not a spy?" Fargo said. "I thought someone said he was a spy."

"Fargo." Allison looked at him. "Didn't I give you a project to do?"

He stuck out his lower lip. "Yes, ma'am." With that, he left the room, mumbling, "Inventory backup lists . . . bah."

"That should keep him busy till we get this sorted out. What concerns me most is really the general, and Graves. The two seem opposed to one another, and I know for a fact Graves has already lied to my face."

Henry looked at her. "Lied to you?"

Carter nodded. "Yeah—he made a call from in here to Washington, D.C. On his cell."

"But you can't call out from Section Five," Henry said.

"Exactly."

Zane spoke up. "Is it possible Graves is the spy trying to find out what it is that Caruso knows before Mansfield does?"

Allison shook her head. "That's plausible. But I don't like it, and we can't know that till we get a better understanding of what's going on before we got dumped with this end of things."

"You're not suggesting we tell Mansfield what's happened."

"I'm afraid so," Allison said. "And I'm aware that he could pull everything and then we'd never know anything."

"Or he'd get mad," Carter said. "Fire me again."

"We need to talk to him first," Allison said. "Zane,

check with security quickly and see if Graves has left yet. I want the two of you to back up whatever it is you have and offload it to something Mansfield's men can't abscond with."

"What are you thinking?"

"I'm thinking we just don't know enough yet to make any judgments on Mansfield or Dr. Graves. We're only guessing this is the same investigator sent by the DoE— but again, no proof. We know there's no backup coming, we know that Graves has lied to us, and we know he has to be the one who's been sabotaging this project from the beginning. What I want is a full briefing from the general, and I plan on doing some calling to see that I get it."

CHAPTᵉR 19

"Allison." Carter rubbed the back of his neck. "I'm not sure antagonizing Mansfield is really the best thing to do. Let's just get Graves and confront him with the evidence. Show him we think he's sabotaged this Caruso's memories. Hell . . . who's to say Graves didn't already know this guy?"

Carter stopped, a small bell going off in his head. He thought back over to the dossiers. Always look for the similarities, the thing that links everything together. If you find that, you might start seeing the signs of the causal chain.

Carter held out his hand. "Allison, Graves's dossier. What were his schools again?"

She opened up the folder and listed them.

"And Caruso's?"

She listed his as well. Nothing similar. "Okay, work experience. Places of employment. Have the two of them ever worked together or in the same place?"

She paused as she looked through the folders and
Zane's fingers flew over keys. He was the one to answer
first. "Both Aircom Graves and John Caruso are listed as
having been employed in several of the government's top
research labs. Caruso worked for the DoE and Graves for
the DoD. But they were assigned to the same locations
three times."

"Okay, so they worked together. I'll lay ten-to-one odds
that these two men knew each other."

"What are you thinking?" Henry said.

"I'm thinking—the general said that when Graves saw
the body he apparently had a change of heart. Now, Mansfield thought it was the shock of actually having to siphon
off the memories of a real body. But what if that wasn't
it?" Carter looked at each of them. "What if he freaked out
because he knew the subject?"

Henry and Allison looked at each other. Allison
frowned. "Do you think he'd tell us?"

Carter shrugged. "Let's ask."

Dr. Graves was just leaving GD when the guards
called him back in and requested that he report to the director's office. He paused at the door, and Carter had to admit
it was probably intimidating to see the director, Henry, and
the sheriff waiting for him.

Allison gestured to the chair she'd moved into the center of the room. "Have a seat, Dr. Graves."

"Is something wrong?" he asked as he walked hesitantly
to the chair, looking at each of them. He visibly swallowed.
"Did something happen with the Brain Box?"

"That's what we'd like to know," Allison said. She
waited until he was seated before sitting forward and clasping her hands in front of her. "Dr. Graves . . . we know you
didn't make a call to Washington to get any data backups

delivered here, high speed or otherwise. We know that because you can't make a phone call out of Section Five."

Carter watched the young man carefully. He didn't seem too terribly surprised. Just . . . resigned.

Dr. Graves nodded. "You're right, Dr. Blake. There aren't any backups."

"You didn't make a backup?" Henry asked.

"Not there," Graves shook his head. "Not for them. I did make one for me."

"The one you thought you'd hidden in the storynest?" Allison said.

That did it. Carter half smiled as Graves's stoic countenance faltered and he stared at Allison. "You . . . you found it?"

"What we found," Henry said as he straightened from his perch by the window, "was a false image. A file with no data in it."

Graves's shoulders lowered. "Then you haven't found it at all. You've seen the same thing I saw—and all of John's memories are still missing."

Carter glanced at Allison, who glanced at Henry, who narrowed his eyes at Graves. "You knew him."

"Yes."

Allison licked her lips. "Are you saying—you didn't create the ghost image?"

"No. It wasn't an empty ghost. Not at first. I copied the data directly from the box to the storynest when I got here. Engineered it so it looked like any of the other memories there so I could store it and view it on my own, before the general got hold of it." He shook his head. "And trust me, you do not want the DoD winning on this one."

"You mean about the singularity?" Allison asked.

Carter waited, watching Graves. The young man looked up at Allison. "I really didn't want any of you to know about that."

Allison nodded. "It took some clearance issues, but I've learned enough. Enough from what Zane was able to translate and from reading about you, and about Jonathan Caruso."

Graves frowned. "I didn't want Mansfield to take a person's memories and make them national security. This whole thing is bullshit."

"Then," Henry said slowly, "you care to enlighten us on what isn't bullshit?"

"Actually—" Graves smiled. "I'd love to." He stood and moved to stand by the window, shoving his hands into his pockets. Finally he turned, glanced at Carter, and looked to Allison and Henry. "You both know that Eureka is one of several high-powered research labs chartered by the U.S. government—each of them conducting cutting-edge inquiries into scientific advancements. Many of these can save lives, and many of them can destroy them. Which all of you have lived through many times, from the reports I've read."

Allison, Carter, and Henry all nodded—Carter the most vigorously, until Allison glared at him.

"I could rattle off the locations, but you already know them."

"I don't." Carter raised his hand.

"Carter, not now," Allison warned.

"These facilities burn billions of dollars in taxpayer money—something the civilian population rarely sees. The government compartmentalizes the findings into two camps—those discoveries that can save lives and advance the development of crucial technologies, and those that can give us a military advantage over our adversaries."

"Mansfield is in the latter one."

"Yes. The Department of Defense. And I work on that side. But John—" He shook his head, smiling. "John worked for the other side."

"The Department of Energy."

Graves nodded at Carter. "Yes. Special Agent-in-Charge Jonathan Caruso. Director of Western Operations for the Department of Energy's Office of the Inspector General. That's a long way from MIT."

Henry said, "You two were friends."

"Yes."

Abruptly Carter heard a buzzing noise. He put a hand to his pocket to see if it was his cell phone. No. No vibration. Two more buzzes and it stopped.

"Is that it?" Allison said. "Is that why you've sabotaged this project from the beginning? Because of your moral dislike? I mean, I can appreciate it if you'd rather not have the general see your friend's memories—that would be something very hard."

"No, no." Graves shook his head. "No . . . I mean, yeah, that's a part of it. But the real tragedy isn't that. It's *why* all of this happened." He took in a deep breath. "Mansfield insisted this was a matter of national security. They tend to throw that term around a lot nowadays. Doesn't mean much anymore. But I guess in his eyes . . . all of this *is* national security."

"Dr. Graves," Henry said. "What was Caruso doing at PNNL? We know it had something to do with the singularity finding."

"Yes, it did. John was on assignment at PNNL, investigating a classified research operation, which you obviously know was the information they got from CERN about the sustainable singularity."

Everyone nodded. This confirmed Carter's theory that the dead investigator was Caruso.

"There had been a lot of infighting between the researchers with the DoE and the scientists with the DoD. I mean, looking at the breakthrough research—you automatically see the good and the bad, and the dual question rose: What would this new technology become? A giant leap ahead of fusion power, or the grandfather of a nightmarish new family of weapons?"

Carter leaned back and crossed his arms over his chest. "Do not like that sound of that."

"See . . . if the researchers determined that the technology had a substantial civilian value, the project would be administered by the DoE. If it was determined to be substantial for the military, then it's the DoD. Ever since the information came to light, there has been nothing but bureaucratic bullshit, official prestige posturing, and the kicker in all of this?"

Carter surprised them all when he said, "Funding."

"Funding?" Henry said. "How do you get to that?"

Carter shrugged. "It's what he just said. You've got a big, huge, really cool invention. Everybody wants to control it. But there's not enough money for everyone to share. So it's all a matter of numbers—to prove which department it can be better used for the dollar on." He looked at Graves. "Am I right?"

The younger man gave him a smile. "Dead-on, Sheriff. It's budget time, plain and simple. And through all the fussing and bullshit, it quickly became obvious to the Pentagon and the energy department that politics were influencing science. That's where John came in."

"They sent him in to investigate," Henry said.

"Yes. They sent him in to get the straight answer, not the bullshit they were being fed by both sides wanting the control and the dollars for funding. This should have been an objective decision—but it wasn't. John had just finished three weeks of interviews, investigations, and report writing at PNNL. He was about to get on an energy department jet to fly here when"—he paused and looked down—"he was killed. I'd talked to John not four hours before, and we were talking about the breakthrough, and about Washington and all the bullshit.

"The next thing I know I'm getting a call from General Mansfield, telling me to bring my Brain Box. I'm shuttled onto a private jet, land at PNNL, and told to harvest my friend's memories."

Carter heard the buzzing again and looked around. It sounded like a cell phone on silent. A few more buzzes and it went off again.

"Mansfield." Allison sighed and shook her head. "I'm assuming something went wrong with John's report? Otherwise, why harvest his memories?"

"All Mansfield would tell me was that he couldn't figure out any of John's notes. Wouldn't let me see them—said they'd been requisitioned by someone higher up on the food chain. And that he probably kept a lot of it in his head. He wants me to make those memories available to him so he can . . . I guess . . . figure out what John's recommendation was."

"You mean all of this is because Mansfield is worried about his bottom line?" Henry rubbed at his face. "I can't believe this."

"I can," Allison said. "We're only guessing, though, at what Mansfield wants. But he's worried enough about it to pull us in on it."

"The rest is as you know it," Graves said. "I wasn't finished with the box—and I thought I could make it work here. But John and I have been friends for over ten years, Dr. Blake. I'm sorry—but I know how he felt about the singularity, and I didn't trust Mansfield. I wanted to see the memories for myself. I also put in for access to John's notes—but I was flatly denied."

"So you hid the backup to look at yourself and use in case Mansfield"—Carter held up his index and middle fingers up into quote marks—"exaggerated?"

Graves nodded. "Only . . . when I went back to retrieve the files, I encountered evidently what you encountered. Empty images. It's gone."

"Did you wipe the Brain Box?" Henry said.

The buzzing started up again. Graves abruptly reached into his pocket, pulled out his phone, and pressed a side button. The buzzing stopped.

"Everything all right?" Carter asked, nodding to the phone.

Graves sighed. "Family." He cleared his throat. "Yes, I did wipe the Brain Box. I'm sorry. It's just that . . . Lucas was a lot smarter and a lot faster than I thought he'd be— and he had that translation program done in record time. And it was going to work. I could tell. I had to stall until I could somehow get hold of a copy of John's notes."

"Do you know where a copy is?" Allison asked.

"Yes and no. He usually kept his notes on MP3 recordings. Used a recorder, which he usually didn't keep on him for security reasons. It was how he did his investigations, and then when he translated them, he had a voice copy of what he was seeing and thinking. But John always backed things up. I wanted to look at the memories as well and see if he could tell me where the backup is."

"You don't think it was with his things after the accident? In his suitcase?" Allison asked.

"I tried. But his things were seized by Mansfield—who has denied access to any of it."

"You don't think," Carter said slowly as he moved from the window, "that the general would . . . fib, do you? Are you afraid he wouldn't be completely truthful about what John found?"

"If it meant the funding being granted to the DoE? I don't know," Graves said. "I work for the DoD, but when it comes to something of this magnitude? This huge of a ground shaker—I'm nervous around men of power."

"Well, I wouldn't call General Mansfield spineless," Allison said. "He's pro military all the way. And I would like to believe he's fair when it comes to things like this.

So if Caruso's notes suggest civilian use, he'd advocate for it."

"You have a better track record with him than I do," Graves said. "I'm afraid we haven't gotten along at all."

"Don't worry." Carter grinned. "Mansfield doesn't exactly play well with others."

"You think Mansfield has access to this MP3 player?" Allison sat back.

"I don't know. No one will tell me."

"So the bottom line here is—the memories are gone."

"I hope not." Graves shook his head. "They have to be somewhere in the system. No one tried to delete them. I mean . . . to delete just those files but keep up the image? What are the odds of that occurring?"

"You haven't been in Eureka long enough," Carter said.

The intercom beeped, and Allison sighed. She pressed it. "Fargo, I told you not to disturb us."

"I know—but the general's in the lab demanding answers, and he's brought someone with him."

"Who?"

"He won't say," Fargo said in a stage whisper over an intercom.

Carter shook his head.

Allison blinked. "What does he want?"

"He wants to see you as soon as possible."

She looked from Henry to Carter. "We'll be right there." She sat back. "Well, time to face the music. We're going to have to tell Mansfield the files were destroyed."

Graves stood, looking a bit too nervous for Carter's taste. "Dr. Blake, there's something I need to go do, an errand. Is it okay if I do that first?"

She shook her head. "I'd rather you stay here, especially if Mansfield's up to something. . . . You've answered a lot of questions I needed answers to, and you've given me a bit more to fight with. What is it you have to do?"

He put his hand over his stomach just as it growled out loud. "I need to grab something to eat. I haven't eaten since last night and I was on my way to pick something up at Café Diem."

She smiled. "Okay. Just get back here so we can put our heads together and find those files. And I'm pretty sure we're going to need your expertise to deal with this new person the general's brought in."

After Graves left, Henry received a page.

"Is it Lucas?" Allison asked.

Henry nodded. "Some results on tests I had the tech run. I need to go take a look at them, and then I'll join you when I can." He excused himself and left.

"You trust him?"

"Who? Mansfield?"

"No." Carter shrugged. "Well, okay, yeah, him, too. But I mean Graves. What he said?"

She pushed back and stood before moving from around the desk. "Everything he said checked out. I did my own preliminary snooping beforehand. And I wouldn't put it past the general to use this as a way of making the numbers work. But I can't help thinking there's something else— something he's still not telling us."

"Yeah, like who keeps calling him." Carter stood up. "He said family. He's got a sister. . . ."

Allison stood as well. "So, you coming with me?"

"Yes—I want to see who this person is he's brought with him."

CHAPTeR 20

"Well," Vincent said with a pause as Zoe stepped into Café Diem, the bell jingling above her. "I'm surprised to see you here," he said as he worked the espresso machine. "Lucas doing any better?"

Shaking her head, Zoe sat down at the counter after looking around for Dr. Graves. Not seeing him yet, she set the folder of her drawings in front of her and looked at Vincent. "No. It looks like a brain tumor—all the symptoms are there. But Henry says he can't physically find one."

"What do you mean, can't physically find one? That's awful. Here." He moved away from her into the pantry and then came out a few minutes later with a brownie on a plate, a fork, and a can of whipped cream. After setting that down in front of her, he held up a finger and then reached under the counter for a small creamer carafe full of warm chocolate.

"Vincent—you got your mojo back," she said, and

started pouring the chocolate over the top. "Though all I really wanted was a coffee."

He sighed. "That's just your conscious mind telling you to be good. But this is what your subconscious wants. Chocolate and decadence. But as for my mojo? No go, really. But after years of doing this you kinda figure out what women really want when they're depressed. Or emotional. Or both." Vincent smiled. "So . . . anything else I can get you?"

"No. Well, maybe a glass of water."

"Sure. You here taking a break?"

"A short one." She finished with the chocolate and then shook the can before spraying the top liberally with whipped cream. After that was done she took the fork and cut herself the perfect bite. "Waiting on someone to show them my drawings."

"Drawings?" He set a water glass in front of her and poured from a chilled metal carafe. "The ones you did with Julia and Fargo?"

"Yep." The brownie was perfectly heated, the chocolate chocolaty and not too sweet, and the cream light and fluffy. Even if Vincent was messing up orders, he sure knew how to make the order special in the end. "Oh, wow, Vincent. . . . This is good."

"Bavarian chocolate. Best there is. And I can make a mean drinking chocolate, too. But only order that when you want to stay awake. For three days." He wiped off the counter with a rag. "Who wants to see the sketches?"

"Dr. Graves."

"The guy here with Mansfield. Saw him walk by yesterday. Very cute."

"He's very nice, yes. He's the one working on the project that Lucas was working on." Abruptly her stomach soured, and she set the fork down. How could she possibly be sitting here, enjoying this good food, when Lucas was lying in a bed dying of a tumor?

A nonexistent tumor, no less.

"What's wrong?" Vincent asked.

The door opened and Zoe glanced over, but it was Jo, looking a little more stern than usual. The deputy nodded to Vincent, then to Zoe, and sat down in the chair beside Zoe. She took one look at the plate of brownie, chocolate, and whipped cream and said, "I want that. But a double."

"Wow." Vincent blinked and turned to fill the order.

"You okay?" Zoe asked, her fork back in her hand and toying with the whipped cream.

"I will be once I down one of those," she said, eyeing Zoe. "Why are you here? Lucas doing better?"

Zoe's appetite once again took a nosedive, and she set her fork down. "Okay. I'll go back to Global."

"No, no," Jo said as the brownie, whipped cream, and chocolate landed in front of her. She dumped the entire carafe on top of the brownie and then buried the brownie and the plate in whipped cream.

"Uh . . ." Zoe pointed at the plate. "Never mind about me. What about you? I've never seen you eat that kind of stuff before."

Jo nearly slammed the can down. "That's because in the entirety of my career in Special Forces, and then here, I have never spent an entire day talking a bunch of crazed, paranoid scientists off the roof."

Vincent snorted. "Oh, you mean the EM Pulse?"

Jo and Zoe frowned at him.

"The Eureka Militia Pulse?" He smirked. "Get it? EMP? They were in earlier—drew up a nice charter and I helped with their logo. Should look good on their new jackets."

"Vincent?" Jo started in a warning voice. "We do not need geeked-out vigilantes right now."

He held up his hand. "It's okay, Jo. I coffeed them all up and got them out of here, told them they'd do best if they guarded the roads."

"Did they listen?" Jo said.

"Wait." Zoe looked from Jo to Vincent. "The Eureka Militia? This is a joke, right?"

"Oh, no." Jo picked up her fork, set it aside, grabbed a spoon, and attacked the mound of whipped cream. "Apparently this town thinks the military being here is because they're going to shut Eureka down due to the economy."

"But . . . but that's crazy."

"I know," Jo said, staring at her dessert. "Carter and I spent most of the early afternoon getting them out of the office and assuring them they're not here to shut anything down or use any mind control on them. Then I spent another hour picking up tinfoil. So"—she pointed at Zoe with her spoon—"don't do any more of those Remote Viewing experiments in the café. At least till Mansfield and his men leave." She took a mouthful of whipped cream and closed her eyes. "Mmmm. . . . This is just hitting the spot."

"Gonna hit your blood sugar alarm, too, Jo," Vincent said as he set a coffee in front of her. "Zoe, go ahead and eat up. You know Henry will call you if anything changes."

Thinking about her pager, Zoe reached behind her and pulled her PDA out of her back pocket. She looked at the device, which resembled the size and width of a stick of gum, and then set it on the counter. There were no messages. "You're right. And I do feel like I'm in the way sometimes. I mean, I'm in for pre-med, but I don't know it all. And I certainly don't know anything about this."

Dr. Graves rushed in at that moment. His cheeks were pink and a slight sheen of perspiration covered his forehead. He looked around and, after spotting Zoe, waved as he made his way over.

"Sorry I'm late. I was in a meeting with the director and your dad."

"Everything okay? You heard anything about Lucas?"

"No, no. Everything's fine as far as I know. They were

going to check on him when I left. Just didn't want to be too late." He looked at the plates of whipped cream and then looked at Zoe. "Hungry? I can get you something a bit more substantial."

"Boy, there is nothing more substantial for the soul than a can of whip and a brownie," Jo said as she again attacked her mound of white fluffy whip.

"Dr. Graves, this is Deputy Sheriff Jo Lupo. Jo, Dr. Graves."

He offered her his hand. "Nice to meet you, ma'am."

She looked at his hand and then looked at Zoe. "He called me ma'am."

"Jo." Zoe arched her eyebrows. "Be nice."

With a smirk, Jo wiped her hands on a napkin and shook his hand. "Nice to meet you, Doctor."

He stepped back and looked at Zoe. "Want to show me the sketches here? Grab something to eat and then head back to Global?"

"Sure." She turned to Vincent and grabbed her dessert. "We're gonna take a table over there."

Vincent nodded. "Two burgers coming up."

Graves paused and looked back at Zoe. "How did he know I wanted a burger?"

"He does that." She smiled at Jo.

Jo turned in her chair, her spoon in her mouth. She pointed at them with the spoon. "I'll be watching you."

Graves turned with her and indicated a chair. "She scares me."

"She does that."

Once seated, Zoe handed him the folder and then proceeded to mangle her brownie as Graves opened the folder. "I'm missing one of these, I think—the one Julia borrowed."

She watched his expression shift from mild curiosity to surprise. His eyes widened behind his glasses, and he sat back and looked at each of the pictures.

She paused, frowning at him. "What is it?"

"I just . . ." He shook his head. "You captured her likeness in each of them. And you saw her?" Graves looked at her. "You actually saw her looking at you?"

Nodding, Zoe took several swallows of her water. "I told you. I did a View and I kept seeing these scenes. There was the snow, and then that argument, and then there where it looks like she's going to hit me . . . uh, him."

He removed his glasses and leaned forward. "Zoe . . . what were you trying to View when you saw this?"

She felt her heart flutter and looked down. She'd told no one but her dad that she'd tried to look into Lucas's head with her Viewing. And now that this stranger was asking her, she felt even more ashamed and embarrassed. "I . . . I wasn't trying to View anything."

"Zoe." His voice dropped and his dark eyes pierced her when she looked at him. "I understand the mechanics of Remote Viewing. I know you have to have a target to actually View. You don't know what it is, only that it's a person, place, or thing. Which were you Viewing when you saw this?"

"I . . . I was trying to View a person."

He sat back suddenly, watching her. "You . . . you weren't trying to look inside the box?"

"What box?"

"The Brain Box?"

She made a face. "Ew? The one with the dead guy's memories? No. I didn't even know it existed until today. I did these yesterday."

"Doesn't matter," he said. "Viewers don't really know their targets, either. Only that it's a person. My God. . . . Is it possible you picked up on his memories in the box?"

She cleared her throat. "No . . . see . . . I kinda did know my target."

He stopped and looked at her questioningly. "Zoe . . ."

"It was Lucas, okay? I was trying to see inside Lucas's head, and all I kept seeing was this girl. Over and over. And I thought it was someone he was seeing at school." She felt her heart skip again. "And then he collapsed like this and I find out he's been suffering from a brain tumor and I felt so guilty—"

Graves gripped the table, his expression playing from shocked, to happy, to concerned. "Zoe . . . I think I know what it was you were seeing. And I don't think Lucas has a brain tumor. I just think, in a manner of speaking, he's got too much on his mind." He held up the pictures. "I think I know how to help both of us. But I'm going to need you to listen to me, and then I'm going to need your help."

"What is it? Do you know who that girl is?"

"Yeah, I do. And she's dangerous." He ran a hand through his hair. "Her name's Dr. Kathryn Caruso. She works for the Defense Advanced Research Projects Agency. Or you might know it as DARPA."

Zoe frowned. "Is this bad?"

"Very bad she's here. She's whom I've been trying to avoid. I'll explain later. And if I don't do what I set out to do, I'm going to end up like John."

Vincent arrived with the orders, neatly bagged and ready. Graves took his and opened his mouth to ask how he knew they were leaving.

Zoe shook her head. "Don't ask. He just does that."

They moved to the door. "I have a lot to tell you on the way back, and you're not going to believe it."

"So this girl in the pictures? Are you saying this Katie is Kathryn Caruso? Who is she?"

Graves opened the door for her. "She's my sister."

CHAPTᵉR 21

Allison and Carter entered the lab to the accompaniment of Mansfield's voice, admonishing Zane and Fargo, demanding to know what progress they'd made.

"You've had more than twenty-four hours already. I expected more from this group and I'm getting tired of all the runaround."

Allison moved to stand behind Zane and a very nervous-looking Fargo.

Carter moved up next to her and put his hands on his hips.

"Dr. Blake," General Mansfield said in a manner of greeting and glared at Carter. "What are you grinning about?"

Allison gave him a furrowed glance and then turned a pleasant face to the woman standing beside the general. Carter looked her over—noticing that her build and style reminded him a lot of Tess's. Tall, slender, with a thin face and long brownish hair, and dressed in a well-pressed pantsuit of black, accented with a purple shirt. She carried a briefcase with her and a slight air of authority. Two of Mansfield's men stood at attention nearby, as if protecting this woman from the others.

When she turned to face him and Allison, he felt as if he'd had the wind knocked out of him. This was the same girl in the memories he saw—and the same woman Zoe'd been drawing.

Allison offered her hand. "Dr. Allison Blake, Director of Global Dynamics."

The woman returned the handshake. "I'm very much aware of who you are, Dr. Blake, and very happy to meet you. Director Kathryn Caruso."

Carter offered his hand to her as well. "Sheriff Jack Carter." He frowned when she returned the shake. "Caruso? Are you related to Special Agent John Caruso? Formerly with the Department of Energy?"

Kathryn's expression didn't falter as she retrieved her hand, her smile maybe a bit sad. "Yes. John was my husband." She gave the general a strange look before directing her attention toward Allison. "I see you've learned the identity of the source of the memories within the Brain Box."

"Yes." Allison nodded, then glanced at Mansfield.

Carter noticed that the general's bravado from moments ago had quieted, though his expression wasn't as calm. In fact, he looked even angrier.

Allison continued. "We have. And I would very much like to give you my condolences on your loss. Are you here in a personal capacity or a professional one, Director Caruso?"

"Both, really," Kathryn said. "And please, call me Katie."

"Allison."

"Katie," Carter said.

"Yes." She gave Carter a nod.

"Dr. Blake, I demand to know how you discovered the deceased's identity. This is a complete breach of protocol," Mansfield interjected.

Allison gave him a withering look. "I thought you might say it was a matter of endangering national security, General." She sighed. "It didn't take much to put things together. It was Sheriff Carter and Deputy Lupo who were the first to discover who he was."

"Carter?" Mansfield moved the full force of his gaze on him.

"Sheriff Carter was a U.S. Marshal," Katie interjected, taking over from Mansfield and, once again, acknowledging Carter with a nod before looking back to Allison again. "Before the general decides to interrupt with any more of his indignant outbursts, I'd like to apologize that this project has interfered with your work here at Global. I'm an avid fan of this research facility's discoveries, and I feel Dr. Graves was both right and wrong to intrude on your hospitality. Once John's—Agent Caruso's—memories were harvested, the general tells me it was Dr. Graves's idea to come here." She looked around. "Where is Dr. Graves?"

"He's out at the moment," Carter said. Red flags shot up all around him. He didn't know this woman, didn't really know Graves, but he sure as hell felt uncomfortable around her. He also didn't like the way she was looking at the lab—or at Zane and Fargo.

Allison spoke up. "Dr. Graves explained to me that since he'd been using the technologies of the storynest, and we are the closest facility to PNNL where the harvest took place, he deduced this was the best place for the translation. And I concur with his decision." She glanced at Mansfield. "We're also more neutral when it comes to the accuracy of reports that could influence where budget funding is spent."

Mansfield's expression faltered from indignant rage, to surprise, then back to just plain anger. "Dr. Blake, I would be very careful about what I said."

Allison bristled. "Oh, drop it, Mansfield. I read the reports, too. And I also have a right to know all the details of what comes across my desk and affects my people—and not get a lecture on breaching national security. So it makes me a little cranky to find out that this whole intrusion is really about funding."

"It's not just about funding, Director." Katie glanced over at the general before continuing. She shifted her briefcase in her hands. "If you know what John was doing, what his investigation was about, then you know he was looking into the misappropriation of officials within the government—between both the DoE and the DoD. It was very important work, and John was very good at what he did. He called his supervisor to let him know he'd made his assessment—and that he wanted to deliver it personally to him."

"Meaning he knew who should get the money and the project?" Carter said.

Katie nodded. "As I said, he was very good at what he did, Dr. Blake. The best. And he always backed up his findings with facts. Unfortunately—" She sighed, shaking her head. "John never was one for keeping things written down, preferring to live inside his head. So that whatever that decision was, it died with him."

Allison looked from Katie to Mansfield. "I understand you have Agent Caruso's notes from his investigation at PNNL?"

Nodding slowly, Mansfield gave Katie a knowing glance. "He talked to you, didn't he? Graves. He's the one who told you most of this."

"Yes, he did," Allison said. "But only after Carter was able to fill me in on a few things."

"Well." Katie sighed and her expression became almost pleasant, as if remembering something fondly. "I must apologize for Dr. Graves. I'm afraid he does have most of the information, but not all of it. His and Agent Caruso's—John's—relationship was a close one at one time. But over the years, working for opposing agencies, I'm afraid their friendship grew strained. Aircom didn't really understand a lot of what John was about, and that caused a little friction in my family."

Carter opened his mouth, and then smiled as he hung his head. The puzzle pieces were falling into place. "You guys are brother and sister."

"Yes. So you see where I find myself torn between the two. I know a lot more of what John was doing over the past three years since taking up his job with the DoE. Spouses talk often. And I feel I know my husband's thoughts much better than Air did."

"Dr. Blake," the general interjected. "Agent Caruso is here to help your people get the memories interpreted. She and Dr. Graves share a similar degree in biomedical engineering, and she has already been briefed on the storynest and has a working knowledge of Dr. Graves's present work on the Brain Box."

Carter frowned at Mansfield. "What about Graves?"

"I want him removed from the project," General Mansfield said with a slight smile. "I feel he's become disruptive, and incapable of carrying through this assignment with an objective eye. I agree with Agent Caruso that her brother's relationship to the deceased has . . . clouded his partiality. Agent Caruso is more than willing to pick up and finish this."

"So you don't think Agent Caruso's relationship to both of these men wouldn't be more of a disruptive element?" Carter asked. "She's worse off than Graves. She was *married* to the victim."

Allison nodded. "I'm afraid I have to agree with Sheriff Carter on this one. I don't want to insult your relationship with your husband, Director, but I don't see where you can be more impartial than Dr. Graves."

"None taken, Allison." Katie moved to the console where Zane sat watching and set her briefcase on top. She opened it and pulled out a binder filled with folders. "But I'm afraid this decision isn't yours to make. The general allowed me to look at the notes John had with him when he died. If I can see these memories, then I believe I'm more than qualified to give the general and the funding committee a correct analysis of what John found." She closed the briefcase and kept the binder in her hands.

"Aw, no . . ." Carter shook his head. "I don't think that's quite the truth." He rubbed the back of his head as he glanced at Allison. She looked pissed. But he wasn't sure if it was at him, Katie, or Mansfield.

"I beg your pardon?"

"You see"—Carter crossed his arms over his chest—"we've seen a small bit of John's memories. And I'm afraid your role in them could call into question any belief that you'd be the one to interpret his notes."

Katie's expression shifted, from innocent widow to an almost curious anger. "You—you were able to translate the memories?"

"A few," Allison said. "There was an accident on the first try, and one of my staff was injured. The second was more successful, thanks to Zane." She nodded to the young man who sat with his arms folded. "We took a small sample and ran it through the new translator. At first the text portions came out as nothing more than name, rank, and serial number—"

"So that's how you knew it was Agent Caruso," Mansfield said.

"Yes. But when the memories were interpolated by

the storynest"—she frowned—"the images we got back showed an argument with a woman—you, Director Caruso. The subject of the argument is unclear, but the emotion behind it feels a lot like fear."

"Are you trying to say my husband was afraid of me?"

"What we're saying," Carter said as he bent forward to get her attention, "is that one of those memories makes it look like you were telling him to lie on his findings. Were you threatening him?"

"Sheriff Carter." Katie fixed him with an intense stare. "Are you a qualified psychiatrist? Or even a psychologist? Are you qualified to give a professional opinion on a technology as new as this—a technology whose application is still in question?" She smiled. "No. You're not. And I'd like it if you stayed out of our way."

Carter opened his mouth, then closed it. She was right. He wasn't qualified to testify to anything like that.

"Director Blake." Katie looked at Allison. "I'd like the rest of John's memories translated, please, and turned over to me immediately. Also all notes, files, and copies of anything you've done here. Oh, and the translation software you created."

Allison looked over at Carter before answering. "I'm afraid we can't."

"Can't?" Mansfield said. It was almost a shout. "Can't or won't, Dr. Blake? It sounds to me like Dr. Graves may have already sabotaged this project by injecting his sensibilities where they don't belong."

She gave him a harsh look before continuing. "You would do well, General, to get the facts before making the conclusions. We can't continue the translation because the information on the Brain Box has been wiped clean."

Both of them blinked in stunned silence. Allison prepared herself for the blowback. It wasn't going to be pretty.

"Wiped . . . clean?" Mansfield put a hand to his forehead. "What does that mean? Did someone here wipe it?" His gaze immediately fell to Fargo, whose eyes grew to the size of golf balls.

Fargo shook his head. "I didn't do anything!"

"Please." Allison held up her hand. "We're still not sure what happened. Apparently Dr. Graves made a backup copy to the Global servers, and it, too, has been removed. We're still looking into what's happened and who could have done this."

Carter hid his surprise at Allison's statement. He realized she was protecting Graves by not telling them he was the one responsible for hiding the files in the first place. And he had to agree—if Katie was whom Graves was hiding them from, he'd have done it, too.

"I'm shocked at the lack of security here," Katie said, her voice tight. "Didn't Aircom make a backup copy when he harvested the memories? Something besides what he made here?"

"He said there was no time." Allison looked at her. "He didn't even know or understand what he was being called in for until he was presented with Caruso's body."

Carter watched Caruso, noticing her complete lack of emotion as she talked about her husband.

"I know the story," Mansfield snapped. "I was there and I should never have listened to him." He shook his head. "I want this facility locked down, Dr. Blake. And I want every employee interrogated, every hard drive, CD, DVD, flash drive seized and searched—"

"No, General," Allison said quietly. "That's not necessary. Mainly because we're talking about petabytes of information. Not something you can copy to any available thumb drive—not even here in Eureka. And level of security notwithstanding, there was no one here besides me, Henry, Zane, Lucas, and Carter who knew about the project at that time."

"You're protecting him," Katie said in a quiet voice. "You're protecting Aircom."

"No, I'm not," Allison said. "What I am doing is trying not to throw my people into more of a panic than they already are. Having the general's men all over the town is already causing a stir, and now that I know that it's over budget cuts rather than national security, I'm more inclined to tell you to pull your men out, General."

"Budget cuts?" He shook his head at her. "You think that's all this is about? It's about the appropriate division of scientific assets, Dr. Blake. This is about putting things into perspective when it comes to scientific breakthroughs that could advance the protection of this nation and not letting them fall into the hands of naysayers and tree huggers."

Carter winced, realizing before the general did that he'd gotten Allison's hackles up. Not something he'd recommend anyone doing.

"General." Allison moved to stand before Mansfield. "If there is one thing I do understand in all this, it's that I personally hope the information and research for that singularity is *not* used for military gain, because when it comes to making the decision between killing millions with it or saving millions, I'm going to pray our government chooses life over death."

Mansfield glared at her for a few minutes before turning to his aide. "Slater."

The man took a step closer. "Yes, sir!"

"Tell your men to arrest Dr. Aircom Graves. I want him brought to me for questioning."

"Yes, sir!"

"Arrest him for what?" Allison said.

"For obstruction," the general said. "You'll be working with Dr. Caruso from now on, looking for those memories, Dr. Blake. You have twenty-four hours. And if you don't find them, then I'll move to take over Global Dynamics and let my people find it."

"You can't do that, General. You have no authority over Global."

"I will by the time I get back, and I'll have Graves in custody. That damn nerd has done nothing but try to sabotage this project from the start. And now you tell me the Brain Box is wiped and you're not looking at Graves as the perpetrator. That tells me you've been compromised, Dr. Blake."

He turned and left the lab.

Katie turned immediately to Zane and started giving him orders to turn over all the data gathered so far, including lab records of computer logs and any security tapes that were kept.

"Just wait a damn minute," Allison said, and moved close to Zane. "I run this facility, Director Caruso, and though you work for Mansfield, I'm not about to just roll over and—"

"Dr. Blake," Katie interrupted with a pleasant smile. "I don't work for Mansfield. As of oh-eight hundred hours this morning, he works for me. I'm the one in charge. So, if you don't mind, I'd like those things I requested. And I'd like to have them sent to your office." She smiled. "Yes, I think your office will do nicely."

Carter rubbed the back of his head again. He needed to excuse himself and find Graves as soon as possible and find out how his daughter was able to draw pictures of this woman—someone he knew Zoe had never seen before—who just happened to be the wife of the dead man and the sister to the man pulling memories.

He needed to find Jo, too. Might be time to break out one of her end-of-the-world guns.

CHAPTᵉR 22

Finding the sheriff's office quiet and empty, Carter went to Café Diem.

Jo waved from the counter. Carter approached her and looked down at her plate. He pointed at it. "What was that?"

"Brownie, chocolate, and whipped cream." She licked her spoon and smiled. "Simple, but satisfying."

"I suppose this is what Zoe calls stress eating?"

Jo swallowed. "Could say that."

"Hi, Sheriff, hungry?" Vincent asked as he came out of the pantry with an armload of stuff.

"No, no . . . I'm looking for Dr. Graves. Guy about yay high? Brown hair? Glasses." He shrugged. "Kinda nerdy?"

"Nerdy cute," Vincent said. "He and Zoe left a little bit ago."

"Zoe . . . and Graves? Together?" Carter looked from Vincent to Jo.

"Relax, Carter," Jo said as she pushed her plate away.

"You read his file. Boring. They're probably being egg-heads together."

Vincent sighed. "They ordered burgers but then had to leave before they could eat."

Carter's phone buzzed at his hip, and he pulled it out. Seeing Allison's name on the ID, he answered it. "Carter."

"Find him yet?"

"No—but apparently Zoe's with him."

"Zoe? Why is Zoe with him?"

"I'm not sure." He looked over at Vincent. "You didn't happen to overhear—"

Vincent nodded. "Said they were on their way back to GD."

"Ah, Allison—Vincent said they're on their way back there."

"Damn," Allison said softly. "If Mansfield's men get him before we do, he'll disappear, Jack. You try calling him?"

Carter blinked. "No . . . did you?"

"I don't have his cell phone number."

"I don't have it—" He looked over at Vincent, who was handing him a small slip of paper. On it was scribbled a phone number.

Vincent shrugged. "Jo gave it to me."

Jo looked over at Carter and glared. "You care to include me in on your little manhunt? Getting a little tired of being left out."

Carter grinned. "Allison, I got his number. You keep an eye out there. I'll give him and Zoe a call." He hung up and nodded to Jo. "You coming?"

She slid off the stool. "Yep. I just need to run over to the office."

"Wait." Carter jogged after her out of Café Diem. "Jo—no big guns."

But she only waved at him as she looked both ways before running across the street to the office.

Carter sighed and pulled out his phone again. The low battery message appeared.

Ah, nuts.

Zoe and Graves sat in her car just outside the entrance to Global Dynamics. She'd seen the added security just as Graves told her to double back. Five uniformed men.

"What's going on?" Zoe turned to look at him, frustrated now that her phone was dead. She'd searched her purse for her PDA but couldn't find it. Had she left it somewhere? A fleeting memory of taking it out at Café Diem came back to her, and she mentally kicked herself.

"I'm glad I suggested you drive instead of me using my rental. I'm pretty sure anything with my name on it's been flagged." He nodded to the front. "What's going on is my sister. Looks like she's managed to take me off the project—or she's in the process of it."

"But why?" Zoe frowned at him. "Air—what's going on? You said she was dangerous, but not exactly *how* she is dangerous."

In the twilight as the sun went down over Eureka, Graves looked even younger than he had before. Zoe wasn't sure if it was his odd boyish charm or the fact that he reminded her so much of her dad with his personality. He was smart, and at the same time seemed naive and a little lost.

"I have suspicions—something John said to me several nights ago."

"You talked to him before he died?" She searched his face. "What is it?"

"He told me he'd found something. Something in his investigation. Something that would probably come between our friendship and his marriage."

"Like what?"

"I don't know. When I got to PNNL—after I'd started harvesting the memories—Kathryn showed up. Started asking me a lot of questions about John's notes. And his investigations. She said she saw he'd called me, and she wanted to know what we talked about." He looked at Zoe with a pained expression. "Zoe—her husband had just died—my best friend—and she was more worried over what we talked about? That didn't make sense. And then . . . when Zane was able to translate a few of the memories before I learned the rest were gone . . . what I saw . . . they were arguing over him lying. . . . And then her voice. I could hear her voice."

Zoe wasn't sure she liked where this was going. "Air—when you talked to John, did he say anything about your sister?"

"He warned me away from her. Told me she was dangerous." He sighed. "And told me if anything happened to him—that I was to find out if she had anything to do with it."

"And what you saw in the memories—you think she *did* have something to do with it? With his death?"

"I think so—something in those memories I saw, that your dad and the director saw. They said it was an accident. He was driving to the airport and suddenly turned into a truck. Could have lost control of the wheel, or he might have been too tired. No one else was in the car with him. I just know that I don't trust my sister right now."

Nodding, Zoe thought back over some of the things Air had said on the drive here, and she watched him. "And you think that somehow, those missing memories are in Lucas's head. They're what's causing him to be sick."

"Maybe. I don't know how or why—I just know he was wearing the halo and he was right there at the nest where I hid them. And if you saw Katie when you tried Viewing him, then you saw what was in there."

"And Lucas has no idea who this girl is?"

"None."

She watched the entrance for a while before speaking again. "How is it you believed me? That I'd Viewed Lucas's thoughts? I mean, I told my dad, and Julia, but even she didn't believe me."

"My family's been involved in government experiments for several generations, Zoe. Remote Viewing isn't that far of a stretch for me. I learned about it mostly from my sister. I mean, she does work for an agency that specializes in defense—no matter how far-fetched the defense seems."

"I still think we need to tell Henry. He could figure out how to get those memories out before they kill Lucas."

"We are. We will. But first I need to see what you saw, and the only way I know to do that is to grab some story globes and have you remember. I might be able to piece enough together to show the general that my sister has something to do with all this."

"This just seems like a really risky thing to do. Let's just go to Henry."

"Zoe—if I go anywhere near that place, I'm going to be arrested and disappear. Not you, nor anyone else, will ever see me again. My sister will make sure of that. I have no idea what she'll make me do. Please. . . ."

"Air—that sounds so paranoid. She can't make you do anything."

"I wouldn't be too sure about that. I heard her tell John in those memories that he would drive into a truck—and he did." He looked at her. "Will you help me?"

"You want me to sneak in there and steal a whole brief-case of stuff and walk back out."

"I would do it myself, but I can't get back in. And if Mansfield gets to me first—I'm serious about disappearing."

"You make her sound so . . . evil."

Graves smiled in the dimming light. "Wouldn't say evil. I'd call her more . . . driven. Misguided? But I'll be right here in case. And then we can take a look at what you saw."

"Okay—but then we go to Henry and get those memories out of Lucas's head?"

"Yes." Graves got out of the car and half ran to the edge of the woods.

With a sigh, Zoe pulled the rest of the way up the drive to the guard post, went through, and parked. Taking a deep breath, she got out of the car and walked up to the entrance like always. The added security demanded to see her ID, which she obliged, and then after a good five-minute wait for them to clear her—she walked in and into the rotunda.

Looking around, Zoe made her way to the elevator and got in and—

Oh no.

She put her hand to her forehead. The storage room Air was talking about was in Section Five. How was she going to get to Section Five with no clearance?

"Hi, Zoe. Going to see Lucas?"

Nearly jumping out of her skin, Zoe turned to see Fargo step into the elevator. She felt a wide grin pull at the edges of her mouth as an idea coalesced. "Oh, hi, Fargo. Yeah . . . I'm heading back to the infirmary. But . . . have you seen my dad?"

"No . . . but he might be with the director in Section Five."

She pursed her lips. "Is there a way you can take me there so I can check?"

"Oh, I don't know. . . . That's a very high-security-level area, and so few of us have access to it."

"I know, Fargo, but I need to talk to him. I've been so

upset about Lucas and I really need to see to him. If you take me, it should be okay. I mean, they trust you."

He smiled and puffed out his chest the way she knew he would. "Well . . . I'm not sure I should do that."

She would tell him she wouldn't leave his side, but that wasn't her plan. Once down there, she had to find the storage room and grab what Air needed. Being with Fargo wasn't going to accomplish that.

"Please, Fargo? A quick look and then I'll be back up to the infirmary to be with Lucas."

He seemed to consider the request, then finally moved to swipe his key card. The elevator began its descent, and Zoe nodded to him. "Thanks, Fargo. I owe you one."

"Naw . . . it's nothing."

"So." She tilted her head toward him. "What's with the goon squad at the door?"

That question lit up his eyes as he looked around—as if there were an invisible person in the elevator with them. "Well, it looks like the general brought in a lady from another agency to take over that top secret project in Section Five—"

"You mean the Brain Box."

"How did you know?"

"Come on, Fargo. It's Eureka."

He seemed to accept that and continued. "Anyway, this new woman happens to be the wife of the dead guy and Dr. Graves's sister. She and the general accused Graves of sabotaging the project—and now all of the important files are missing. So the general issued an arrest warrant on Graves. He's to be taken into custody on sight and interrogated. They'll find those missing files." He smiled. "And I'm going to help."

"You are? How?"

The elevator doors opened, and Zoe stepped out into the familiar dark corridor. She'd been to Section Five before—

more times than she really wanted to. She just didn't have the authorization to get herself there.

"I plan on calling Graves—we're friends now. He trusts me. And then I'm going to get him to tell me where he hid the files and then lure him here so that the general can take custody and I can show them where the files are." He beamed. "I'm hoping that'll show them I had nothing to do with this case. Not a thing. I didn't touch anything."

"And if you solve it, then you'll be redeemed."

"Yeah, that's one way to put it. But I—" He stopped and reached into his back pocket, pulling out his Global PDA. He looked at it. "Oh no, the director wants me. I've got to get back upstairs."

"Well, I know where the lab is. I'll just go take a quick peek and then leave."

"Okay . . . but just don't touch anything, okay? And stay out of the general's way," he said as he got back on the elevator and disappeared.

"Uh-huh," Zoe said as she turned in the direction of the lab, and just past that, the storage room. But first, why not take a peek in the lab?

CHAPTeR 23

The sun had nearly set when Carter and Jo arrived at Global. He noted the added security outside the front gate—and the front door. And it took a little longer to persuade Jo to leave her extra gun in the car. Ten minutes of security bull and they were finally in the building, heading across the rotunda to the elevator, when he saw a familiar face.

"Sheriff Carter." Director Caruso met him and Jo in front of the elevator. She looked at Jo. "And you must be Deputy Sheriff Jo Lupo. It's a pleasure." She extended her hand.

Jo looked at it as if the woman had handed her a skinned frog.

Taking her hand back, Caruso looked at Carter. "Have you caught Dr. Graves yet?"

"No, ma'am." Carter shook his head. "But I'm not exactly looking for him to arrest him."

"Those were the general's orders, Sheriff."

"Maybe." He gave her a stiff smile. "But you can ask Mansfield or Director Blake—I don't follow orders all that well."

"Sheriff, my brother wiped John's memories off that Brain Box for what was probably some misguided moral dilemma. If we can't find them, he will pay for his mistake—whether you approve or not."

He crossed his arms over his chest. "Director—your husband just died. He was a good friend of your brother's. And I find it odd that you seem completely non—" He snapped his fingers and glanced at Jo. "Non—"

"You don't care," Jo said in a bored voice.

Carter straightened and grinned, holding his hands out to his sides. "Doesn't it even bother you that there might be private memories of the two of you? Something you might not want people like Mansfield seeing?"

Caruso shrugged. "It's all part of the job, Sheriff. I'm willing to do what it takes to protect my country. Why aren't you?"

He shook his head. "What is this really about, Director Caruso? What's in your husband's memories that you don't want anyone else to see?"

"Sheriff." Caruso's voice was smooth. Controlled. "There's nothing in my husband's memories I'm afraid of. My concern right now is for my brother."

Jo spoke up. "You mean you think your brother wiped the Brain Box. Or maybe he saw something, or knows something you don't want him to."

Caruso spoke in a soft, lilting voice. "Air hasn't been himself since he saw John's body. I think the shock of seeing his best friend dead was too much—and then being told to take those memories like that. I'm not sure that was the wisest thing General Mansfield could have done."

The elevator opened. A few people got off as Carter,

Jo, and Caruso stepped inside. She pressed the button for Section Five and swiped her key card. "We're all traveling to the same place?"

Jo glared at Caruso. "You know, I'm not buying this whole willing-to-air-your-dirty-laundry-to-the-military bullshit. And you seem very well-adjusted for someone who just lost her husband."

"The women in my family are very resilient. Also, I don't think your opinion of me means a damn thing, does it, *Deputy*?"

Carter winced. He feared for Caruso's life for saying that.

"My brother knows where the files are. Once he's brought in for questioning, I'll have the means to extract that information."

Something in the way she said that bothered him. "How is getting Aircom in here going to find the files? He insists he doesn't know where they are, either."

But Caruso only smiled. "His memories will know, Sheriff."

Carter glanced at Jo. "Director—you aren't planning on using the Brain Box on your own brother?"

"Why not? If he hid the files, we'll see where. Once we find him."

The door opened and Caruso stepped out. Carter pointed up. "We need to go to the infirmary. Just hitching a ride."

The doors closed and Carter did an involuntary shudder.

"I hate her," Jo said.

"Yeah. Me, too. And I'm thinking her brother's not that crazy about her, either. Unfortunately he's not answering his phone, and Zoe's is going to voice mail."

"And her pager?"

Carter dug into his back pocket and pulled it out. "Left it at Café Diem."

Once back up on the main floor, he and Jo found Allison in her office.

"Carter—did you get hold of Graves or Zoe?"

"No." He shook his head and told her what he'd told Jo. "I was wondering if you could, like, switch on a GPS tracking system. Maybe pinpoint them?"

Allison shook her head. "That only works if they have the GD pager on them or their phones are turned on. If Zoe's phone is dead and you have her pager, then there's not much we can do to find them. Unless she's in a building on the GD grid. Then she can be identified through DNA."

"What about Graves?" He shrugged. "He's a government employee. Don't you, like, LoJack everyone?"

Allison smirked. "Only you, Jack."

Carter's eyebrows went up.

"I don't like that woman," Jo said. "She's a textbook sociopath."

"You mean Director Caruso?" Allison nodded. "I'd have to agree with you, Jo. It's like . . . the fact that we're talking about her husband's private memories means nothing."

"Well, sociopath or not, she just threatened to use the Brain Box on Graves when he's brought in," Carter said with his hands on his hips.

That got Allison's full attention. "What? She can't be serious."

"I think she is. And if she gets permission to use it on her own brother—"

"I honestly don't think that's the type of woman who gets permission on anything, Carter. My assumption is she'll use it whether he's willing or not."

Jo looked at Carter. "Can I shoot her?"

He paused and then pointed at her. "Ask me that later."

Allison sighed. "Stop it, you two. This is serious. And it's not helping us or Lucas. We've got to get this whole thing out of GD." She rubbed at her brow. "Caruso insisted she take a look at my personal computer and server. Accessed my files and scanned everything. I feel like I've been invaded."

"Where's Jenna?" Carter looked around, suddenly remembering Allison had brought her child.

"I sent the babysitter home. No use worrying about shelves when we're stuck in another crisis of national security," she said, her voice dripping with sarcasm.

"So what do we need to do?" Jo asked.

"Jo, at this point"—Allison shrugged—"I'm open for suggestions. We have searched every possible place that data could be—I mean, it's not a small amount. Not that easy to hide. And it's just not here. It's not in the Brain Box—that was the first thing she took a look at. I'm almost afraid to admit the memories are gone—completely wiped."

Carter pursed his lips. "Would that be such a bad thing? I mean, what if they are? And they can't make heads or tails of Caruso's notes? If a decision can't be made, what would happen?"

"Well." Allison looked from Jo to Carter. "I think the worst case here would be that another investigator would be discharged to redo what Caruso was doing. For a timing issue, I know that budget requests are due at the end of next week—I had to fill out those for Global Dynamics. My assumption would be that the decision to fund the project period would be shelved until the next year."

"Which means neither the DoD nor the DoE can get hold of the funding or the project." He shrugged. "Maybe—if Graves did actually wipe out the memories—that was his plan? Maybe he just thinks funding it period is a bad idea?"

"You think he really sabotaged this, Carter?"

Jo shook her head and answered before Carter could. "He might have—and I don't know him—but after meeting the sister"—she looked at Carter—"I think it might be a good idea for me to check out this Kathryn Caruso."

"I doubt you'll find that much on Director Caruso," Allison said.

"Oh, just watch me."

Fargo knocked on the door and stepped in. "You wanted to see me, Director."

"Yes, Fargo, come on in."

Fargo smiled when he saw the sheriff and Jo. "Oh, hi, Sheriff. Hi, Jo. Zoe's looking for you."

Carter, Jo, and Allison exchanged looks. "You saw her?" Carter said.

"Yeah. She wanted to see if you were here, so I took her down to Section Five."

"How long ago?"

Fargo turned an odd shade of red. "Well . . . that was just before the director paged me, and then I bumped into Julia and she wanted to talk and she apologized for accusing me of taking her Remote Viewing notes and so we started a makeup kiss—"

Carter held up his hand. "Okay . . . that's plenty. I don't need a blow-by-blow. Was Graves with her?"

"No. She was by herself. She said she was going to check down there and then go to the infirmary."

"You didn't see Graves?"

"No. Why . . . ? What's wrong?"

Allison pushed her intercom. "Henry—you there?"

"Yes."

"Zoe with you?"

"No, she just left. Came in to check on Lucas and then said she needed to go home for a bit. Is something wrong?"

Allison looked at Carter, frowning. "No. She was by herself?"

"Yes."

"Thanks, Henry. How is Lucas?"

There was a pause. "No change, but if I can see you and if you can find Carter—"

"Right here, Henry."

"Good. I want to show you both something."

"We'll be there in a bit." She switched off. "So Zoe came in alone."

"And left." Carter shook his head. "So where did Graves go?"

Allison grabbed her tablet and closed her laptop, preparing to head down to the infirmary. "I'm assuming he's hiding, if he got my message. But I don't know why Zoe was here without him if they left Café Diem together."

Carter and Jo followed her out to the elevator, with Fargo trailing behind.

"Jo—go see what you can dig up on Caruso. I'm going to head down to the infirmary with Allison."

"On it," Jo said.

"Hey, Allison." Carter touched her shoulder.

She stopped and turned to look at him.

He paused. "Uh . . . about that LoJack comment. You don't really do that—do you?"

But Allison only smiled, patted his shoulder, turned, and joined Jo at the elevator.

Air had been right—going back through security had been easier, even while carrying the briefcase. They'd opened it up, taken a look, and passed her on through.

Graves was still at the woods' edge when she drove down. He got in the car and reached for the briefcase. When he saw two, he paused. "Zoe . . . why did you get two?"

"Well . . ." She winced. "I went to the lab just to take a peek in, and there was nobody there. The Brain Box was out in the open and it looked like it'd been unplugged, so I—"

He opened the larger briefcase fast and pulled it into his lap. She couldn't really see while driving but he flipped on the overhead and she could tell he was looking at the octagonal box. "Damn her. . . . She's swapped out the drive."

"Is that bad?"

"Means she's planning on running it through several different scans. I'd swear there was nothing on it—but you never know."

"So this one doesn't have a drive in it?"

"No." He packed it back up and set it in the back floorboard. "And once they see it's gone, they'll run the security tapes and know you took it, Zoe."

She shrugged. "I've stolen worse . . . trust me."

He opened the second briefcase under the light and looked at the rows of deactivated storycatchers.

Zoe snickered. "You do know what those things caused a while back."

"Yes, but I don't plan on using them the same way," he said as he closed the briefcase. "Good, you got a halo as well. Now all we need is a quiet place to work."

"We can go back to my house. I'm sure S.A.R.A.H. won't mind the company."

"Sarah? Is that your mom?"

"I guess she thinks she is sometimes. And if it wasn't Fargo sounding like a girl, then I wouldn't mind. S.A.R.A.H. is the house AI where Dad and I live. If I tell her to, she can lock things down so no one can find us."

"Um . . . it sounds interesting, but I'd really rather not put my life into something that someone else could override." He sighed. "Can you think of anywhere else?"

"A hotel room."

He didn't look very happy with that idea, either.

"I know—we can go to Lucas's house."

"What about his parents?"

Zoe shook her head and closed the briefcase. "It's perfect. They're out of the state right now—I've been calling them to let them know how Lucas is doing. But I have a key and I promised them I'd check on the bird while Lucas is at GD. No one would think we'd be there."

CHAPTER 24

People were busily working as Carter and Allison entered the infirmary. Lucas still rested on the main examination table, a mask over his face and several round disks taped to his forehead. Julia was there applying more to his temples and smiled as they approached.

Henry stepped up and nodded to Carter. "You met Director Caruso?"

"Yeah . . . feels like I still need a shower, too."

"She's intense," he agreed. "And I've been able to keep her out of the infirmary computers. But she's got the highest-level clearance I've seen, and it's only a matter of time before she comes in here and starts demanding to take these systems offline for her searches."

"She can't do that. You have patients depending on them."

"Tell me about it," he agreed. "And the last thing I want is for her to stick her nose into anything I'm doing. Espe-

cially when it comes to what I'm about to show you." He
nodded to Julia. "We're putting magnetic sensors on Lucas
so that we can use his magnetic field to read and measure
what's going on in his mind. Not really reading his synaptic impulses but more of understanding his thoughts."

"Thoughts have a pattern brain wave," Allison said.
"Did you find something?"

"I did." He half smiled and pointed to two monitors.
"The levels of readouts on the left monitor are from Lucas's basic brain waves. His normal EEG pattern."

Carter nodded. He couldn't really understand what the
squiggly lines meant, but he'd seen them before on EEG
machines.

"The monitor on the right shows those of the deceased,
John Caruso."

The second set of patterns was very different.

"Wait, Henry, how are you getting John Caruso's brain
activity? He's deceased. There's no activity in the brain to
measure, much less an actual brain."

"Both of these are coming from Lucas, Allison. Both
his, and Caruso's."

Carter and Allison both blinked and came forward.
"How . . . how do you know that's his?" Carter asked. "I
mean, how do you know that that is Lucas's and that one's
Caruso's?"

"If there is one thing Dr. Graves is, it's thorough. His
harvesting technology didn't miss a thing—not only did
it capture the synaptic cry, but it also recorded the actual
brain waves present at the time. The translated sample was
large enough that I could run it through several brain pattern enhancers and simulate a brain wave using the patterns I found in those memories. This is the pattern I got."
He switched Lucas's brain waves to a new one. And the
new one matched almost exactly to the one Henry claimed
was coming from Lucas.

"Henry . . . that's incredible," Allison said.

"Incredible." Carter grinned. "You're a genius. Henry—what you're saying is that John Caruso's memories are there." He pointed to the image on the screen.

"Wait just a minute." Allison frowned at Carter and then at Henry. "Are you saying the files we're looking for—the memories—are in Lucas's brain?"

"Yes," Henry and Carter said in unison.

Henry held up his hands. "Remember the blast from yesterday? If Graves had already copied the raw data in its untranslated form into the storynest, and then Lucas was wearing the halo in a receiving capacity—"

"Then those memories transferred directly to him," Allison said as she put a hand to her chin. "It does make sense. They were in their native state, and the translator program was already set to take in that proprietary signature. So the missing memories are with Lucas, and that's what's causing it to look as if he's developed a sudden brain tumor."

Carter pursed his lips. "Is this possible?"

"It's actually pretty easy to understand, Carter. Our memories are stored in the cortex." Henry reached down to the keyboard in front of the monitors, and the image with Caruso's activity disappeared. In its place was displayed a side section of a brain. "Think of it as our memory room. It's where we store our experiences. Lessons. Poignant moments in our lives—instances that define who we are."

"Kinda like that drawer in the kitchen." Carter looked from Henry to Allison. "You just kinda throw things into it."

"Kinda," Henry said. "When we're young, that cortex is an empty room, or drawer. It craves experiences, sensory mainly, to help us learn and grow. We learn through the cortex what objects are, and that information is stored in our long-term memory. As we grow, our capacity to retain and store information decreases, and finally diminishes. Which is why many of the elderly have trouble remembering things that are new, but can still retain memories from their childhood."

"You mean the drawer—or the room—gets full," Carter said.

"Yes. There is a theory, though unproven, that we are already genetically predetermined to remember a certain amount of things." He snapped his fingers. "Like a hard drive. You have stored memory and temporary memory, like with the buffer Zane first used to test the translator on. Temporary would be stuff we learn for a test. Something we know on a subconscious level we won't commit to the long term. Some things will stick, but most won't."

He pointed back at the cortex. "Think of that temporary memory like a waiting room outside your main memory room. When he received that shock and apparent download, the memories immediately dumped into those buffers—or his waiting room—a room not big enough to handle that much information at one time."

"And in order to retain as much of that memory as possible, his cortex created a secondary waiting room," Allison said.

Henry pointed at her. "Right—but it needed space to do that, and it's using the permanent memory to do this. My theory is that the shadow I'm seeing branching out from the cortex is that extra room. And it's expanding, chewing up other areas of the brain in order to retain the new information." He looked at both of them. "I think one of two things is going to happen. Either Lucas's brain will eventually dump the information out of short term, which might actually dump a lot of his long-term memories with it—or, Caruso's memories will replace Lucas's long-term memories."

"You mean he'll have two sets of memories?" Carter asked.

"More like bits and pieces of both," Henry said. "Lucas would completely lose the use of his cortex. It will be like reformatting a hard drive. Permanently."

Allison shook her head. "Henry, we have to get those memories out of there. Somehow dump this extra room his brain has set up. If Mansfield even gets wind that that's where the missing data went—"

"I know," Henry said, holding his hands up. "I just haven't figured out how to get it out. It was shocked in— like a high-speed transfer. In a burstlike pattern. In order to reverse the process, you're talking about pushing the information back in from Lucas's brain. There's no way to actually make that kind of thing occur. We'd end up frying his central cortex."

Carter pursed his lips as he looked around the lab. A thought occurred to him. "Henry . . . you said the transference happened because of the shock he received and the fact that he was wearing the halo."

"That's right."

"A lot of people got shocked yesterday. And a lot of people have been acting kinda freaky—well, freakier than normal. You don't think anyone else ended up with some of Caruso's memories?"

Allison turned a concerned face to Carter. "That's a good question. The town's power grid is tied directly the generator here in Global. If something happened here, it could have traveled out much like information traveling through a network."

"I don't think that happened," Henry said. "But— given what we've learned so far about what Caruso was doing and his possible state of paranoia and distrust . . . I wouldn't be surprised if his emotions had somehow filtered out to the town."

"Which would explain people's sudden unwarranted distrust of the military being here," Carter said. "You plug in a worker for the Department of Energy investigating improprieties that may or may not have been initiated by the Department of Defense—add in lots of soldiers, and we get a mild case of mob rule."

Allison looked at him with her eyebrows arched, a half smile on her lips. "That . . . was impressive, Carter."

He grinned at her. "I have my moments."

Henry turned, sighing. "With the other Caruso going through the records and crawling all over the data so far, if she's good, then she might come to the same conclusion that this is where the missing memories went."

"I don't know, Henry, this is quite a stretch. Even I'm not sure I believe it." She moved to the side table and looked at a binder resting there. Carter recognized it as the same one he'd seen Julia holding the day before. She opened it and began thumbing through it. "These are Julia's notes." She stopped on one of the pages and blinked.

Glancing over at Carter, she picked up a wrinkled sheet of paper, her mouth open. "Carter . . ."

Moving to her, he came around the side and peered over her shoulder. He recognized it as one of Zoe's drawings—the first one she'd done of the mystery woman's face.

"What is it?" Henry joined them and then whistled. "If I didn't know any better, I'd say that was Kathryn Caruso. Who drew this?"

"Zoe did," Carter said as he took the piece of paper. "She did this yesterday afternoon during one of those Remote Viewing sessions. I was going to tell you—this is where I'd seen Kathryn Caruso's face before. Zoe was targeting Lucas for Remote Viewing. Only she called it something else."

"Well, I'd say she was successful," Allison said, looking back at the likeness. "That's nearly a perfect shot of her."

Henry leaned in over Allison's shoulder. "Carter, are

you saying that Zoe tried to View directly into someone else's mind?"

Sighing, Carter nodded. "I thought it was all mumbo-jumbo . . . but she even named one of the drawings she did *Katie*."

"Kathryn Caruso," Allison said.

"What do you mean, *one* of them?" Henry turned to face him. "She did this more than once?"

"She showed them to me last night. I thought she was tuning in on a movie she'd probably overheard when she fell asleep in front of the TV." He sighed.

"Jack . . . this is incredible," Allison said. "To do this with only a few Views?"

"So you think she really was looking into Lucas's head?"

"Carter." Henry glanced at Allison. "It looks as if Zoe was trying to Remote Influence, which is part of phase four techniques. I think I touched on this yesterday at Café Diem. It was theorized that if a person was able to go to target on call, why not actually go *into* target? Why not study another person from the inside? Experiments were conducted in secret to perfect the art of Remote Influencing. Trying to remotely brainwash someone into doing something they would never do."

"You're not serious." Carter grinned again. The grin dropped. "You are?"

"Yes—it was rumored the government actually influenced a number of foreigners to do things, commit unspeakable crimes, that then made it easier for our soldiers to step in and correct the situation." She looked at Carter. "Set up a scenario that put our government in power from the actions of a few others."

"Exactly," Henry said.

"But that whole project was dismissed. The funding was cut and it was turned over to us."

"It was turned over to Dr. Schmetzer, but if you remember from Eureka history, the project was still being looked into as part of Section Five before it was closed. They still ran experiments here in Remote Influencing." Henry sighed. "I finally got access to Schmetzer's notes. Their findings trained six individuals in the late eighties before it was shut down."

"Why was it shut down?" Carter asked.

"Because apparently the participants all turned on each other." He took the piece of paper and looked at the drawing. "They became paranoid and power hungry."

"Where did you get this information, Henry?" Allison looked at Carter and then back to Henry.

Henry turned and retrieved his tablet from the other workstation and handed it to Allison. "It's all there. I've been going over a lot of Schmetzer's notes, preparing the class I wanted to teach. But when I got to the part about RI—I almost couldn't believe what I read. None of the subjects were prone to irrational behavior. Each had been carefully screened for possible psychosis that could compromise the testing. And then, suddenly—" He shook his head.

"What?" Allison said.

"One broke into the house of the other and they stabbed each other. The other four panicked, and then one by one they each died within a week. One drove his car into a brick wall accelerating to sixty-five miles an hour. Another walked out in the middle of rush-hour traffic in front of a bus. Of the final two, one of them stalked the other and shot her in her home in Connecticut."

"And the last subject?"

"He mysteriously died about five years ago. Eyewitnesses say he walked off of a forty-story building. Never looked back."

Carter frowned as he looked at Allison, who was looking over the tablet and then to Henry. "You're not gonna . . . ah . . . teach this to high school students . . . are you?"

"Oh, hell no, Carter. Combine that information with what's happened with Caruso's memories, and I'm convinced the mind is a place we really have no business in."

"Especially since it looks as if Carter's daughter had a knack for this." She looked at Henry. "So you think Zoe tapped into those memories sitting in Lucas's extra room?"

"Maybe. I can't say. I would like to talk to Zoe about these, see what method she used. Either way, we can't let Mansfield or Caruso find this or they'll somehow think that Zoe has the missing memories."

Allison nodded. "Especially not after Carter heard her threaten to use the Brain Box as an interrogation device."

"What?" Henry said with a surprised expression.

"Dr. Blake?" Fargo's voice preceded him into the infirmary, where he nearly barreled the three of them over. He was out of breath and wheezing as he tried to tell them something.

Allison laid the tablet on a table and moved around Lucas on the bed. "Fargo—what is it? Please don't tell me Mansfield's causing another problem."

Fargo shook his head quickly. "No . . . not . . . Mans . . . field. . . ."

Carter sighed. "Fargo . . . just spit it out. You did not run that far to get to us. The elevator's just around the corner."

"I wasn't . . . in the elevator," he said.

"Fargo, I think it's time we put you on a strict exercise and eating program," Henry said. "It's obvious your health is suffering."

The young man immediately straightened and looked at Allison. "I was in the storage room like you told me, and was inventorying."

"You were taking inventory," Allison corrected.

"Right."

"The point?" Carter prompted.

"Ah. One of the briefcases is missing."

"Briefcases?" She frowned.

"Of storycatchers."

That set off a red flag. She reached out and took his shoulders. "Fargo, are you sure?"

"Yes, I did a physical count earlier today, and when I went back, there was one missing."

"Oh jeez." Carter sighed, immediately thinking back to the last memory issue they had when Tess introduced the damn things. "How many are in a briefcase?"

"About two dozen, and then each contains a halo."

"So you can view the memory." She turned to Carter. "Who would want the storycatchers? All they do is collect memories. And they only hold one at a time."

"Who knew where they were?"

"Anybody that worked on the time capsule. Oh, and Graves did. I showed them to him earlier," Fargo said.

All eyes fell back to him again. He took a step back. "What?"

"You showed him where the storycatchers were?" Allison said.

"Well, yeah. He didn't take them or anything. He hasn't even been back in the building since he left."

"How do you know that?"

"Because Director Caruso told me. She was standing outside the door of the lab and asked me about Dr. Graves."

Carter leaned forward and pointed to the door. "You saw Director Caruso outside this lab? When?"

"Just now. Before I came in."

Henry, Carter, and Allison all stared at him. "What was she doing?" Carter said.

"Just standing there with her eyes closed. She asked me about Graves, and then where the bathroom was."

"Just great," Allison said. "If she overheard us, she'll

report everything back to Mansfield, and she'll twist it to support DoD supervision."

"Well, if Graves hasn't been back in the building, and Caruso doesn't know where they are, then who took the catchers?" He looked at Allison.

She shrugged. "Or why? What's the point?"

Carter snapped his fingers. "Jo and Vincent said that Zoe was showing Graves her drawings. What if he came to the conclusion that Zoe has Caruso's memories and not Lucas?"

"And he's going to use the storycatchers to see them?" Allison frowned. "He'd have to persuade Zoe to take them—she's the only one who's been in the building since Graves left."

"Graves wants to see those memories," Carter said. "And I'd bet anything that he knows something—something he suspects is there and doesn't want anyone else to see. Especially Mansfield."

"Or his sister?"

"Could be. Either way, getting Zoe to help wouldn't take much. She was trying to explain why she'd been seeing that woman's face, and if Graves could give her an explanation other than Lucas was seeing someone at school—"

"Then she'd be more than willing to help Graves."

"Yeah, but"—Carter winced—"won't those catchers still delete memories?"

"No." Henry shook his head. "Fargo solved that problem."

Fargo smiled.

"Yeah, but Fargo caused the problem to begin with."

Fargo frowned.

"Well, I'm more worried about what the living Caruso is doing. I'm heading down to the lab to check on Zane to see what's going on. Fargo, come with me. Carter, where would Zoe go with Graves to look at those memories?"

"Uh, I don't know. I can check the house."

"Do that. Henry—"

"I'll see what I can do about removing the memories. And I'll call if there's any change."

Carter took a lingering look at Lucas before heading out the door to the elevator.

CHAPTeR 25

The exterior lights came on as Zoe pulled up at Lucas's house. She and Graves got out of the car. He carried the briefcases in his hands as she used her key and then entered a pass code into the keypad by the front door.

"Lights," she said, and the foyer lights as well as the kitchen and living room lights came on.

It was a modest house, with modern fixtures set in here and there. Though its technology was not nearly as advanced as S.A.R.A.H., Lucas's father had installed many modern conveniences, masking them behind more classic features.

A bird squawked from a cage in the corner of the kitchen. Zoe approached the African gray and eyed the food and water bowls. It also looked as if Lucas hadn't bothered to change the paper at the bottom of the birdcage in days.

While Graves set the briefcase on the kitchen table, Zoe

busied herself refilling the water and food and decided against cleaning the birdcage floor. That was Lucas's job. He could do it once he was out of GD.

After checking all the locks, Zoe joined Graves at the table. Aircom had set about dissecting the halo and five of the storycatchers. Apparently he'd had his own tool set with him as well, as she looked at it on the table next to him. Glasses pushed up on his forehead, he narrowed his eyes as he pushed at something with a very tiny Phillips head.

Zoe watched him intently. "You and your sister ever get along?"

"When we were kids, sure. She's about five years older than me," he said as he chewed on his lower lip. "John and I met at a seminar at Johns Hopkins—and somehow we clicked as friends. Two geeks lucky enough to be noticed by the government."

"Just on different teams? Him at the DoE and you the DoD?"

"Well." He smiled. "Kinda. John and I stayed friends through most of it, always trying to show ways the two agencies could work together."

Zoe nodded. "So how did your sister get into this?"

Graves reassembled one of the catchers and moved to the next. "Katie and John met the first time I brought him home to Connecticut for Christmas. It was puppy love at first sight. What I'd planned on doing with my best friend was pretty much put on hold as those two made doe eyes at one another."

"You're smiling."

"Oh, it was a good thing once. We were a government family; his was a government family. It was the perfect match. We'd lost our mother at a young age. He'd lost his mother." He gave a small laugh. "I don't remember really when it changed. I just know the last two times I'd seen him—John was distracted. He was upset about something but he wouldn't tell me what, said he suspected something, but he didn't have proof."

"Never said what about?"

"No." Graves finished another catcher and set it down before picking up a third. "That was about the time he got the assignment over at PNNL to investigate something important there. Katie called me several times, demanding I tell her what John was doing, but A"—he glanced at Zoe—"I didn't know what he was doing because there were just certain things you didn't talk about, and he and I respected our NDAs."

"NDAs?"

"Nondisclosure agreements. And B, I wasn't too happy about the way she spoke to me. Katie had . . . sort of changed over the years." He picked up a fourth catcher and opened it, tinkering inside. "Become distant. More secretive. You know, she was even assigned here in Eureka for a time, but I wasn't sure what for. Neither was John." He closed that one up and looked at each of them. "That should be enough for what we need to do."

"What exactly are you doing to them?"

"Changing the frequencies." He held up one of the catchers. "Reprogramming them to pick up John's memories and not yours."

"Yeah, 'cause I'm not sure I want any more of my memories in that whole storynest thing."

"So let's give it a try." Graves handed her the catcher and then pulled out a sheet, the one of the woman with her hands on her face. "Let's start with this one."

"Okay." Zoe stared at the catcher as she'd done months before. "And I just tell you what I saw?"

"Yes."

She did as he asked, recounting every small detail she could remember. When they finished, she started looking around the papers of her drawings. "One's missing."

"Which one?"

"Well, two, actually. The first and the last one, the one I did in the infirmary. I thought I'd gotten that one back. On the first one I wrote *I love you* on the bottom of it."

"Fargo had that one—that's where I first saw what you'd done. And now I have it." He pulled the folded sheet of paper from his back pocket and set it on the table.

"Fargo had it?" She sighed, rolling her eyes. "Knowing him, he probably wanted to use it as proof that I failed one of the Remote Views."

Graves grabbed for the halo and slipped it over his temple. Looking at Zoe, he picked up the first globe they'd used and activated it. "Here we go."

It appeared that Zane and Kathryn Caruso were at a stalemate when Allison and Fargo walked into the lab. Zane was seated behind the storynest terminal, his arms crossed over his chest. Dr. Caruso stood facing him on the other side of the terminal. Two armed guards stood to either side of Director Caruso, though neither had his weapon drawn.

"What's going on in here?"

Zane spoke a beat before Director Caruso did. "She took the Brain Box."

"I needed an accurate copy of everything on the Global Dynamics system so I can do a thorough check of all the files, so I merely removed the hard drive. But I left the box here."

Allison put her hands up as she stood between the two, positioned to Zane's right. "Stop. Both of you. Zane."

"This woman came in here and had me forcibly removed to the rotunda. When I came back, the Brain Box was gone. Then she comes in here again and demands she get a copy of the storynest, and if I remember Dr. Fontana's orders, the storynest contains private memories from the residents of Eureka that are not the purview of any secret government agency."

"We are not a secret government agency," Director Caruso insisted. "This . . . boy . . . is in my way and I have asked him to move and unlock this system several times. If he does not, I will have these men arrest him."

"No, you will not," Allison said firmly, and noticed Fargo giving a little arm pump from the side of her peripheral vision. "I am the director of this facility, and all actions you take, regardless of who ordered them, go through me. Do I make myself clear?"

"You are no longer in charge, Dr. Blake. General Mansfield has—"

"Acted out of line, Director Caruso." She pointed to the storynest. "That machine is not a part of the GD network. Therefore it is not a part of what you do and do not have access to. The memories stored in that matrix are not for anyone but the people in Eureka, and I will not allow you to make copies so you can freely take a look at every individual in this town."

"I am shocked that you would think I am capable of such a thing."

"Director Caruso, you just lost a husband—and from what I can see with my own eyes, your brother has shown more of an emotional reaction at John's death than you. But you do seem hell-bent on getting at whatever his decision was on where the funding for the singularity would go. I propose that since the investigator was your husband, I stand by my earlier assessment that your presence here constitutes a conflict of interest, and I intend to make a few phone calls over your head to have you removed."

Caruso's eyes narrowed as she watched Allison. Allison was shaking from her head to her feet. Yeah, she was upset, but she was also pissed off. How dared this woman come in here and start demanding to pick apart GD's accomplishments? As far as she was concerned, Mansfield was only using Caruso as a tool to gain access to what he couldn't comprehend.

And that was the end of that.

"You've overstepped your bounds, Director Blake. I will be back with the general, and I will have access to the storynest."

"Zane?" She didn't look at Zane when she spoke.

"Secured, Dr. Blake." He smiled. "I'm afraid only I have the password and security codes. Oh"—he nodded to empty table where the Brain Box had been—"you already took that, so I'd say you're done in here."

But Caruso didn't leave. "Where is my brother?"

"I don't know where Dr. Graves is, Mrs. Caruso."

"*Director* Caruso."

"*Director* Caruso." Allison crossed her arms over her chest to match Zane's stance. "Now, if you would please leave my lab, I would greatly appreciate it. And you can take Mansfield's puppies with you."

Caruso turned and stalked out of the lab, the uniformed men glancing at each other before following her.

Once the door closed, Allison turned and grabbed hold of the storynest console. Her heart thundered in her chest and she was more than a tad close to fainting. Just . . . not in front of Zane.

"Dr. Blake, are you all right?" He was beside her, his hand on her arm.

She patted his shoulder. "Yeah . . . I'm fine."

"You are more than fine. You were great, Dr. Blake!" He almost cheered her.

"I don't think I've ever seen you that mad, Director," Fargo said from his place in the corner.

"Well, Fargo, I've been madder. But what irritates me more is that Mansfield's allowed someone that close to the subject in this facility. And she thinks she has the right of access to anything without going through me first. And I don't like it when they take property that doesn't belong to them—that Brain Box is part of Dr. Graves's research and we need it back."

"She kind of reminds me of Eva Thorne," Zane said as he sat back down.

"Yeah, well." Allison nodded. "There's a dark secret behind Director Caruso's mask, same as Thorne's. Only whereas Eva's was a tragic secret, I somehow suspect Kathryn Caruso *is* the tragic secret."

"Oh, she's tragic all right," Zane said. "Too bad she's hot, too. Hot and damn scary."

She smirked at Zane. "Henry copy you on what he found wrong with Lucas?"

"Yeah, he did." Zane shook his head. "I was trying to go over all the possibilities when *Director* Caruso walked in."

"Henry said it wasn't possible to retrieve those memories the same way they got there."

"No, and using Graves's harvester probably won't work, either. I mean we could use it to harvest them, but it's not built to erase them. They'd still be there."

"Well, the storycatchers erased everyone's memories. Why not use them?"

"Thought about that, too." Zane glanced at Fargo. "Everyone affected had an open neural connection to the storycatchers. We don't have that kind of conduit. And the memories erased by the storycatchers were random. Don't want to take a chance that you'll delete not only Caruso's memories but Lucas's, too."

"Well." She sighed. "Keep thinking. Henry's going to consider options as well. But if you can wire the harvester to extract only Caruso's memories from Lucas, do that."

"Sure. But it'd be a lot easier if I had Graves here."

"We're trying to find him. But don't stay up too late—

you need sleep. Otherwise you won't be able to think. Or at least get something to eat."

"I might go grab a bite over at the café," Zane agreed. "See if I can find Jo."

"Jo's helping Carter look for Graves right now," Allison said on her way out. "And make sure this lab is locked down. I don't want her trying to get back in."

Fargo followed her out. "What about me?"

She paused just outside the door and pursed her lips. "Fargo . . . go check on Director Caruso. And let me know exactly what it is she does."

"You want me to spy? I can get into trouble for spying."

"I want you to watch." She arched an eyebrow.

"Yes, ma'am."

Allison grinned as she moved to the elevator. The door opened and she stepped in, calling out to Fargo, "Let me know if that woman so much as blinks."

CHAPTER 26

"B.A.R.A.H.!" Carter called out as he half ran down the steps of his home.

"Good evening, Sheriff. Would you like dinner tonight?"

"No, no." He paused, trying to remember what he'd done with the bags Vincent had given him. Had he left them at GD? "Uh . . . Sarah, has Zoe been home since this morning?"

"No, Sheriff, she hasn't. Should I check her present location?"

Carter paused. "Ah . . . can you do that? I mean, I think her cell phone is dead."

"Not a problem, Sheriff. Zoe is at Lucas's house."

"She by herself?" He moved into the kitchen and poured himself a glass of orange juice.

"No, Sheriff. She is with Aircom Graves."

He swallowed the juice in one gulp and then pressed his fingers to the bridge of his nose. "Ah . . . brain freeze."

"Would you like for me to ring the residence?"

"No, no. I'll get out there."

His cell phone buzzed in his back pocket. He didn't glance at the face, just opened it. "Carter."

"Hey, you need to stop telling me to look up all these government spooks," Jo said over the tiny speaker.

"Jo, you found out about Katie Caruso?"

"Oh, yeah, I did. Broad's as creepy as they come."

Looking around the kitchen, he grabbed an apple from the pantry as S.A.R.A.H. opened the door. "Tell me."

"Ever heard of DARPA?"

He stopped in midbite of the apple, his teeth buried inside the juicy middle. He wrenched his teeth out. "Yeah. I have. That's the Defense Advanced Research Projects Agency. Don't tell me she works for them?"

"Yep," Jo said, accenting the *P* at the end of the word. "Her formal title is Dr. Kathryn Caruso, Director, TCTO, DARPA."

"TCTO?"

"Transformational Convergence Technology Office. Wow. Who writes this stuff?"

"So she's a director like she said. But why would DARPA send out any kind of liaison to work with Mansfield? Especially on this?" Though he'd already figured that out in the back of his head. This wasn't about the budget placement anymore, but about the singularity discovery.

"Don't know. Both of her parents are deceased; her surviving brother is Aircom Graves, whom we've already met. Ph.D. in bioengineering, similar to her brother. Recruited out of college, same as him. Hired over into the DoD for a while. After that, she's been with DARPA ever since."

"Nothing shady or completely off the charts?"

"No . . . well . . . there's this tiny little mention of being involved in a project called Helix about fifteen years ago. She was twenty. Worked with a Dr. Romey Schmetzer."

"Schmetzer." Carter frowned. "Henry mentioned a Dr. Schmetzer. Does it say what the project was?"

"You're gonna love this, Carter. She worked on the Helix project, Remote Viewing."

He sighed. "Oh, for the love of . . ."

"Yeah, I know. I was curious about that myself, so I pulled records on the parents."

"And?"

"Nothing. I can't find anything at all on them. I can see were they were born. Lived in Connecticut. Mother was killed in a home invasion robbery back in 1989. Father died from heart failure in 2001. But there's just nothing there under employment history."

"It means they were government employees," Carter said as he ate half the apple, chewing around his answers to Jo. "Which makes sense with both kids in government as well. You have legacy families. Well, not much there. S.A.R.A.H. says Zoe and Graves are over at Lucas's. I'm heading there now. Get there soon as you can."

"Can I bring a gun?"

Graves was visibly shaking once he finished viewing all five of the storycatchers with the halo. Zoe watched him turn pale and then remove the device and place it on the table. He took his glasses off and set them next to the halo and just stared at the table.

"Air?"

He shook his head slowly. "I—" Graves rubbed at his face before looking at Zoe. "I can't put the pieces together— not like I thought I could. It's all so disjointed—"

"Well, something's got you upset. I mean, look at you." She reached out and touched his arm. "You going to be okay?"

Nodding, Aircom put both of his hands on the table,

palms down. "I always suspected my sister was capable of things. What I mean is—she was always strong and took charge. When our mother was killed, she took charge of the house and practically raised me. Took care of Dad. She didn't fall apart, just always seemed to be waiting. Asking questions, talking to Dad about his work."

Zoe looked at the halo. "Air, what did you see that I didn't?"

"I think you did see it, Zoe, but it wouldn't have made any sense to you. It was the argument, between her and John. He mentions an acquaintance of our parents who jumped off a building when I was about twenty-five. I remember John talking to me about it—wanting to know how well Katie knew him. I told him there wasn't much there. The guy just committed suicide."

"But—" She watched him as she picked up the halo. "John didn't think so?"

Graves focused on her. "Tell me what you see."

Nodding, she placed the halo over her head, setting it along her temple. Within seconds her mind's eye displayed scenes as if from a movie, only she was looking at them through someone else's eyes. The woman was there like before; her expression showed a mixture of anger and sadness. It looked as if they were outside somewhere. There were trees behind them, their trunks covered in thick green moss.

The grass around them was green, the sun high.

The woman was half yelling, half talking to Zoe.

". . . never let me explain anything. You always buried your head when it came to me, came to what I went through. He was a monster—he killed our mother. He deserved what he got."

"What is there to explain, Katie?" came a man's voice from somewhere around Zoe's ears, and she assumed this was John Caruso. "You just admitted to me you killed a man. You fucking pushed him off that roof."

Her expression hardened as she stood her ground. "I never touched him."

"No? I guess not. You and that stupid-ass Jedi mind shit you were into before we met. You had Weaver so paranoid he actually believed you were in his dreams, Katie. He came to me and declared he had proof you were responsible for Fern's death—and then he threatened me, that if I didn't swing things his way in this investigation, he'd expose you." Zoe could see hands to her sides gesturing to Katie. "What am I supposed to do with this, huh? I come to you thinking Weaver's just some nut off his rocker—and you tell me he's right?"

"John, there is no way he can prove any of it. All you have to do is put him in your report. Just discredit him."

"You want me to lie?"

"You won't be lying. Weaver *is* a nutcase. He's narcissistic as well as paranoid. And if you prove that enough of the researchers representing the DoE were the ones using their clout and posturing to delay any reliable research on the singularity, Washington will grant the project to us."

There was a long pause, and Zoe wondered what John had been thinking at that moment. Here was his wife, who'd just admitted to killing a man, telling him to lie on her behalf. Finally he spoke. "I don't know you anymore, Katie. Air was right—you've lost your soul to your job. You want me to lie, to falsify my report, to bend things your way—for what? So you can get your hands on the singularity to make your Juicebox? No, Katie. I'm not going to do it."

The scene changed at a dizzying speed as John turned and began walking away from Katie. Zoe saw a building with glass doors. But she could hear Katie behind her.

"John . . . you don't know what you're doing," came the voice from the back of Zoe's head. "You're making a big mistake. You won't live to regret it."

When the image faded, Zoe removed the halo and stared at Graves. He was looking at his hands, still splayed palm down on the table. "But . . . I didn't see all of that the first time. I only saw pieces—"

"That's because you were only viewing pieces. But the memory was there in your head—you just couldn't access it."

"Air, did she threaten her own husband?"

"I think she killed him, Zoe. That's the memory I saw when I went back into the lab when Lucas was taken to the infirmary. I didn't know what to do or who to go to. I needed to see more—I needed to translate all of it. But the memories were gone from the storynest. I panicked, thinking the electric shock had dumped them.

"So I falsified the information on the Brain Box to buy time—to figure out what to do and find the data."

"And now you think those memories are in Lucas's cortex?"

"Yes. I think Katie's here because she's afraid of what we'll find in John's memories. We may even find out she was responsible for his death."

"Air, he was hit by a car, remember. That's what you told me."

"Was he?" Graves reached into his tool kit and removed a flat, silver box, the size and look of a cigarette case. He took a small cable from inside a pocket and hooked it into the side of the halo, then held it up for her. "I made a copy of what Lucas translated—just in case something like this happened. Zoe, he turned *into* an oncoming truck. The others haven't seen this. Look for yourself—was this an accident?"

Zoe took the halo again and set it back on her head. She

closed her eyes and again her mind's eye shifted to midafternoon. It was sunny and she was driving. The windshield wipers were busy sloughing water from the glass, and the sky overhead was threatening. She could hear John's voice and see a man's hand on the wheel in front of her. "Katie—we've already been through this. I'm heading back to Washington to put the report together and I'm not going to lie. Once I've delivered my findings, I'm going to launch an investigation into Dr. Fern's death, and into Tom Weaver's as well. I don't know how you did it, but I'll find out. You practically confessed to having a hand in Fern's so-called suicide. Look, I'm hanging up. Those papers are real. . . . I want a divorce. And whatever you do, do not drag Air into this."

She saw a cell phone in his right hand. He closed it and tossed it on the empty passenger seat. Zoe saw his right hand go to the radio and start punching buttons, but she could see through the windshield as well.

Zoe saw the truck coming in the other lane. There weren't any other cars on the road. The rain slackened. Visibility was clearing.

And then suddenly he gripped the wheel with both hands and turned *into* the truck moments before they passed each other on the narrow, winding road.

She yanked the halo off and tossed it on the table. "Okay—I'm going to throw up."

Graves jumped up ready to help, but she shook her head as she braced herself against the table.

Graves said quietly, "It looked like he committed suicide."

"Yeah, which doesn't make a damn bit of sense since he just told her he wanted a divorce." She took in a deep breath and ran both of her hands through her hair, pulling it back. "It sounded like she was trying to coerce him into doing things her way. And it makes sense now why she's here. She doesn't want any of this seen."

Graves shook his head. "If this is just what you picked up from Viewing Lucas's surface thoughts, then I can only imagine what else is there. Katie's afraid all of this will expose her. I know my sister, Zoe. She'll do whatever it takes to protect whatever it is she values most."

"I hope that's you?"

"I doubt it. She and I haven't exactly gotten along in the past ten years. But this explains a lot of John's odd mood swings in the past three months." He smiled softly. "You know, he called me right before he left. Wanted to get a beer at Chadwick's. Said he had a lot to tell me. Now I'm guessing it was about this."

"Aircom, we need get this stuff back to GD. Get past those guards somehow and show my dad." She stood and went for her purse to get her phone. Unfortunately, it was dead. "Someone at GD needs to invent a twenty-year battery for cell phones."

"What, and put the whole cell phone battery business under?" Graves packed up the globes and halo and retrieved his glasses. "Maybe we can call your dad from here? Tell him to meet us so he can see this? Maybe he can get me past the guards at GD—even call Dr. Blake."

"Yeah, that's what I was thinking." She frowned as she looked out the window past Graves.

He narrowed his eyes at her face and turned as two headlights moved closer to the house. "Are we expecting company?"

Zoe immediately jumped up and looked outside just as the floodlights illuminated the side and front. "I don't recognize that car, Air."

"Shit." He started looking around the kitchen. "Where is the light switch?"

"Lights off," Zoe said aloud, and the lights abruptly went out. "I don't know what good that's going to do us because whoever is in that truck knows we're in here now."

"Is there a back way out?"

"Back way to where? We're technically past the city limits. We need my car to get back to GD."

"Or we can sneak out, wait till they leave, and then come back for the car."

The headlights pulled into the driveway behind Zoe's car. She reached out and grabbed Graves's arm and pulled him to the back of the kitchen. There was a utility room that led to the garage, which doubled as Lucas's personal lab. If they could get through the land mine of Lucas's stuff out there without making noise, there was a door on the opposite side they could exit through. Double back and then get the car.

But as she pulled Graves to the side door, a voice shouted from outside. "Air? I know you're in there. We need to talk."

She turned a concerned face to him as she felt his shoulders sag. "Is that who I think it is?"

"It's Katie."

"How the hell did she find us?"

Graves sighed. "She Viewed us, Zoe. She freakin' Viewed us."

CHAPTᵉR 27

Café Diem had a few regular evening customers when Zane stepped inside. Vincent waved from behind the counter, and he spotted Jo taking a to-go cup from Vincent's hand. She was nodding and saying, "Uh-huh," as he gave her a quick kiss on the cheek and stood beside her.

Vincent turned to Zane. "The usual?"

"Yeah, only double it. I'm starved." He looked around. "You seen Carter?"

"Not yet. But since I've just about seen everybody else in here tonight, I'm still waiting."

Nodding, Zane doctored his coffee as he waited for Jo to get off the phone.

"Right, right. And you're sure about this . . . ? Okay. . . . No, I owe you on this one. Take care. Bye." She disconnected and turned to look at Zane. "This day just keeps getting better and better."

"What?" he said as Vincent set a cup of coffee in front of him.

"This Caruso woman? You met her yet?"

He nearly snorted into the hot beverage and nodded, setting it down. "Oh, yeah. Real piece of work. To quote an old movie, you could freeze ice on her ass. She wanted access to the storynest. I said no. I think she threatened me."

"What'd she say?"

"Oh"—he shrugged—"she said she'd get her way, whether I cooperated voluntarily or not. But that was before Dr. Blake pretty much put her in her place." He shrugged. "I mean, she told Carter she was going to use the Brain Box on her own brother."

"Well, I just got off the phone with the deputy sheriff over in Richland."

"Washington?"

"Mm-hmm . . . and apparently there was a pretty big commotion surrounding our John Caruso."

"Well . . . yeah. According to what I've learned, Agent Caruso was there to investigate inconsistencies in PNNL's research findings on the singularity discovery."

Jo frowned. "Yeah, all that. But Caruso had a bunch of the scientists there angry with him—especially Kathryn Caruso. She was there lobbying heavily for the project to be funded over to the DoD. Several of the workers there were eyewitnesses to the two of them arguing. Which of course caused even more of a commotion when it was revealed they were married."

"So she's officially with the DoD?"

"She's officially employed by DARPA, which is a subagency of the Department of Defense."

Zane's jaw dropped. "What the hell? She's DARPA?"

Jo's smile was priceless. "Thought that'd get your attention. I told Carter about it, too, but what I haven't told him, which Wellman just gave me, was that he heard from two of the scientists that Kathryn Caruso was there to see how the singularity could be used in a project she was calling Juicebox."

"Juicebox—wait—I've heard that somewhere."

"Yeah, it's a project—and it had John Caruso pissed off. And one of them swears he heard John telling Kathryn he'd rather see the whole project shelved before it went to the DoD."

"But no one ever found out what this Juicebox was, except for Caruso?"

"Uh-huh. So I'm thinking John Caruso was killed for what he knew as well as for holding the financial future of that project."

Zane sipped his coffee. "Great theory, Jo, but killed by whom? The guy got into a fight with an eighteen-wheeler."

"Yeah, in light rain, no traffic on a four-lane highway. What are the odds of that happening?"

"What are the odds of it *not*? Look, Jo"—he shrugged—"I think being her husband's killer is something anyone that meets this woman would like to see her go to jail for—she doesn't exactly win friends. But that'll be hard to prove unless you can find evidence of tampering with the car. And unless you can prove motive and come up with substantial evidence, then the Richland police aren't going to spend the man-hours or forensics to go over the mangled wreck to find that."

"I know that." Jo stood and smiled at him. "But she doesn't."

"Jo—what are you thinking?" He narrowed his eyes at her.

Jo's phone rang. She retrieved it, checked the caller ID, and rolled her eyes.

Who? Zane mouthed.

But Jo only answered it. "What, Fargo?"

Zane watched as Jo's expression turned from irritation to concern. "What . . . ? When?"

His own phone buzzed. It was Henry. "Yeah."

"I need you to see about reconfiguring the Brain Box to harvest the overloaded memories in Lucas's cortex. His condition is worsening, so I told Allison we'd at least go with getting all the memories out, Lucas's and Caruso's, before we decide on how to delete them."

Zane stood. "I'll get right on it. I've already been working theories in my head—but I'm going to need Director Caruso to bring the box back in."

"I'll call Allison and see if she can put some pressure on Caruso. I'll meet you in the lab—where are you?"

"Café Diem."

"Can you pick me up something? Tell Vincent—"

But Vincent was already setting two to-go boxes in front of him. "Got it, Henry. I'll be right there." Zane hung up and gave him a broad grin. "Vincent, you're amazing."

Vincent smiled. "I know. And I'm also making up for the orders I got wrong this morning. I'm thinking if I make up enough, I can just erase it from the akashic records."

When Zane frowned, Vincent shook his head. "Never mind."

Jo hung up and turned to Zane. "Fargo just tracked Caruso pulling up at Lucas's house. He can't get hold of Carter. I was on my way there." She held up her coffee. "Just needed a recharge and a place to call Wellman."

"The sheriff's probably ignoring Fargo. You heading out there? Without backup?"

"Oh, I'm the backup. You heading back to GD?"

"Yeah, Henry needs me in the lab. Said he's got some ideas he wants to run by me." He grabbed the to-go boxes. "Be careful, Jo. That woman is dangerous."

She slipped her weapon from the holster and held it up. "So am I."

Graves put a finger to his lips as he and Zoe moved into the garage. He'd pulled a small penlight from his back pocket as they tried to maneuver through the strewn junk.

Zoe made a mental note to scold Lucas about this mess—once he was better—and vowed to drag him out here and clean this place up before his parents got back.

"Aircom—I know you're in there. We seriously need to talk. You have something I need."

Biting her lower lip, Zoe stuck close to Graves as they made their way slowly around the piles. Twice she'd nearly knocked something over. If she did, the sound would instantly give them away. Caruso'd been outside circling for a good ten minutes now. Luckily the house security wouldn't allow her access—but that wouldn't work in the garage.

They were two feet from the door when Graves's head connected with something hanging from above. He reached up to disentangle himself from it, but his elbow connected with a shelf.

"Watch out!" Zoe heard herself hiss just as the metal shelf came down on top of them.

The crashing noise seemed to go on forever as Zoe tried to back away. The top of the shelf caught her back and sent her forward on top of the couch she and Lucas had made out on so many times before leaving for school.

She heard the garage door open as she tried to pull herself up. A sharp burning pain made her hiss—if felt like the edge of the shelf had scraped along her back through her shirt. When the lights came on, she saw Aircom on the ground buried beneath the shelf and everything that had been on it, including a lot of heavy metal pieces.

He wasn't moving.

"I knew you were here," came the woman's voice. The voice from the memories.

Kathryn Caruso stepped inside from a side door. She held a gun in her right hand, pointed down. She looked at the mess and spotted her brother underneath.

In what could have been misconstrued as a filial moment, she picked her way through the debris and reached in to touch his neck. She almost visibly sighed. "He's alive."

"You don't want him dead?" Zoe heard herself say.

Kathryn focused her attention on Zoe. "You're the sheriff's daughter. The one that was Remote Viewing, peeking into things you have no business in." She stood and pointed to the pile. "Amateurs. Dig him out. I need him awake when we leave."

Zoe didn't question it. She had a healthy appreciation for guns. Wincing from the pain along her back, she started pulling stuff off Graves. He lay on his side, blood running from a head wound on his left temple. "He needs medical attention."

"He's fine. And it won't matter. Finish up before your father gets here."

"Dad's coming?"

"Sheriff Carter is a lot smarter than people here realize," she said with a bored expression. "I did my homework on him. U.S. Marshal. Damn good at what he did. He'll figure it all out, but by then it'll be too late."

"You killed your husband, didn't you?"

"You watched the memories." Kathryn sighed. "You shouldn't have done that. I thought I'd only have to deal with my little brother. He was never supposed to get involved in this. If Mansfield hadn't brought him in, he'd still be safe in his little lab in Washington." She moved the gun. "Hurry."

As Zoe was moving the debris, she realized the briefcase Graves had been holding had slid, or he'd pushed it, beneath another shelf. Only the edge was evident, and if she was careful to pile stuff on it . . . "What do you plan on doing?"

"I need to know where the rest of the memories are. I understand you had a few. And he brought the storycatchers with him to see." That was when she started looking around. "Where are they?"

"What storycatchers?"

Kathryn aimed the gun at Zoe's head, then moved it quickly and aimed it at Graves. "Don't play with me, Zoe. Where are the catchers you took from GD?"

"They're in the house. We saw you coming and came out here. We didn't have time to pack them up." She heard the waver in her voice and was sure Kathryn heard it as well. The subtle telltale hint she was lying.

"Then once you get him up, we can go back through the house on our way to my car and get them."

Zoe was nearly done with moving the stuff that had been on the shelf; now she needed to move the shelf off him. Having helped Lucas move things around in here before, she knew it was much heavier than it looked. With a scowl at Kathryn, she said, "I could use a little help."

"Oh . . . no." Kathryn shook her head, keeping the gun level. "You're a hefty, strong-looking girl. You can move it off him."

Hefty? Zoe frowned as she glanced down at herself. "I'm not hefty," she muttered as she put her shoulder into it, then pushed and heaved until it finally budged. Flipping the thing to the side made an even louder noise as more items fell from various shelves on the walls.

Graves was exposed now and she bent down over him, touched his face. "Aircom? Can you hear me?"

He stirred, blinking slowly. His glasses had been knocked off and were a few inches away, one of the lenses smashed. With a low sigh he turned and looked up at her. "I—I don't feel so good."

"You're going to feel even worse if you don't get up," Kathryn said.

Graves closed his eyes. "Now I really feel bad."

"You know too much, brother. It's all a matter of national security."

"The only thing I know is that you killed John because you didn't want him to turn in his report."

"I was nowhere near John when he hit that truck. Idiot was tired. I told him not to leave—to wait until he had a night's sleep. But he didn't listen to me. He never listened to me." She shook her head. "But that's not why you can't survive this, Air. It's because you know about the Juicebox."

Zoe frowned. That word had been used in the memories, but she hadn't known what it meant, and she was pretty sure that Graves didn't know, either. His sister was assuming a lot.

Graves pushed himself up, leaning heavily on the hip-high set of wooden shelves lining the back wall. Blood trailed down the left side of his face and over his forehead. It was still bleeding as he stood and he put his hand to it gently, staring at his fingers when they came away red.

"Head wounds always bleed the worst," Kathryn said. "Now, get yourself out of that mess. We need to grab the catchers and leave before the sheriff shows up."

Zoe caught Graves's questioning glance, as if to say, *Where are the catchers?* But she couldn't tell him outright, so she made a show of putting her shoulder under his right side and pulled his right arm around to her other shoulder. "I told her the catchers were still inside where we left them. She wants to get them on the way out."

"Where are we going?" Graves asked, leaning on Zoe. She was pretty sure he was making his injury seem a lot worse than it really was.

"To a place where no one will find the bodies. Cover story is that the two of you ran away together."

Zoe huffed. "No one's going to buy that. I love Lucas."

Graves chuckled softly. "Well, thanks."

"No offense, but I think you're a little too old for me,"

she said, trying to lighten her own mood. She was sure her dad would come through that door at any moment. Expected it. But when they'd reached the kitchen door and she was preceding Kathryn in, her expectations plummeted.

What she should have been expecting was Dr. Graves's resolve to live.

Once they were inside the washroom, Graves abruptly came to life, spun, and landed a well-aimed kick into his sister's midsection. She expelled air as she fell backward on the concrete steps as he bolted in, slammed the door, and turned the dead bolt.

"Go!" he yelled out and shoved at Zoe to head into the house.

They were halfway through the living room to the front door when the shots rang out behind them. Zoe glanced back to see the door burst in. Kathryn had apparently shot at the knob and then kicked it in. The whole scene would have been an "oh, cool!" moment if they hadn't been running for their lives from a crazy woman.

Graves took her hand and half pulled her to the front door, crouching. She crouched as well. But when they got to the door, it was locked. He looked at her. "Key?"

Her eyes widened. "It's in my purse—which is in the garage."

"Then I suppose this is the end of the road for both of you," Kathryn said as she came up behind them. Both stood, raising their hands as she leveled the gun. "And since I didn't see the catchers on the table, I'm assuming they're in the garage, where I can look for them once I dispose of the two of you."

CHAPTeR 28

Carter arrived at Lucas's house just before Jo did. He
spotted Zoe's car and an unfamiliar black SUV behind it in
the drive. He knew Lucas's parents weren't home, so who
else was in the house?

When Jo pulled up, her headlights off, his hackles rose.
Jo did that only if she didn't want someone to know she
was near. He got out of the car and pulled his gun, but kept
the safety on just as Jo joined him and motioned to stay on
the road side of the sheriff's car.

"Got a call from Fargo—he said Kathryn Caruso was
here."

"Fargo called you? Why didn't he call me?"

He could see Jo's smirk in the floodlights from the
house. "Oh please, Carter. Any opportunity to call me?
And besides—he said you had your phone off."

"I do?" He pulled it out of his pocket and checked
it. Dead. Slipping it back inside, he watched the house.

"Seems all quiet in there. Though I doubt she's in there having tea. And the fact that Zoe's in there, too—"

"Makes you a little too involved. Let me move in closer first and take a peek."

"Jo?"

"Yeah?"

"Don't shoot first, okay? Think of Zoe?"

She nodded, waved at him, and then crouch-ran to the house, keeping just outside the illumination line of the flood-lights. Carter watched with a pounding heart as she moved quickly to the front window and ducked under. He watched her strain her neck to look up and into the house.

Jo ducked back down and shook her head—

—just about the time shots rang out from the garage.

Carter ducked down on instinct, seeing Jo flatten herself out as well. He could hear commotion in the house, then loud voices. He half crouched, half crawled to the front of the sheriff's vehicle and watched Jo repeat her previous move.

This time she pointed to the front door.

Someone was at the front door—but who? Zoe and Graves or Kathryn Caruso?

Carter half crouched as he hurried to take a position behind Caruso's SUV. He leaned out to look at Jo and mouthed, *Who?*

Jo pointed at him, and then motioned her arms as if cradling a baby.

Zoe was at the door. He looked back to Jo and nodded, then pointed at her, pointed at his eyes, and then pointed at her again, asking her if she had a good view.

She gave him an okay.

Carter took in a deep breath and yelled out, "Zoe, are you okay in there?"

There was a pause before he heard her voice. "Yes, Dad. We're fine."

"Dr. Graves?"

Another pause. "Alive, Sheriff."

"Dr. Caruso—you do realize you're under arrest for kidnapping if you don't let those two walk out of there."

"I'm afraid this is bigger than both of us, Sheriff Carter," came Kathryn's voice. "They can't live after what they've seen."

"You kill them, you go to jail for the rest of your life, and then national security won't be something you'll have to worry about anymore." He motioned for Jo to go around the back. She nodded and disappeared.

"You killed your husband over the checkbook, Kathryn."

Another pause. "I'm sorry, Sheriff, but I was nowhere near my husband when he had the accident. That's not something I can be tried for."

"Well, maybe you weren't near him when he swerved into that truck." Carter crouched and moved up to a position behind Zoe's car. If he moved his head at the right angle, he could see just inside the window. Tom and Graves were standing just at the door as Jo said. "But if you've seen the few memories we've already viewed, then you know we've all heard your voice threatening John, telling him to swerve into that truck."

He waited for the pause, and then, "And?"

"And—there is always forensics. Yeah, see . . . I have a few friends over in Richland . . . so I called them and told them I thought that scientist's death was sabotage. Well, they went and pulled John's wreckage from the dump and found some interesting stuff."

"You're lying, Sheriff. They didn't find anything."

"Oh . . . well . . . see, they faxed that forensics report over to Dr. Blake at GD. And she's the one who showed it to me and sent me out here. We think that besides ordering your husband to kill himself in those memories, you also tampered with his brakes. And she's sure that's what Dr.

Graves discovered as well. Your brother already expected it. Only he didn't know how to prove you were guilty. So he was hoping there was something in John's memories that proved what you'd done."

"You're bluffing, Sheriff. Just buying time."

"Well—" Carter said as he continued watching Graves and Zoe. He leaned out just a bit to see if he could get a straight shot at Dr. Caruso. But he just wasn't close enough. "I checked some things out for that day—the roads weren't slick and the traffic was light, and even the rain was spotty. But it's a major truck route, and it has stretches of road where one side is solid rock and the other a drop-off. Now"—he crawled a bit farther and looked inside the window, unsure of where Jo was—"seems to me a scientist would know how to calculate miles by the amount of brake fluid there was in a car, and figure out when the brakes would fail. Me personally—no clue. So I asked my friend to check those brakes out."

"There weren't any fingerprints. . . . You're just trying to goad me."

"Haven't gotten the results back on the prints, Dr. Caruso. This isn't a forensics TV show. Doesn't happen that fast. But they were able to tell that the level of brake fluid in a rental car that was checked out and topped off was incredibly low for a three-week stint.

"In other words, someone had to have pulled a specific amount of fluid out of the reservoir, taking the chance that John wouldn't make it once those brakes failed." He leaned up against the house on the garage side of the window. "Tell me, Dr. Caruso. Is anything really worth the life of another human being—especially your husband's?"

"My, that's one hell of a story, Sheriff Carter. You should write for television."

"Well, it's easier to prove this than to believe you simply used your mind to make John kill himself. They call that Remote Influencing, don't they?"

"That's very true—no one's going to believe it, are they? And though your forensics story is very imaginative, it's complete bullshit. I do my job well, Sheriff Carter. I've been good at what I do. And I've never failed. Everything I've ever initiated—every project, every mission, every job—I have always succeeded. And I wasn't about to let John ruin that for me or for the defense of this country."

Carter heard it in the inflection of her voice. That instant of decision that shooters, kidnappers, assassins, all of them have when they make a swift decision. He'd been up against it before. And knowing that Jo would have caught it as well, he realized he had only seconds to react. "Zoe! Air! Duck!"

There were two shots, from two different guns. He heard Zoe scream, and his heart sank into his throat. He ran to the front door and kicked it open. Luckily, Zoe and Graves weren't directly behind it.

Graves was on top of Zoe, shielding her behind the coffee table. Caruso lay on her front, the gun still in her hand. Carter kicked it away and, with a glance at Zoe to make sure she was moving, reached down to check Caruso's pulse.

Strong and even.

"Oh, I didn't kill her," Jo said as she came from the kitchen to the living room. She held a really big gun. When did she get that out of her car? "Rubber bullets. Been wanting to try these out for a while."

Carter sighed and pulled his handcuffs out and cuffed Caruso's wrists behind her back. "Why did you fire two shots?"

"I didn't."

Carter looked around. "I heard two." Once done with Caruso, he moved around the coffee table to Zoe, who nearly leaped into his arms. They sat back on the couch together as her shoulders shook against him.

Graves grunted as he moved to stand up. Carter winced at the blood on the side of the man's face. "Sheriff, my sister fired the other shot." He nodded to Carter's right. He followed the gesture to see a bullet hole in the wall to the right of the window. Just about in the spot he'd been crouching.

She'd known exactly where he was. It was only Eureka's enforced building code that saved him from a bullet hole.

"Oh, God," Zoe said in his arms. "Of all the things I've experienced in Eureka, I'm thinking that was the worst."

"I'm so sorry, Zoe," Graves was saying as he plopped down on the couch beneath the window. "I knew she wasn't right in the head. I just didn't know how bad it was. I mean, she was going to kill us."

"Nah," Carter said, shaking his head. "She still needed the memories I'm assuming you copied from Zoe?"

"I think they're still in the briefcase," he said. "In the garage." He took in a deep breath. "Sheriff, did you really call your friend in Richland and have them pull John's wreckage?"

Carter pursed his lips. "Uh . . . about that. I made that up. Though I think I now have enough motive to have that done. But"—he watched Graves's expression—"I'm also thinking we wouldn't find any tampering at all by your sister, would we?"

Graves shook his head slowly. "No. She's very good at what she does, Sheriff. It's just that I've never been able to really pinpoint"—he sighed—"what that is."

Jo's phone rang, and she answered it. Looking at Carter, she said, "It's for you. It's Dr. Blake."

Carter didn't want to dislodge Zoe, who was fastened at his hip. Graves stood and passed the phone to Carter. "We got her."

"I heard. Look, let Jo handle that. I need you and Graves

back at GD as soon as possible. Lucas is dying. We've got to get those memories out of his head and figure out a way to delete them. And we need Caruso to tell us where she put that Brain Box."

Carter glanced at Graves and then down at his daughter. "Oh. Right. I'll find it." He hung up and tossed the phone back to Jo, who caught it in midair. He gave Zoe another squeeze and kissed the top of her head. "Would either of you have the Brain Box?"

Zoe winced. "Yeah. It's here."

"Good. We need to get back to GD."

She released him, her eyes wide. "Is it Lucas?"

"Yeah." Carter stood and helped Zoe to her feet. "Dr. Graves, go get the storycatchers."

"I know where they are." Zoe stood and picked her way past Dr. Caruso and out the door to the garage.

"You know you'll never be allowed to view those memories," Kathryn said from the floor.

Jo pursed her lips and stepped on the woman's back. When Caruso made a painful noise, Jo put her hand to her mouth and frowned. "Oh, I'm sorry. Was that you? Thought it was the rug."

Carter frowned at her and watched as Zoe returned with a briefcase in her hand. She set it on the coffee table and opened it, revealing a case full of tossed storycatchers and a halo as well as a flat metal device. "Okay, it's all there. You two ride with me. Jo, take Miss Thing here back to the office and lock her up. Oh, and I suggest leaving the cuffs on."

"With pleasure."

Carter hustled them all into the car and headed to GD.

After about ten minutes, Carter looked at Graves in the backseat. The young man looked worried. "Dr. Graves? You okay? I'll see if Henry can take a look at that cut once we get to GD."

Graves looked at his reflection in the mirror. "Oh . . . thanks, Sheriff. I was just thinking . . . this was too easy."

Zoe turned in her seat from the front and faced him. "You call that easy? Hey, look, you might deal with guns in your face in your everyday life. Not in mine."

"No . . . that's not what I meant." Graves looked directly at Carter via the rearview mirror. "Kathryn has never been a simple person—nothing's ever been that cut-and-dried with her. With all the planning she's done in her life, all of her achievement, the thought that she'd recklessly come after me—us—brandishing a gun and threatening our lives—"

Turn the wheel.

Carter was listening to Dr. Graves. Heard what he said—but there was another voice. A softer one inside the SUV. Like a song on the radio with the volume turned too low. He reached out and checked to see if the radio was on.

It wasn't. "Doesn't feel right, does it?" Carter said when Dr. Graves paused. He still heard the voice—and was almost sure it was Allison. "Hey, does anyone have a working phone? Is it on?"

Dr. Graves shook his head. "I left mine at GD."

"My battery's dead," Zoe said. "And I don't know what I did with my PDA."

"Oh." Carter nodded. "I have it. Yours and mine." He started shifting in his seat to reach his right hand into his back pocket to pull the PDAs out, his left on the steering wheel. He, too, had had that feeling. "Air, you suspect your sister did something?"

Turn the wheel.

"Yeah . . . I do."

Carter saw a bridge coming up and applied the brakes as he pulled the PDAs from his pocket. He tossed them into the passenger seat.

"What do you think she did?" Zoe asked.

Turn the wheel.

Dr. Graves sighed. "Zoe, I don't know. I know my sister is capable of a lot of things. Right now I just want to get back to GD and help Lucas."

The SUV's headlights narrowed the path for Carter as he moved the vehicle onto the bridge, a ravine looming below them. The water was still pretty high given the time of year, and he was sure it was ice-cold water.

"You think she'll still try to have you arrested?"

Turn the wheel.

Something formed in the rain in front of Jack, past the foggy windshield. Was that—

"I'm afraid she'll do something—Sheriff Carter?"

"Dad! Why are you—"

"Sheriff—look out—"

He turned the wheel.

CHAPTᴇR 29

The infirmary was filled with people, several of them doing their best to try to replicate the Brain Box harvesting technology. Allison stood to the side, out of everyone's way, as she watched Henry and Zane do what they could. Lucas was in worse shape now, Henry having explained that the memories were not only losing integrity, but spreading out from the cerebral cortex and into the occipital lobe.

"If we don't get those memories out of there, eventually it'll spread to his hippocampus, and if that's damaged—"

But Allison already knew that answer. "Lucas will lose the ability to form new memories. If he survives, it'll be like having Alzheimer's."

Henry had nodded. "We need that Brain Box here so we can at least harvest what's there."

"And then what? How do you delete the memories? You've already said you can't use the storycatchers or the storynest because with those you can't pick and choose the memories. They're randomly deleted."

"Allison." Henry put his hands on her shoulders. "We're doing the best we can with what we've got. We're hoping that with the Brain Box back here and Dr. Graves's expertise on this, we can figure something out. Zane's been working round the clock to figure this out, too."

She checked her watch again. "I know. I just can't understand what's taking Carter so long. He has Graves, Zoe, and the box. He should have been here over an hour ago."

Henry's response became little more than an "uh-oh" when Allison turned to see General Mansfield strolling purposefully into the infirmary. He looked as if he were about to explode. "Director—you care to tell me why one of my top people has been arrested and confined to the city jail?"

"General, would you care to tell me why one of your top people tried to kidnap and kill Dr. Graves and Zoe Carter?"

The expression on the general's face wasn't as readable as she'd hoped it would be. He did open his mouth to protest, closed it, and then said, "Dr. Caruso did say you would accuse her of that. But the report I was given was that Dr. Graves stole the Brain Box in a feeble attempt to prevent your team from translating the information inside. And he coerced a poor, innocent young girl into following him. Sounds to me like he should be the one in jail, not Dr. Caruso."

"Well, that part about the Brain Box isn't true because Director Caruso already removed the hard drive," Zane said from where he sat. "The box, as it is, has no memories to translate."

"General." Allison crossed her arms over her chest, looking up at him. She was tired, hungry, and worried sick over what was keeping Carter and the others. "For your information, if Dr. Caruso had been completely honest in her report to you, you'd know the box is useless. But we do have a theory on where those memories went."

Allison moved past him to Henry's terminal and sat down. She called up her personal login and waited for the system to retrieve the records she'd been working on.

Mansfield was right behind her, looming. "Where are Agent Caruso's memories?"

Ignoring him, she brought up Kathryn Caruso's files—a real pill to get ahold of, but she now owed a favor to a friend at DARPA—as well as the files on a recently submitted project. She motioned for him to come around her and pointed at the screen. "General—what's Juicebox?"

The general's reaction couldn't have been better if she'd planned it. His eyes widened as he leaned in, reading the proposal. He glanced around, reached out, and quickly shut the monitor off. In a tense and very angry-sounding voice, he whispered, "Who else knows about this?"

"Just Henry and I."

He looked at her, his expression unreadable. "What do you want?"

"Answers, General. But first we need to find Carter, Graves, and Zoe. Once we find them"—she glanced at Henry, who stood by her side—"I'll show you where the memories are."

Carter decided at that moment in time that nothing else hurt worse in the universe than a headache. And there was no comparison to the one he woke up with. For several minutes, he tried to remember what it was he'd drunk the night before. He hadn't had a beer in a while, and not many since taking the job as sheriff of Eureka.

Was it something he'd eaten, then? Or maybe something

S.A.R.A.H. had fixed him, like one of her cold remedies gone bad. Whatever it was, it had taken up residence behind his eyes and wasn't letting go.

When he moved to get out of bed, something prevented him from rising. And there was a smell—was that gasoline? He tried opening his eyes, but they stung and he let out a serious moan as the pain in his head abruptly traveled all the way down to his toenails.

"Oh . . . ow," was the best he could do as he somehow got his arm to his eyes and rubbed at them with the back of his forearm sleeve. Squinting, he was able to make out a spiderweb.

No . . . not a spiderweb.

As his vision came into sharp focus, he realized he was staring at a cracked glass window. A windshield. And there was something red splattered on it.

Whatever kind of morning this was starting out as, he hoped the day would be a lot better.

"Uh-Sheriff Carter! Are you all right!"

Waking up to a man's voice completely threw him off his game. He twisted his head around to look.

He was in the sheriff's car. In the driver's seat. The passenger-side window was missing, with no glass left around the edges.

"I, uh . . ." he heard himself say. "I'm not sure. . . ."

Then, like a douse of cold water, his memory came back to him. The Brain Box. Caruso. Storycatchers. And—

"Oh my God." He remembered the bridge. The car blew a tire when he swerved and then they were airborne, going over the side and then— "Zoe? Are you all right?"

"I'm fine, Dad," came Zoe's voice from somewhere. "But it looks like we're down in the ravine, and still a good way from GD."

"Oh. That's nice." He felt a hand on him from his left but couldn't turn his head that way.

"Sheriff, I need you to move your left arm—yes, like that. I'm going to reach around and release your seat belt. Try to put your hands up or you'll land—"

The belt released with a click and Carter felt himself fall up, smashing his head on the roof of the SUV.

Ow.

And there was water. Ice-cold. Rushing into his nose and mouth.

He sputtered, trying to get away from it.

"On your head," Graves finished. "Sorry. . . . I think the buckle was damaged and ready to give anyway. Just move your head to the left so the water doesn't—that's good."

"Uh-huh." Carter moved himself along; the pain that'd moved from his head to his toenails was now dancing around in every muscle as he pushed and twisted himself out of the driver's-side window, his body starting to shiver as he realized he was soaked, and cold, and very uncomfortable. He grabbed hold of Graves and Zoe until he was kicking free and then settled back on the cold wet ground. The stars were high and bright and he thought he saw Cassiopeia.

"Dad?" Zoe came into view, followed by Graves. Graves held a penlight into their faces, casting them in ghastly shadows. They both looked a bit banged up, Graves now sporting another cut to his face while Zoe looked almost immaculate. "You okay?"

"I think he hit his head pretty hard on the windshield."

"I'm fine, I'm fine." Carter moved to his left, intent on sitting up but only managing to lie half on his front with his butt in the air. "Maybe not."

"Dad . . . just lie still."

"No . . ." He pushed himself up to a sitting position and looked up again. He could just make out the bridge they'd fallen from. A long way above them. "Wow . . . that was a long drop."

"It's surprising we're alive," Graves said. "Why did you veer off the road like that?"

Carter rubbed at his face. It felt as if he were hearing and seeing from a long way off. "I veered? I thought— there was a girl up there. I saw her there." He reached out as if to touch that memory. "And then I heard someone telling me to turn the wheel."

"Damn her." Graves shook his head, sighing.

"You really think this was your sister's doing?" Zoe said.

"I'm positive. Like I said . . . her getting caught like that was just too . . . easy. Somehow she got into your dad's head. She's never been able to get to me, and you evidently weren't an option. So she went after the most pliable mind."

"Thanks," Carter muttered.

"Sorry, sir—I didn't mean—"

"Yeeuah . . ." With a grunt, Carter pushed himself up into a standing position. The gully and brush around him tilted just a little in the moonlight and he stumbled. Graves and Zoe moved to him, and each took an arm. "Wait. . . . Is the Brain Box still good?"

"It's . . . okay," Graves said. "I should be able to fix it, but we're going to have to try to get to GD on foot. Sheriff . . . you okay?"

"No one has a cell phone?"

Zoe shook her head. "Well, mine's at the bottom of the water over there, with the back end of the SUV. You got yours? Or the PDAs?"

"Ah." Carter frowned. "I tossed the PDAs into the seat."

"Great," Zoe said. "Then they're either buried under the car or underwater. And I'm not sure we can find them in the dark."

Graves said, "Is there one built into your car?"

Carter shook his head. "Only works if the car's running," he looked at the upside-down vehicle. Buried up to the middle of the driver's seat under water. "I don't think it's running."

"Look," Graves said. "Normally, I wouldn't recommend you moving. We could be compromising your C-spine. There could be a neck or back injury we just can't see. But we need to get to GD." He stepped away from Carter and held out his hands to make sure the sheriff was going to remain upright. That was when Carter noticed the two briefcases beside them.

"You think you're up for this, Dad?"

"Well, yeah, why wouldn't I be?"

"Maybe because you're leaning at a funny angle?"

Carter nodded, but the movement tilted him off balance. He felt his knees buckle as he lost balance and landed on all fours, his stomach rolling. "Okay . . . I think I'm going to be sick."

"Concussion," Graves said. "Not a good one, either."

Carter looked at him sideways, tilting his head as Graves knelt down next to him. "There are good concussions?"

"What I mean is, you need medical attention. We all do. Zoe's got a pretty nasty cut on her back from the shelf, and one on her hand from the glass. But we don't have any way of contacting them."

"Well," Carter said as he decided that it would be better to lie down on his back. Once he succeeded in doing that and not throwing up, he stared at the stars. "The phones are powered by batteries, right?"

"Yeah," Zoe said.

"So . . . do we have something that'll do the same thing? Work as a recharger? The car battery, maybe?"

Graves abruptly slapped his hand to his forehead. "Of course, the battery powering the Brain Box is basically a phone battery. If I can figure a way to hook it up to one of the phones, then we should get a charge and a signal."

Carter nodded to himself. "Yeah . . . you'll need tools, won't you?"

Graves's shoulders slumped. "Yeah . . . I will. But they are underwater, too."

"What are we gonna do?" Zoe asked.

"Hello!"

Carter looked at Zoe and then at Graves. "Either one of you hear that? It wasn't just me?"

Zoe spoke up. "Yeah, I heard it. Air?"

"Yeah." Graves turned and stood up, looking around. "Should I answer back?"

"Hey, anyone alive down there?"

Carter moaned. "That's Mr. Burns's voice."

Zoe turned to him. "The guy with the shed in his backyard?"

"Yeah . . ."

Air held up the flashlight and waved it. "Hey! Yes, we're here. We need help!"

Zoe stood as well and hugged herself with her arms. "Is it me? Or is it just strange that we crash in the middle of nowhere and someone finds us?"

Carter heard the snap and crunch of several sets of boots approaching to his left. He narrowed his eyes as the same group of people he'd seen at the sheriff's station emerged from the roof.

And all of them wore tinfoil on their head.

Graves shook his head. "Well"—he pointed—"that's not something you see every day."

"You haven't been in Eureka long enough," Carter said as he struggled to sit up. Seth Osbourne moved forward quickly as the others joined in to help right the sheriff on his feet. As they all swarmed around, checking out Zoe and Graves, Carter grinned. "You guys see the accident?"

Seth beamed. "No, sir. The deputy gave us a call—we were out patrolling the roads and she told us to be on the lookout for you." He pointed to his head. "And she told us to wear our protection." He tapped the metal on his head. "Said there might be mind waves out tonight."

Zoe looked around. "Who are you guys—and what's up with the tinfoil?"

Carter grinned. "Zoe, Aircom, I'd like you to meet the Eureka Militia Pulse."

Graves grinned. "EMP. Nice."

CHAPTᵉR 30

"Damn it!" Zane said as he angrily ran his hand through his hair. Fargo nearly jumped out of his skin. He'd been double-checking Zane's calculations for a possible way of deleting the memories from Lucas's cortex.

So far, every idea simulation Zane had run gave a 90 to 92 percent probability that Lucas's own memories would be wiped. This whole thing was too close to Fargo's own experience with the storynest.

Dr. Blake and Dr. Deacon were with Lucas in the infirmary. Graves and the sheriff hadn't shown up yet.

"What?" Fargo barked back. He hated it when Zane got so overemotional.

"This just isn't possible. You can't just pick and choose which memories to delete. I don't care that the storycatchers were doing it—it was still random. Memories can't be sorted by any known scientific way. I won't be able to tell whose memory is whose."

Fargo knew he was right, and was very happy that the director hadn't assigned him that job to do. "Too bad we don't make backup copies of our memories. Like on a spare disk. Then you could just overwrite and restore."

When Zane didn't answer, Fargo turned in his chair and looked at him. He did not like the look on Zane's face. "I was kidding. You can't really do that."

"Why not? We have a way of putting the memories back. And the problem isn't that we can't wipe them; it's that we can't single them out. Why not try that?"

Fargo rolled his eyes. "So, when did Lucas come in and get a backup done of his brain?"

Zane lowered his shoulders and hung his head. "You're right. I'm so tired I'm not thinking straight."

"Maybe I should run by Café Diem and grab coffee?" Not that Fargo really wanted to. He just wanted to get away from Zane.

"Yeah . . . that's actually a good idea. I'll . . . I'll keep working on this."

Fargo practically ran out of the lab. He checked his phone messages once he had a signal again and stepped off the elevator. He put the phone to his ear, calling Vincent to put in an order.

He stopped in the center of the rotunda as Vincent answered. "What is it, Fargo? It's very busy tonight."

Standing outside was a crowd of crazy-looking people with tinfoil on their heads.

"Fargo?"

"Vincent! We're under attack!"

Sheriff Carter limped forward and banged on the door. He was bleeding and his clothes were ripped and dirty.

"And they've got Sheriff Carter!"

On the other end of the phone, Vincent called out. "Jo— EMP found the sheriff!"

* * *

Carter wasn't too happy with the fuss made over him when several of Mansfield's men half carried him into the infirmary.

Henry and Julia confirmed he had a slight concussion, as well as a few bruises and contusions that smarted when Julia applied alcohol. Graves was given a few stitches to his forehead before he, Fargo, Zane, and Henry brought as much of the equipment of lab 511 as they could into the infirmary so Graves could adjust and set up the Brain Box.

Wanting to be as much a part of what was happening as he could, and feeling rather out of place dressed in the GD scrubs Julia had given them to change into because their clothes were wet, Carter got out of bed once Graves announced he had the Brain Box online with a new hard drive and the harvester running.

Henry and Zane wheeled the machine over to Lucas, and Carter watched in lurid fascination as they attached electrodes to his forehead, neck, and temples and behind his ears. When they were done, Lucas looked more like a science experiment gone wrong.

"I can't promise that any of the modifications Zane and I made to the box will delete the memories after we copy them. As things stand now, there is the possibility we could delete everything or nothing." He looked directly at Allison. "Are you willing to take that risk?"

She didn't hesitate in her answer. "He won't survive if we don't do something—just push the button, Aircom."

"Glad it's not me," Fargo muttered.

Graves sat at the Brain Box console Zane had converted for him that connected the machine directly into GD's network. Henry gave Graves a nod, and the box lit up along its edges. He hadn't actually seen the box in action, and Carter was a bit underwhelmed. The whole process seemed almost—anticlimactic.

After twenty minutes of very little conversation, save Fargo's periodic informative percentage count of the memories being harvested, Graves finally announced that the transfer was complete. He powered the machine down. "The machine is reading that all the data is there, and then some. Did it delete them?"

They all waited as Henry initiated another portable brain wave scan to look into Lucas's cortex.

Carter strained to see the screen as line by line the scan appeared. It didn't look any different than it had before.

Zane swore and turned away. Allison sighed, putting her hand over her face, and Zoe pressed herself closer into Carter's arm. He could feel her pain, and it hurt him as much as it hurt her.

"What happened?" Mansfield asked. He'd kept quiet in the far corner, nodding only when Graves announced he had the memories.

"Nothing was deleted out," Allison said, lowering her hand. "The machine is basically built for copying, but not for deleting. I'm sure if given time, we could come up with a combination of the storynest and the Brain Box that could delete the memories—but we just don't have it."

"I'm afraid we've got no choice but to revert to the last resort," Henry said.

Carter looked over at him. "Last resort?"

Zane shook his head. "I don't want to risk that, Henry."

"We don't have a choice, Zane. His brain is going to pretty much turn into mush if we don't get those memories out of there."

"But you're talking about wiping out everything, and then reloading?"

"Wait. . . . What?" Carter said. "You make it sound like he's got a computer for a brain."

"Basically we all do," Henry said. "The human brain is, in theory, a hard drive. You have long-term memory, which is the memories written to the hard drive, those you keep and never lose. You have sensory memory, and temporal memory, which can be seen as inputs from other sources."

Carter frowned. "You mean like having hard drive space and RAM?"

Henry nodded. "Well, yeah. RAM is the short term, which is where most if not all of Caruso's memory was stored."

Carter frowned at them. "If you're serious that it's like a computer, then why don't you just kill the power?"

Everyone looked at Carter as if he'd grown a third eye. He looked back at them and even felt Zoe pull away from him. "What?"

"Carter, you hit your head harder than we thought," Allison said. "You can't just kill the power."

"Why not? You just said it's a lot like a computer. What happens if a computer loses power? You lose everything you had in your RAM. Stuff on the paste board, programs you had running if the information isn't saved. So if you just restart—"

"Carter, that's enough. You realize you're talking about killing Lucas."

"No, I'm not." Carter shook his head.

Graves straightened, his brow knitted together. He looked at Henry. "Therapeutic hypothermia."

Henry's attention snapped to Graves, and the two of them locked on to each other. "That might work—and it would be the best bet in preventing brain damage."

"That's what I was thinking—" Graves put his fingers to his lips. "A neuroprotectant—but usually it's done with cold packs—"

"No—that's too slow. We're already running out of time—"

Carter held up his hand. "Whoa—what are you two talking about? Therapeutic hypo-what?"

Henry turned a patient smile to Carter. "Hypothermia. Lowering Lucas's body temperature. Your idea of killing the power to Lucas's brain—it might work. But to shut his brain down we're going to have to slow his heart rate. We'd need to freeze him—getting his heart rate down to ten to fifteen beats a minute."

"That's pretty damned dangerous," Allison said in a warning tone.

"I'm open for options," Henry said.

"I'm not sure I understand the need to freeze him," Carter said.

Graves turned to him, his expression one of enthusiasm. "Colder patients have better brain function when their hearts restart. There are dozens of stories out there of babies or children falling into frozen lakes who are subsequently recovered, with a heart rate of two beats a minute, and ultimately survive with no neurological deficit."

"Wait. . . ." Zoe looked at Graves and then at Henry. "You *are* talking about killing him."

"Just stopping his brain functions long enough to expunge the temporary memories," Henry said.

"We just need to get him cold quick." Graves looked around the room.

"What about the cryogenic bed you put Fargo in?" Carter said. "When he had that mummy's curse."

All eyes turned to look at him again.

Carter looked at all of them, his hands on his hips. "Okay, you're all going to have to stop looking at me like that."

Henry laughed out loud. "No, Jack—it's perfect. Julia, I need you to grab a few techs and get the cryo bed wheeled in here. Zane, I need you and Graves working together with me and Dr. Blake on monitoring all of Lucas's vitals."

Everyone started moving quickly, and Carter waved at Henry. "What do you want us to do?"

"I want you to pray."

Half an hour later, Lucas lay still inside the same glass hooded bed Fargo had been in some time ago. Carter and Zoe stood nearby, looking down at him, while Zane, Graves, Henry, and Allison monitored screens near the Brain Box.

"We're at eighteen beats per minute," Graves called out.

Henry nodded. "Let me know when we get to ten."

Carter turned and looked at Henry. "And then what?"

But Henry didn't say.

"Fifteen," Graves said.

Zoe chewed on her lower lip but didn't let go of Carter.

"Twelve."

Carter looked from Henry back to Lucas's face, just visible in the frosted glass.

"Ten."

"Allison . . ." Henry looked at her.

She closed her eyes.

Carter looked at them. "What?"

Alarms went off suddenly and he and Zoe moved back, looking around the room. "What—"

Graves spoke up. "It's okay—we just have to make sure he doesn't go into cardiac arrest. That was an alarm to let me know it was possible."

Zane nodded his head. "All brain functions have stopped."

"Oh my God." Zoe put her hand to her mouth. "Is he dead?"

"Actually, he's not," Zane said slowly as he stared at the monitor in front of him. "He's just in a very deep, very cold coma. Henry, I'm at thirty seconds."

"Initiating restart," Henry said.

The alarms went off again.

"Shit." Graves jumped up. "Cardiac arrest—"

"It's okay, Dr. Graves," Henry said. "Already initiated defibrillation from here. Heart rate is?"

Graves sat back down and looked at his monitor. A wide smile broke his concerned expression. "He's at . . . he's at twenty beats per minute." Looking over at Zane, he said, "This place is amazing."

Zane shrugged. "It's Eureka."

"Temperature climbing, heart rate getting strong . . ." Henry said. He smiled at Carter. "He's back."

Carter and Zoe moved closer to the bed and looked down. Lucas's eyes were fluttering open, and he looked around. Spotting Zoe, he smiled. "Hey . . . I'm sorry I didn't . . . call you. . . ." He paused and looked around him. "Why am I all icy?"

She put her hand on the glass and wiped away a tear. "It's okay. Really."

"Let's check the scans again," Henry said, and a light came on inside the bed's chamber. All eyes turned to the monitor behind Henry.

The area that was shaded before was now clear.

Zoe cheered and hugged Carter. He nodded to Henry and then to Graves.

Henry sighed and turned to Graves. "Dr. Graves—you have your memories back in their box."

"And you have Lucas back." Graves stood and moved to Carter, offering his hand. "That was a brilliant idea—and not one I believe I would have thought of."

Allison moved to join them, looking down at Lucas and smiling before looking up at Carter with an unmistakable look of pride. "Yeah, he does that."

CHAPTᵉR 31

S.A.R.A.H. said.

Carter yawned as he came into the kitchen, showered and dressed in his uniform. He'd been forced to take yesterday off to recuperate from the car crash and was ready to get back to work. He hadn't been expecting Henry to be over so early, though.

Since the sheriff's car was at the bottom of the ravine, he was going to need a ride.

"Hey, Carter, you up?" Henry called out from the stairs.

"Yeah."

"Come out here for a sec."

Carter went to the pantry and grabbed his cub of coffee, prepared by S.A.R.A.H., before moving up the stairs and outside.

The air was chilled and he shivered, then stopped in his

tracks at seeing his vehicle parked where he always parked it. "Wait. . . . Henry . . . this can't be the same one."

Henry, dressed in his oil-stained overalls, shook his head as he shoved his hands in his pockets. "No. We keep a couple of them between GD and the garage. I tuned this one up yesterday. Going to pull the other out today and work on it."

"Really?" Carter moved around the vehicle, his coffee in his hand, his other hand in his pocket. "I thought you'd be spending your time working with Graves to view those memories on the storynest."

There was a very long pause.

"Carter, about that—"

He did not like Henry's tone. Carter had bent over on the other side to look at the tires and now popped up over the hood to face Henry. He took one look at his face. "No . . . no, no, no . . . don't tell me."

"Yeah," Henry said. "I'm afraid so."

"When?"

"Yesterday when we got in. Allison was ready to shoot someone." Henry sighed. "They must have come in right after we left. Brain Box, all the notes, everything from the past two days, all gone. Wiped off the GD servers. Allison can't even find it in her Section Five archives."

"And Dr. Graves?"

"Can't find him. I tried calling his house, but the number is out of service."

"Son of a bitch," Carter said as he pulled his hand from his pocket and put it on the side of the hood. "They did it again."

"Kathryn Caruso is gone as well. There's no record of her arrest, and Lucas said his family's house is just fine. Could never tell anything ever happened inside."

"So they're covering it up. All that work that Graves and Caruso did—and they're going to cover it up."

"They've also restricted all access about the singularity. Any blogs that even mentioned it? Gone." Henry sighed. "I had a feeling something like this would happen."

"What do you think they'll do with Graves?"

"I don't know. Lucas can't remember any of it."

Carter straightened. "So all of this happened yesterday?"

"Yeah. And the only reason we didn't call you was because S.A.R.A.H. wouldn't let us. Not sure if she was just being protective or receiving an order Fargo swears he didn't send. Either way—" Henry tossed the keys over the hood at Carter. Carter caught them in his free hand. "We're meeting with Mansfield in Allison's office."

"Really? Mansfield's still here?"

"They left him out, Jack. And he wants to talk to us. Me, you, and Allison."

Carter opened the door and slipped into the driver's side. "Okay, but I have one place to go first."

"Where's that?" Henry said, getting into the passenger side.

Carter set the coffee in the holder and cranked the SUV. "It's Muffin Monday."

The air in Allison's office was more than oppressive as Carter entered, Henry behind him. General Mansfield was already there, his hat resting on Allison's desk. Allison sat behind her desk and gave the two of them a forced smile.

Carter realized she was upset.

Mansfield stood by the floor-to-ceiling window looking out over the rotunda. It was early, and most of GD's employees were trickling in.

"Morning, General," Carter said. He held up a bag. "Muffin?"

The general shook his head. "Now that we're all here—"

He turned and looked at Allison. "Ever been to Niagara Falls, Dr. Blake?"

"Yes. I went there with Nathan before we were married."

"I love that place. The majesty, the raw power of nature . . . all there in a single place. You can feel it when you stand out on one of the overlooks, the spray drenching you in a matter of seconds. The sheer force of the water and the wind . . ."

Carter glanced at Henry, who took one of the seats opposite Allison's desk and moved it out so that he could sit and face the two of them.

"What about you, Dr. Deacon?"

Henry cleared his throat. "It's one of the great natural wonders of the world."

"Natural, you say?" Mansfield shook his head. "How do we know that for sure? Who's to say some prehistoric creature didn't shift a pebble that eventually diverted the river to that spot to carve out what we see today."

"Any way you look at that," Henry said, "it was still caused by nature. Living creatures in their own habitat, doing what they do best."

"Yes. That's true. But I would beg to differ with you, Doctor, on many levels. We're all responsible for the state of our lives—how we work, who we hate, how we treat others—but there are only a select few who are responsible for the larger picture. The macrocosm as it envelops everyone's small worlds."

Allison pursed her lips. She was impressed with the general's use of some words, but he wasn't staying in form, and he was confusing her. "General . . . everything's gone. All of it. Even Graves has disappeared. What did they do with him? Why are we here?"

"I sometimes stand there looking out at the people, not the falls. Watching them, and knowing that they have no idea of the decisions that are made behind closed doors. The near disasters and Earth-destroying catastrophes that occur every day." He turned from the window and looked at her. "Many of them right here in Eureka."

Carter watched the general, noticed the way he shifted his arms and hands. Sometimes he kept them behind him, sometimes in front. But he always looked as if he were alert, at attention, always watching. He wanted to ask him if this monologue had a point.

"You know about the other high-end research facilities in the states. That Eureka is the best of all of them. Most of the weapons we use to defend this country, as well as others, originated here in Eureka."

Henry leaned forward. "General—is this about Juice-box?"

Mansfield held up a finger. "You're going to be patient and listen to me for once, Dr. Deacon. All of you are. You know that the research that is generated from here, as well as places like PNNL and Area 51, are all reviewed by committees. Dr. Aircom Graves sat on one of these committees. They argue, fight, squabble, pore over what deserves better funding and what doesn't. Sometimes things like Dr. Fontana's storycatchers that were given a pass in so many of these committees are revisited by Graves. An admirable idea."

Henry and Allison nodded, though it was Allison who spoke. "Dr. Graves shared his original vision for his Brain Box with all of us."

Mansfield stepped into the center of the room. "I know Graves has told you about the work Agent Caruso was doing for the DoE at PNNL—about the bureaucratic bullshit, posturing, and downright falsification of research."

"He didn't mention the details—just that Caruso was working to discover the truth, and that what he found could influence whether the project of the sustained singularity was handled by the DoD or the DoE."

"I'm impressed. The boy knew more than I thought." He inhaled deeply.

Carter pulled a muffin from the bag, rattling the paper, and winced as Allison cut him a look.

Mansfield continued. "Like the committees I told you about, those who know about DARPA and its purpose understand the similarities."

"Yes," Henry said. "They commission projects, but they don't do the hands-on work. They conceive of an idea, figure out exactly what it needs to do, set the specifications, and establish a cost framework. Once that's done, they set it out for bid."

"Correct," Mansfield said. "So you can see why ideas are very valuable within DARPA, and a lot of those ideas or proposals are classified. Most of them on a need-to-know basis.

"One of the things we're been trying to create is a small, high-output power system. Something that can sustain itself even under high usage."

"You're talking about a micropower source," Henry said. "Something like that could power an armored suit and not be dragged down by the drain of the suit itself. You need something the size of a . . ." His eyes widened. "A juice box."

Mansfield smirked. "Sometimes it amazes me how you scientists can label the most amazing things with mundane inane ridiculousness."

"Let me understand this. . . . Someone is thinking of using this sustainable singularity . . . making it a microsingularity . . . and creating the juice box from hell," Allison said.

Henry stood. "The military possibilities for that would be . . . monstrous. Forget a suitcase nuke. . . . You could make a lunchbox nuke, or even a purse."

"The proposal for this kind of thing surfaced when we first heard of CERN's discovery. It's something that's been waiting in the wings for some time." Mansfield looked thoughtful.

"And the DoD would love to have the funds allocated to bid on that project," Allison said. "And John Caruso found this out?"

"He found a leak in certain channels—bribing, behind-the-scenes pandering—and he discovered that the leak was his own wife, Kathryn Caruso."

Carter put the rest of the muffin back in the bag. He felt as if the wind had been knocked from him. He sat forward. "General—you knew all this. That Kathryn was dirty and that John paid the price. You knew John confronted her, didn't you?"

"I only had bits and pieces from witnesses. John wouldn't tell me—I'm DoD and he didn't trust anyone with his findings. Unfortunately, when he was killed, I requi-sitioned his notes, but there was nothing there about the leak, his wife, or Juicebox."

"You brought Graves in to use his box," Henry began. "Because you needed to know what happened. You . . . really weren't worried about the budget."

"I was. I am. But if John had discovered improprieties with a DARPA agent—to me that was a matter of national security. We put a lot of manpower and dollars into that agency. I demand that they represent themselves as beyond reproach."

Carter felt really bad. He—as well as Henry and Allison—had misunderstood Mansfield's actions.

"It never occurred to me to check to see if Graves had a relationship to the two. Aircom and Kathryn kept their personal lives very private. I realized something was wrong when I saw his reaction to the corpse." Mansfield shook his head. "At first he didn't want to do it, but I ordered him to, or I would lock him away for a very long time. He did as he was told, like I said, admirably. But then before we arrived here I discovered that Caruso's notes were missing."

"And you assumed Graves had them."

"Yes, I did. And the more he seemed to delay the project, the more it looked as if he knew something. At the time, I didn't know if he was working with Kathryn or that it was Kathryn who'd taken the notes. No one did. But now I suspect that Graves did, and he wasn't just looking to preserve his friend's memories; he wanted to see for himself what the truth was."

"Do you know what the truth is?" Carter asked.

Mansfield fixed him with an unreadable stare. "No. I don't. I've been told not to talk about this again. To be a good soldier. And I've been warned not to interfere."

Allison frowned. "Then why did you just tell us about Juicebox?"

"You made a promise to deliver those memories. And you did. I promised I would tell you."

"But—" Henry looked around. "You didn't have to tell me. Or Carter."

Mansfield glanced over at Carter. "Carter's a former U.S. Marshal. He's good at finding things that go missing." Nodding to each of them, Mansfield took up his hat, placed it on his head, and left Allison's office.

Allison leaned forward on her elbows. "What did he mean by that?"

Carter shook his head. "I don't know." He reached in and retrieved his muffin. "I just don't know."

Henry stood. "Neither do I. But I'll say this." He looked at each of them. "I'm rethinking any classes on Remote Viewing."

*　*　*

Sitting at a table at Café Diem, Zoe carefully peeled the paper away from the oversized chocolate chip muffin. She was aware of Lucas's eyes on her, and she could see his smile just past the chocolaty goodness. Finally she lowered the muffin. "What?"

"I'm sorry."

"Lucas—you've said that about a thousand times already. I'm the one who's sorry. I tried snooping into your thoughts, looking at your brain. And I had no right."

But he shook his head. "And why did you do that? Because I wasn't talking to you, Zoe. I wasn't communicating with you like I should. I just"—he sighed and folded his arms on the table—"I was just embarrassed."

"Look." She set the muffin down completely and reached out to take his hand. "Please, don't ever think that I would think less of you, okay? How many mistakes have I made here in Eureka? How many mistakes are we going to make out there in the world? A lot, Lucas. Just please"—she leaned in close to him—"If you ever have doubts, or feel scared, or even need someone to talk to—talk to me, okay?"

He gave her a half smile.

"We have to trust each other, Lucas. Without trust—" She sighed. "We build up these stupid ideas in our heads. So . . . trust?"

He nodded before he half stood, put his hands on the table, leaned in, and planted a kiss on her lips. She felt her heart thunder against her chest and reached up to twist his curls into her fingers.

"Hey, hey . . . not so early in the morning," Vincent said as he moved closer and set two coffees down. The couple parted and Lucas returned to his seat. "So, you two good?" He pointed at each of them.

Lucas grinned. "Yes, we are. I make a promise never to

shut her out again. As long as she makes a promise never to poke around in my head again."

"That is so a deal," Zoe said as she took up her coffee. She stopped as she smelled something different about it. "Wait. . . . Vincent . . ."

"Oh, that's mine," Lucas said as he moved the cup in front of him closer to her. "I wanted to try the chai."

She set it down and looked up at Vincent. "I thought you'd made a mistake again."

He pointed at her. "Don't start, or I'll cut your break short." With that, he flipped the towel over his shoulder and moved away.

When she looked back at Zane, he was smiling. "What was that? Vincent's never messed up an order."

"I love you, Zoe, mind reader."

She leaned in close. "And I love you, Lucas, memory keeper."

Vincent waved at Carter as he entered Café Diem. "Come in for more muffins, Sheriff?"

"Maybe," Carter said.

Zoe was sitting at a table with a much-improved Lucas. Zane sat at the counter eating breakfast.

"Hey, Sheriff, you look better today," Zane said.

"And I feel better," Carter said. He glanced back at the couple. "Looks like Lucas is better, too?"

"Yeah . . ." Zane nodded. "He's still a little fuzzy on it all, but they've been talking all morning." He hopped off his stool and motioned Carter to follow him to the door near the pantry. There he pulled an envelope out of his back pocket. "I found this on my desk yesterday, when I discovered everything was gone. It was for you."

"Me?" Carter opened the flap and pulled out a handwritten note on plain white paper.

Carter,

I don't know what'll happen, but rest assured, I'll continue to fight to see that this machine is used to help law enforcement catch criminals. I don't know that we'll ever see each other again, but I wanted to thank you for not giving up on me.

Aircom Graves

Carter refolded the paper and slipped it back into the envelope. He'd been in law enforcement a long time—he knew, understood, and respected the power the government had and wielded on a daily basis.

Yet all of that might had always ridden on the shoulders of Mansfield and a select group of individuals. It humanized it for him. To talk to Mansfield was to talk to them.

But he'd never seen anything like this. Everything magically returned to the way it was. It was almost like what Henry and Zane had done to Lucas. Rebooted. Restarted. Returned to normal. And what happened was erased.

But this time it wasn't Mansfield. It was something else. A lot more powerful, and a lot more mysterious.

"Even the security tapes are wiped," Zane said. "It's like if I hadn't seen that note, I'd have thought I'd dreamed the whole thing." He looked down. "You think Graves is still alive?"

Carter reached over to his left to the three-tiered iron service and plucked up a chocolate chip muffin. He held it in his hands and nodded. "I believe he is, Zane. I think he'll do what he says in that note."

Everything pointed to Kathryn Caruso's influence, whether that was through her job or through Remote Influencing. If she had influenced her husband to hit that truck, or made Carter drive off that bridge—she could have gotten rid of her brother at any time.

Either she cared about him and wanted to protect him, or Aircom had a way to avoid his sister's wrath.

Carter could believe the latter. Kathryn Caruso didn't have a caring bone in her body.

With a smile at the muffin, he said, "I think he'll do what he says he'll do. He'll do the right thing." Carter glanced at Zane. "And I'll do what I do."

Before he could bite into his muffin, Zoe came up beside him and gave him a tight hug. "You okay, Dad?"

He set the muffin back down and turned to return the embrace, kissing her on the check. "Yeah—I'll be better."

She searched his face. "He'll be all right, won't he?"

He looked past her to Lucas. "He's a growing boy—and he doesn't remember anything—"

"No, Dad." She lowered her voice. "I mean Air. He'll be all right, won't he?"

He should have known Zoe already knew what'd happened with the Brain Box. He nodded as she pulled back. "Yeah. I do. I think he'll be fine. So"—he shrugged—"you and Lucas are much better now? You going to do any more Viewing into other people's heads?"

Zoe gave him a soft smile. "No. I've sworn off it for a bit." Her smile faded. "I don't think we need to know what other people are thinking—unless they tell us. Thinking I was looking into Lucas's mind—I saw things that weren't even his. And I assumed I knew what they were.

"It's like you said before about how evidence without context—isn't evidence. Looking in from the outside, you can't really know unless you ask. You have to trust." She reached out and hugged him again. "And trust is something you earn. I won't take it for granted ever again."

Carter returned her hug again and grinned before they pulled away. Her eyes were red-rimmed as he looked into them. "I know sometimes I have to trust you, Zoe. And I'm only human—I'm going to doubt on occasion. Just like you will with friends, and boyfriends."

"I know, Dad. And I love you."

"I love you, too." He grinned as she stepped back, grabbed a towel from the counter, and moved to bus a table.

Carter picked up the envelope, folded it, and slipped it into his back pocket before grabbing his muffin and heading out into the October morning.